Praise for the novels of Lee Tobin McClain

"[A] magnetic second-chance romance…. McClain pits her charming, authentic characters against the realistic problems of everyday life, making for a story that is deeply emotional but never soapy. The welcoming community and beautifully described scenery of Teaberry Island only enhance this cozy romance. Readers won't want to put this down." —*Publishers Weekly* starred review on *The Forever Farmhouse*

"Lee Tobin McClain dazzles with unforgettable characters, fabulous small-town settings and a big dose of heart. Her complex and satisfying stories never disappoint." —Susan Mallery, *New York Times* bestselling author

"Fans of Debbie Macomber will appreciate this start to a new series by McClain that blends sweet, small-town romance with such serious issues as domestic abuse…. Readers craving a feel-good romance with a bit of suspense will be satisfied." —*Booklist* on *Low Country Hero*

"[An] enthralling tale of learning to trust…. This enjoyable contemporary romance will appeal to readers looking for twinges of suspense before happily ever after." —*Publishers Weekly* on *Low Country Hero*

"*Low Country Hero* has everything I look for in a book— it's emotional, tender, and an all-around wonderful story." —RaeAnne Thayne, *New York Times* bestselling author

LEE TOBIN McCLAIN

the bluebird bakery

HQN

ISBN-13: 978-1-335-42743-4

The Bluebird Bakery

Recycling programs for this product may not exist in your area.

For questions and comments about the quality of this book, please contact us at CustomerService@Harlequin.com.

HQN
22 Adelaide St. West, 41st Floor
Toronto, Ontario M5H 4E3, Canada
www.Harlequin.com

Printed in U.S.A.

To Kathy Ayres, who's helped me
improve countless stories including this one.

the bluebird bakery

PROLOGUE

Fifteen years ago

TAYLOR HARP WAS fifteen years old when she learned that, sometimes, it was better to be the smart one than the pretty one.

"Let's go, Savannah, you're going to stay with me." Mrs. Williams, Mom's best friend, tugged Taylor's sister toward her Lexus.

Aunt Katy put an arm around Taylor. "Come on, honey. You'll be living with me."

Taylor leaned in, welcoming the comfort of her beloved aunt. And then she processed what the two adults had said.

Shock and pain tightened her chest as she looked at her younger sister, gorgeous even with the tears that had streaked mascara down her face. Taylor should have told Savannah not to wear mascara to their mother's memorial service. She should have done a lot of things differently, she saw now, but it was too late.

She stuffed down the pain and welcomed the anger that rose in its place. Mrs. Williams and Aunt Katy wanted to separate her and her sister? How could they even think that, today of all days? "We need to stay together," she said, stepping forward to take her sister's hand.

Taylor was older by a year and wiser by a lifetime. She wasn't always crazy about her sister, but it was her job to take care of Savannah. It had been that way for most of their lives.

She wasn't going to cry. She was *mad*, not sad. Except when she looked at her sister's tear-streaked face.

Today, when they'd just laid their mother, Birdy, to rest, was not the day to neglect her duty to her sister. "We're staying together," she repeated with more force in her voice.

Savannah gripped Taylor's hand so hard it hurt.

"You can't stay together," Mrs. Williams said briskly. "Everything has changed, and we need to deal with it. Your aunt works too much to get Savannah to all her pageants."

Taylor opened her mouth to make the horrible suggestion that she would come and live with Mrs. Williams, too.

Seeming to read her mind, the woman shook her head. "I can't take both of you, so don't even ask."

Aunt Katy looked like she was about to cry herself. "Savannah could stop competing—"

"She needs to stay visible so she can get more modeling gigs." Mrs. Williams's voice was sharp. "Birdy left nothing. You know that."

Aunt Katy bit her lip and reached out to brush back Savannah's blond curls. "You can visit. A lot." Then she turned and patted Taylor's shoulder. "And you're so good at math, you can help me with my tax business."

Taylor tried to maintain her anger, but it was turning into a stone of despair, pressing down on her. If Aunt Katy was giving in to awful Mrs. Williams, that meant the adults had already discussed this. It meant this separation was inevitable. That was a new word she'd learned by eavesdropping on Mrs. Williams's phone conversation. "It was *inevitable* she'd take her own life one day," Mrs. Williams had said.

Taylor swallowed hard and kept a grip on her sister's hand. "If you ever feel like Mom felt, you come to me," she whispered. She'd learned online that depression ran in families, and Mom had definitely been depressed. "Whatever it takes, you hear me? Come to me, or I'll come get you, wherever you are. Do *not* do what she did."

Fresh tears rose to Savannah's eyes and spilled over. "You, too," she choked out. "If you ever feel like…" Her voice rose to a squeak on the last words.

"We have a train to catch." Mrs. Williams took a tissue and tried to wipe Savannah's face, then gave up and grasped each girl's wrist, yanking them apart like they were beads on a child's plastic necklace. "You can call your sister tomorrow, after the pageant."

Aunt Katy pulled Taylor into a side hug, her warm softness comforting. "Come on, we'll stop at the bakery and get cupcakes on the way home."

Seriously, their mother had just died and Aunt Katy was offering cupcakes? But Taylor bit back the snarky remark. Aunt Katy was sweet, and really, cupcakes were as good a comfort as anything else would be.

"I want a cupcake," Savannah croaked out.

"No cupcakes for a pageant princess. Your dress is already tight." And with that, Mrs. Williams opened the passenger door of the Lexus and half pushed, half lifted Savannah inside.

Mrs. Williams must have seen something on Aunt Katy's face, because her own expression went sour. "It's not our fault, it's Birdy's," she said. Her voice was harsh, but at the end, her face sort of caved in, her mouth twisting. She hurried to the driver's side of the car and got in. Before Taylor could catch her breath, the car had squealed out of the parking lot, taking her sister away.

Taylor watched the Lexus until it blended into a traffic jam of other vehicles. She kept squinting, trying to see it long after it had disappeared.

"Come on, honey." Aunt Katy took Taylor's hand, even though Taylor was way too old for that, and they headed down the street toward the small apartment that would become Taylor's home for the next however many years. Until she was eighteen and on her own, she guessed.

On the way, they stopped in front of the neighborhood bakery. As they walked inside, the checkered tablecloths and sweet-smelling cookies and happy chatter washed over Taylor. They gently soothed, for just a moment, the hole in her heart.

CHAPTER ONE

Present Day

IT WAS 5:00 A.M., and US Army Staff Sergeant Cody Cunningham—*retired* Staff Sergeant—had given up on trying to sleep.

No surprise there. He hadn't really slept, not for more than a few hours, since he'd been found wandering just outside of an enemy camp, naked and with no memory of what had happened to him. If he slept, the demons lurking near his conscious mind might make their way in. Whatever part of his brain controlled sleeping didn't think he could tolerate that apparently.

At least here, on Teaberry Island in the Chesapeake Bay, he had a few friends, a few loved ones and a place to stay.

Temporarily.

He made sure that his nephew was sleeping and that Betty, who lived next door, was awake and available if the boy needed her. Then he slipped out of his newly-wed brother's home and walked the short distance to the island's main street. As he'd expected, it was deserted. Except...

There was a light on at the Bluebird Bakery.

He walked by, staying in the shadows out of habitual caution he couldn't seem to shake. When he saw the Help Wanted, Housing Included sign, though, he couldn't resist stopping to study it.

Sudden movement inside the bakery let him know that his presence had been detected, and he backed up.

"Who's there?" A woman flung open the door, saw him and stepped backward, shock warring with simple dislike on her face. "You scared me. What are *you* doing here?"

He blew out a sigh and scanned Taylor Harp, the instant assessment another habit from his combat days. She stood in the doorway of the bakery, a hand propped on either side of the frame as if she were a bouncer ready to physically block him from entry. Silvery moonlight washed over her hair, tied back in a practical bun. Her wide, happy smile had captivated him when she'd visited the island as a teen, but now those full lips had turned downward into a frown. "I couldn't sleep," he admitted.

"Some of us wish we could, but we have to work." Just like the last time he'd spoken with her, at the end of their high school acquaintance, she was as disapproving as an old-fashioned schoolmarm.

Prettier, though.

She started to close the door, from which wafted the smells of bread and cake baking. Familiar, good smells. They drew him like a fish to bait, a bee to flowers, an enemy soldier to a decoy. "Wait, Taylor."

"What?"

He gestured toward the sign. "That job, have you filled it yet?"

She snorted. "No. No one of legal age to work nights has applied. Doesn't help that I can't pay much, even though housing's…" She trailed off and studied him. "Why are you asking?"

He shook his head. "I'm looking for work, and a place to stay, but I know—" He paused. His therapist said he shouldn't automatically discount opportunities. "Is there any chance I could apply?"

"Are you *kidding* me?" She squinted at him like he was a two-headed rockfish. "You want to work night shift at a bakery?"

"Never thought about it before. But I was a cook in the army."

"Oh, my lord, that's right. That chef show." She shook her head. "You were funny."

He'd definitely been more lighthearted back in those days. Quick with a joke or quip. The military channel show had gone viral, army chefs competing for silly prizes. It had eased the monotony of wartime and entertained the troops.

And then everything had blown up. Literally.

He hadn't cooked since then, aside from fixing breakfast for his nephew or heating up a can of soup.

"You're not seriously thinking—" Taylor broke off, still staring at him like he had a few screws loose.

Which, in fact, he did. "No. It could never work," he said.

"No," she agreed.

He breathed in the smell of baking bread and looked at her. "Could it?" he asked.

"No," she said firmly, and shut the door.

TAYLOR SHUT THE door and then leaned back against it, willing herself to settle down after the shock of seeing Cody Cunningham. How could he still be so appealing, with those eyes that seemed to see right into her soul? How had he gotten even *more* handsome than when she'd seen him, at a distance, on her friend Mellie's wedding day?

She was half waiting for Cody to knock again or try to open the door. That was what he'd have done when she'd known him as a teenager.

And Taylor, foolishly, would have opened the door and invited him up to her apartment above the bakery for breakfast, because she'd have hoped against hope that he wanted *her*, wanted to be with her, cared about her.

When, of course, it was always about Savannah.

Cody didn't knock, and when she peeked out the window, she saw him disappearing down the street. She blew out a breath and headed back to the oven to check on twenty loaves of teaberry sweet bread.

Savannah.

The sight of Cody had brought her sister to the forefront of Taylor's mind, and now she was stuck there. Where was Savannah now, and how was she doing? Why hadn't she been answering Taylor's calls?

Even though the island was distant from the everyday world in some ways, accessible only by boat, old-fashioned, they had the internet and cell phones and news, at least most of the time. There was no excuse for Savannah to be out of touch.

No excuse except that she was ashamed of the way she was living. Taylor, having spent her adolescence under Aunt Katy's influence, was the wholesome type: be strong, do your duty, go to church. Savannah had lived in a different, more glamorous world, with completely different values.

Taylor didn't judge her sister, or not too much. She prayed Savannah hadn't descended to the dark place they both feared after losing their mother to it. Surely, whatever had caused Savannah to pull away from Taylor, she'd land on her feet and get back in contact, just like the other times she'd run into some kind of trouble.

Taylor straightened and went to the window, looking out into the now-empty moonlit street. She was half glad, half sorry that Cody was gone. What had the world come to, when a heroic and decorated veteran was seeking a job as a night shift baker and wanted to live in an apartment above the shop? Cody should have come home to more fanfare.

She looked inside, tested her feelings the way you'd poke at an old scar. Did she still feel *that* way about him?

Slowly, she walked back to the kitchen and washed her hands. She'd been rolling out dough for cinnamon rolls, and now she touched the big sheet of it with one finger. It had gotten dry while she'd been talking to Cody, so she dipped a brush into the pot of melted butter and re-coated the sheet. Today's customers would find the rolls a bit richer than usual, which wouldn't arouse any complaints. People didn't come to the Bluebird Bakery for diet fare.

She looked at the clock and started sprinkling the streusel she'd already prepared onto the dough. She added nuts to one half. Ideally, she'd have made two separate batches, one with nuts and one without. She'd probably sell out of these by 9:00 a.m. But she didn't have time to do it all. There were still scones and muffins to get ready before the bakery opened at six thirty.

Which was why she needed to hire a night baker.

She yawned and stretched, rolling her shoulders. It was a good problem to have. She'd moved to Teaberry Island and started the bakery on way too little capital and an intuition that it would go well, that it was what the island needed. The island had a lot of teaberry bushes and was named for them, but aside from ice cream, no one had capitalized on the unusual minty, root-beer-like flavor.

She'd worked her fingers raw for the first two years, selling all the standard bakery hits but also developing recipes for teaberry scones and muffins and cakes.

It had paid off. Not only during the tourist season, but the rest of the year. She'd had a steadily growing customer base. She'd hired summer help, a high school and a college student, and she'd kept the high school student on to help on weekends and the occasional weeknight. A friend's daughter who had a cognitive impairment and a temperamental senior citizen worked for her in a random way, too.

But since she'd put out feelers about distributing teaberry baked goods more widely, she'd started getting off-island orders. More than she'd expected. Now she *really* needed a night baker.

She was on her way to achieving her fondest goal. Not just owning her own bakery, not just scratching out a living, but making a huge success of it. Enough that what had happened to her and Savannah would never, ever happen again. Enough that she could take care of Savannah and maybe, one day, the kids she desperately hoped to have, without the constant dark cloud of financial and emotional disaster following her around.

She could do it, but she had to have help.

The fact that she'd had exactly one potential applicant, and it was the man who'd come close to breaking her heart…well. It was par for Taylor's course. She put it out of her mind and focused on her baking.

SAVANNAH HARP WISHED this party were over.

She smoothed down her sparkly dress and waved away the caterer's assistant, who was circulating with a tray of champagne glasses. She was new enough to all of this to marvel that there was a caterer, in her own apartment, overlooking the bright lights of New York City.

Well, not *her* apartment, but Rupert's. She straightened her back and moved through the room, making sure people felt welcome. She'd spent way too much time feeling unwelcome herself, after her mother had died. She was a natural at making sure that no one else felt that way on her watch, that no one was off in a corner by themselves, feeling shy.

Or feeling a desire to steal the silver, said her more skeptical side.

No one's going to steal the silver. These are your friends. Well, Rupert's friends. Whatever. The forty or so guests were all as well off as Rupert, with no need to put an expensive knickknack in their pocket.

She greeted Clint Fitzgerald and his wife, whom everyone called Cookie. Clint and Cookie were some of the nicer of Rupert's friends. They sometimes asked Savannah about herself and whether she missed the pageant world, which she definitely didn't.

It was what everyone knew about her: that she'd been a beauty queen. First Runner-Up in the Miss Maryland pageant three years ago. One of the oldest near-winners, at age twenty-six.

She hadn't quite made it. Just as she hadn't quite made it in the competitive world of professional modeling, not after a few promising gigs as a kid. She still had hopes, but not as many as she used to have.

Savannah was fairly sure Rupert had tried and failed to date Miss Maryland herself, but the woman was a medical student and on her own path. Whereas Savannah had had no path planned after pageants, aside from some vague idea that she'd get back into modeling. She was nothing like her sister, Taylor, who'd always had a dream and pursued it relentlessly.

That was just one reason Taylor held her in low esteem.

"Come here, sweetheart," Rupert said from the bar area, where he stood talking to another man. His voice was soft, but nonetheless, it was a command. "I want you to meet someone."

She approached the two men. Rupert was still handsome at fifty-three, a silver fox, fit from tennis and weight training at the gym. At the height of his powers professionally, too, doing whatever he did with hedge funds to make possible the swanky apartment and expensive parties. And her, she guessed, though she could have been swept away by a much less affluent man who'd offered her a home and a sense of direction.

"This is Alistair McVeigh," he said, and the man, whom she now saw was a little older than Rupert, smiled and gave her a quick appraisal. A network of broken blood vessels across his nose and bags under his eyes suggested some hard living.

She made small talk, something her beauty queen education had taught her to do, but Alistair didn't seem interested in getting to know her as a person. Nor in talking about himself, surprisingly. He looked expectantly at Rupert.

"Alistair has had a difficult trip in from LA," Rupert told her. "Why don't you go back to his hotel with him and help him settle in?"

The clinks of glasses, the sparkling laughter around them seemed to fade. So *that* was what Rupert wanted. He was doing it again. She glared at her so-called fiancé.

Alistair let his hand rest on her hip, then slide down to cup her butt.

She gestured for Rupert to look, telling him with her eyes that he needed to *stop his handsy friend right now.*

But, big surprise, he didn't do a thing to help her. She moved away from the man, bumping into Rupert and causing him to spill a few drops of champagne.

"Watch it," he said, his voice cool. His eyes on her were steely, letting her know he meant more than the spilled champagne.

How had it evolved to this? He was supposed to make her into a top model, or, barring that, send her to acting school. "I need to talk to you," she said.

For a moment, she thought he wouldn't go, but he nodded. "Excuse us a minute," he said to Alistair.

He guided her to a corner of the living room. Outside the window, the expanse of city lights suggested freedom, opportunity, fun.

"What's the problem?" he asked as if she were a teenager who wouldn't do her homework.

"I told you I'm not doing that again." It was the third time he'd tried to set her up with one of his business acquaintances. The first time, she'd fended the guy off in horror and taken a cab home to a penitent Rupert, who'd said he hadn't known what the guy meant to do.

The second time, he'd made sure *she* had had enough to drink that she was in a pliant mood, and he'd orchestrated an encounter in one of their spare bedrooms while a party similar to this one, but a little drunker, took place in the apartment. Things had gone far enough that she felt sick, not just physically but about herself, when she finally flung the guy off her. She'd rushed to the master bathroom and thrown up.

She'd laid down the law the next day. She wasn't a possession to be shared with his friends or brokered as part of a deal. And when were they going to talk about acting school? A wedding date?

Now, clarity so bright it nearly blinded her shone from the tasteful mood lighting and the single, gaudy chandelier.

Rupert wasn't going to marry her, and he wasn't going to send her to acting school. And he wasn't going to stop offering her up to his friends. "I'm not doing it," she repeated.

Rupert crowded her against the wall like he used to do when he wanted her. She'd liked it, liked that he knew how to take charge and she didn't have to make decisions. She liked that he was older, too, probably because she'd never had a father.

Now his aggression had a different feel. "Look," he said. "You have nothing. You earn nothing." His words were a little slurred. "You do what *I* say."

Did she have a choice? If she made a scene, shouted out what was going on, one of the partygoers might take pity on her. They might call the police or give her a ride somewhere.

But where would she go?

She looked around and spotted Clint and Cookie, whispering together while looking in their direction. Cookie's facial expression was avid, curious, not compassionate.

No help there.

Despair and darkness rose up inside her, the kind she fought each day but a million times worse. Rupert was right. She did nothing, earned nothing, *was* nothing. Nothing but a former beauty queen.

And now, apparently, she was on the path to becoming a high-end hooker.

She thought of the sleeping pills in her medicine chest. There were plenty of them for her to end it, and knowing the danger, she kept three quarters of them locked in a drawer, the key hidden in yet another room in the house. Her thought was that the time it took to hunt down the key and unlock the extras would stop her from doing the unthinkable.

Although it obviously wasn't unthinkable. She'd accumulated the pills, after all, and not for no reason.

If you ever feel like Mom felt, you come to me.

She'd remembered Taylor's words so many times, but never with so much of a notion that she might need Taylor's help to stop her from swallowing a handful of pills.

Rupert waved to someone behind them, and she felt that possessive hand on her rear end again. Not Rupert's. Alistair's. "She's ready to go."

The clinking cutlery and the laughter and the murmur of conversation went on. Cookie and Clint were out of sight. None of the guests were paying attention to the hosts' little drama off in the corner.

A caterer's assistant gave them a quick, curious glance, but when Savannah caught her eye, she looked away.

Savannah was on her own, and three paths opened up before her. Least resistance: go with Alistair and playact her way through an encounter that made her cringe even thinking about it.

Excuse herself, go to her bathroom and swallow enough pills to at least knock herself unconscious.

Or think of Taylor and be strong.

She was out of practice at that last option, but she managed to channel her sister and swatted Alistair's hand away. "I'm not going anywhere with you."

Alistair and Rupert exchanged glances. Alistair looked affronted, and Rupert looked angry. Alistair turned and disappeared into the small crowd.

"If you don't go with him, you're out on the street. Tonight."

"You can't do that to me." Savannah reeled back and stared at him. "I live here."

"You live here because of my generosity, which has just about reached its limits. You go with him or you leave. And don't come back."

He looked…smug. Like he knew she didn't have the courage to leave and couldn't make it alone.

Taylor wouldn't put up with this. "I'll get my things."

His mouth dropped open.

She spun, went to their bedroom and looked around wildly, her heart hammering. Was she really going to leave him?

Maybe so. She unzipped her dress and stepped out of it, threw on a sweater and jeans. She fumbled around her underwear drawer, found the three one-hundred-dollar bills she kept for emergencies, and slipped them into her shoe. Then, from the back of her closet, she grabbed the go-bag she always kept ready. It looked like a big purse but was packed with compactly folded spare clothes and her important papers. She'd started keeping it after her last relationship had gone bad.

So on some level, she'd known this might happen.

She slipped on a warm coat and emerged from the bedroom to find Rupert standing outside, arms crossed. "You're not leaving."

"If the choice is being pimped by you or leaving, then yes, I am." Maybe he'd change his mind. Maybe he actually cared for her.

His jaw squared. "Then use the back door. And I'll take that." He tried to pull her purse off her shoulder.

She clutched the strap and stepped back. "No way! That's mine."

"Everything you have is mine." His voice held a sneer.

"Rupert, please? I need my ID." And her credit cards.

He let go of the strap. "Okay, but I'll be canceling your cards within the next ten minutes, so don't even think about making a withdrawal."

She stared at him, pain and sorrow pushing their way through her anger. "Don't do this, Rupert," she whispered. "I want to marry you. You know that. I don't want to be with other men."

His mouth twisted into more of a sneer. "You're nothing. Beautiful, but nothing."

The words hammered at her, and she thought again of the pills. She should have thrown them into her bag, but it was too late.

Tears blurred her eyes, but she brushed them away and spun toward the back door. The servants' door. Fitting, since a servant was all she'd ever been to him apparently.

And then she was outside on a cold night with nothing, almost, and no place to go.

Except to Taylor. Somehow, she had to get to Taylor.

CHAPTER TWO

CODY WAS PUTTING the finishing touches on breakfast omelets for himself and his nephew when he heard Alfie shout from upstairs.

"Mom! Dad!" Feet thundered down the stairs and the front door opened at the same time that voices sounded outside.

Doughnut, the chubby, vaguely-basset-hound-type island dog Ryan and Mellie had taken in for the winter, thumped his tail but didn't get up.

Cody turned down the heat, put a lid on the pan and walked to the window. Sure enough, his brother Ryan had just climbed out of Digger Hampton's pedicab and was hugging Alfie. Mellie was right behind him, and the three joined in a family hug.

That was nothing to take for granted. Until a short while ago, Ryan hadn't even known he had a son. Mellie had kept the news from him for various reasons, and once the truth was out and they'd worked through all that, they'd rekindled their relationship and married. Cody had offered to stay with Alfie during their two-week honeymoon, which they'd spent snorkeling and relaxing and sightseeing in the Algarve region of Portugal.

Cody had expected them to spend the night where they'd landed, in New York, and take the ferry to the island later today. He'd expected to enjoy a little more time hanging with Alfie and figuring out his options.

Oh, well.

He turned the heat on the breakfast all the way off—sitting there getting cold wouldn't be good for the eggs, but oh well to that too—and strode out into the yard. He shook Ryan's hand, gave Mellie a side hug and picked up suitcases to carry inside, nudging Ryan away from the heaviest ones. "You've been exerting yourself, man," he said, raising an eyebrow. "I haven't. Let me get those."

Once the luggage was inside and Digger was paid and tipped and waved away, they all gathered in the kitchen. Cody toasted bread, and cut the omelets into pieces and poured coffee and juice.

Doughnut came to sit at Mellie's feet, and she reached down and petted him. "I feel like I'm still on vacation," she said, stretching and eyeing the breakfast with an appreciative smile. "You stay as long as you want, Cody."

Cody looked at her quickly to see if she meant it.

Ryan noticed. "For real, man. Stay on with us."

Ryan, whose background with his biological and foster families was even more chaotic than Cody's, definitely got it. Being a foster kid could make you sensitive to that feeling of being kicked out of a home, or of being unwelcome in one.

And Cody appreciated the offer but didn't want to horn in on this newly formed family. "Thanks, but I may stay with Betty."

Ryan frowned. "Not sure that's going to work. She's renting the farmhouse out to a family while she and Peg go on their trip, isn't she?"

"Is she?" Cody had heard something about that but was hazy on the details. He was hazy on a lot of things these days. And he'd never been as close to their foster mother as Ryan had been.

"Sit down and have some coffee," Mellie said. She pulled out a bakery bag and waved it around, tickling Cody's nose with the fragrance of something fresh and sweet. Tickling his mind's eye with the memory of Taylor Harp's exasperated, un-made-up morning face. "I had Digger swing by the bakery on the way home. Didn't realize you'd be up and cooking already."

"Uncle Cody's a good cook," Alfie volunteered through a mouthful of omelet.

"That he is," Ryan said. "Always has been."

It was true: when the three foster brothers had come in late and hungry, Cody had always been the one to make them bacon and eggs or a bunch of sliders. He'd even learned to make fancier dishes, enchiladas and chilaquiles and Bolognese sauce, just because he'd found cooking fun and relaxing.

They talked generally then, about the trip, the travel, what Cody and Alfie had done in the meantime. Cody could read between the lines of his brother's and Mellie's comments: they'd had a wonderful time together, getting to know each other in their new roles as husband and wife.

Mellie and Alfie went off to dig through the suitcases to find the gifts they'd brought home, and Ryan and Cody cleared the table and washed dishes. "So, what are you gonna do now?" Ryan asked bluntly. No polite beating around the bush.

Cody appreciated that. "I'm not staying here, if that's what you mean."

"You can, man. We have Alfie, anyway. It's not like we have privacy."

"Yeah, but you need time to be a family."

Ryan started to protest, but Cody waved off his words. "And you have two bedrooms. We all need more space than that."

"I get it. But you're out of the army for good, right?"

Cody nodded as regrets started to swamp him. He'd loved being in the military. The army had given him a great life.

Until it hadn't.

He dried off the last pan, leaned against the counter and gestured toward the bakery box. "I talked to Taylor Harp this morning."

"When and where?"

"Don't worry. I made sure Alfie was sleeping like a log, and I texted Betty so she'd know I was out walking." He and Ryan and Mellie had agreed beforehand that was okay. One of the benefits of living on a small, safe island where people looked out for each other. "I walked downtown, and the bakery light was on. We talked a little."

"Yeah?"

He nodded. "She has a job opening."

"Hey, that's right," Ryan said. "A night baker. She can't find anyone. Are you thinking..."

He shrugged. "I would, but she's not exactly a fan of me."

"Because of Savannah." It wasn't a question.

"Yeah."

"Still…there's an apartment with the job, right?"

"Yeah."

"Might be worth convincing her to give you a chance. A cooking job for a night owl, with an apartment, seems like a no-brainer."

It did. Cody knew that. He wasn't normally a person to believe in signs from God, but this situation was a little too perfect to be an accident.

Perfect, except for the fact that Taylor hated him. Maybe it was time to straighten that out.

TAYLOR WASN'T ENTIRELY surprised when Betty, who ran the market next door, stopped in at the bakery on Saturday.

It was the day after Taylor's predawn conversation with Cody, and as small as Teaberry Island was, word was getting around. She'd already heard from two customers that Cody's brother was back from his honeymoon, so Cody wasn't needed as a babysitter anymore. He would probably be looking for a job on the island.

Someone else had mentioned that Cody couldn't stay in Betty's house, since she was renting it out while she was on her bucket list trip to Paris.

Taylor figured all of that was the likely reason behind Betty's visit, even though the woman pretended she had other ones. She had a library book for Taylor to return. She was putting in an order for supplies for the store, and did Taylor need anything? What kind of baked goods did Taylor think she should get to welcome the family of long-term renters who were arriving on Monday?

Taylor answered patiently, knowing Betty would get to the real reason quickly enough. She did. "So, what do you think about hiring Cody and having him take the apartment upstairs?" she asked.

"I think it's a bad idea." Taylor got busy bussing the tables that held the morning's last dishes and napkins.

"I thought he'd stay on with Ryan," Betty said, pulling out a chair and sitting down, "but he doesn't want to."

"We can't all have what we want." Taylor banged a couple of plates into her dish tub harder than she should have, making a clatter.

No way was she hiring Cody and letting him move in. The very thought of it made her chest feel hot and her fingers and toes feel cold.

Cody had had an effect on her from the moment she'd met him, that summer she and Savannah had spent on the island. She'd even gotten the feeling he liked her back during the two weeks that it was just her and Aunt Katy in the rented beach house. But, of course, as soon as Savannah had arrived, Cody had pushed Taylor aside and rushed to her sister, and they'd been inseparable for the rest of the summer.

Not that Taylor was surprised by that. She was used to Savannah getting all the boys. She hadn't let herself feel more than annoyance. She'd known she was too driven for a serious relationship, or at least, she'd thought so back then. She'd had plans.

But Savannah hadn't. Savannah had been looking for a man to save her since their mother's death, and she'd settled on Cody, who was only a boy, as a possible candidate.

When he'd taken advantage of Savannah, it had been a sobering experience for Taylor. She'd thought Cody was basically a good guy. And he was, in most ways. It was just that you couldn't trust men, even the nice ones.

Savannah hadn't learned the same lesson. In fact, Cody had been the first in a long line of men taking advantage.

Although Taylor felt Savannah had been foolish, and probably a willing participant, she still didn't forgive Cody for hurting her. Hurting Taylor, too, if the truth be told. No way was she giving shelter and a job to that man.

"You need the help." Betty watched Taylor wipe down tables. "You shouldn't be doing that kind of work around here. You should be in back making plans for those big orders you were so happy to get."

A knot formed in Taylor's stomach. Betty was right. Taylor had bitten off more than she could chew, making that big sales push to wedding planners and restaurants on the mainland, but the truth was, she hadn't expected so many to take the bait.

It was a good problem to have, she reminded herself. Really good. She'd manage somehow. "Things will get better once Misty gets back from her family trip."

"Okay, but she has school, and she's too young to work nights. She's not going to solve your problem."

"I have Ruthie to help with the cleaning. And I might ask Lolly to work more."

"You know that's not enough."

Taylor grabbed the broom and started sweeping the floor. She'd have to mop, too. Clean up in the back, and get set up for a whole day of baking the next day.

"You have no other applicants," Betty persisted. "And Cody is well qualified."

"He isn't a baker," Taylor said.

"He's *baked*," Betty said. "And you don't have room to be picky. No one else on the island is an experienced baker, either."

"I know, but… I just don't think I can."

In truth, she'd expected more of the islanders to apply, but as Mellie had pointed out before leaving on her honeymoon, Taylor was still a newcomer. She'd been on the island for two years, but she didn't know the island culture well. Most everyone was set in their ways, set in their family businesses. It wasn't as if there were a lot of idle housewives looking for night work. If anyone was willing to get up that early, they'd fish, make some real money.

Taylor had thrown in the apartment to sweeten the deal because she owned the building and she couldn't afford to pay much above minimum wage. But anyone who lived on the island was already settled in a house, with their family. And visitors, the few there were during the off-season, were on vacation. They didn't want to work nights in a bakery.

Cody was pretty much perfect, and he was pretty much the only option.

But her heart railed against hiring him, sheltering him, *seeing* him all the time as she'd have to if she gave him this opportunity.

Betty was glaring at her. "Listen to me, girl. If you're going to be a successful businesswoman, you have to get over this personal stuff. You can't let emotions run your business."

"Says the woman who shoved her own business into someone else's hands for three months last year." Then Taylor clapped her hand to her mouth and sat down across from Betty. The woman had been a mother figure to her since she'd arrived on the island, something she'd sorely needed since her own mother had abandoned the role. She was grateful to Betty, grateful beyond words. There was no call to be rude. "I'm sorry. It's not the same."

"Not really, but you're right. I shouldn't have curled up and forgotten about the business when Wayne died. I'd be in a better place financially if I hadn't done that. And emotionally, too. It doesn't do any good to wallow in your feelings. Didn't do me any good as a new widow, and doesn't do you any good as a…" She paused and looked at Taylor blankly. "I don't even know what it is between you and Cody. But letting it fester inside you isn't moving you forward."

"It's not anything *between* me and Cody. It's the way he hurt my sister."

"Not only that," Betty said as if Taylor hadn't spoken, "but it sounds like Cody will be on the island for a while. And it's a small place. You're going to see him all the time. If you hire him, you'll at least know what's going on with him. It'll be on your own terms."

Taylor thought about that. Thought about not hiring Cody, and seeing him everywhere, anyway, but unexpectedly. "If I hired him, I could put him on my own schedule. Is that what you're saying?"

Betty flashed her a grin. "Seize control, girl." Then her expression sobered. "You have the chance to be great. To put our island on the map, like Smith Island did with their cakes. Rival them, even."

"I don't know about that. They're already the state dessert of Maryland."

"They're the state cake. Who's to say we can't have the state pie?"

Taylor cracked up. "That's way bigger a delusion of grandeur than I'm capable of having. Mine is more like, I can make a go of this bakery and support myself?" *And Savannah if she needs it.* "How come you're so gung ho for Cody to work here, anyway? It's not all about me reaching for the stars. It can't be."

"I *want* you to reach for the stars and to make it," Betty said. "I like you, Taylor. I see a little bit of myself in you. The good and the bad. The talent and the emotional undermining of it."

"Wow." She'd never thought she was emotionally undermining herself. And she'd certainly never thought Betty had done that.

"How are you going to fill those orders without help?" Betty asked, her voice reasonable. "And how are you going to get help without Cody?"

Taylor bit her lip, thinking.

"Besides," Betty said, her voice softening, "I'm his mom in every way that counts. Something happened to Cody overseas. I don't know what it was, but it cut a piece of his soul out of him. I'd like to see him get that back."

That made Taylor curious, but she didn't ask questions. She didn't need to be wondering about Cody and his past.

Betty waved a hand around the bakery. "This place is special. Working here might be just what he needs."

That made Taylor happy, even as her thoughts swirled. She wanted the bakery to be a place of healing and was pleased that Betty saw it that way. "I'll think about it all," she promised as Betty stood.

"Good," Betty said. "Don't shoot yourself in the foot because of hurt feelings or a grudge you're holding."

"You're right about that." But Taylor had the feeling she *would* be shooting herself in the foot, some way. Whether she hired Cody or whether she didn't.

CHAPTER THREE

HE WAS OUT of other options, Cody reminded himself as he headed back in the direction of the Bluebird Bakery on Sunday afternoon. He had to convince Taylor Harp to take him on as an employee and tenant or leave the island.

Teaberry was one of the few remaining inhabited islands in the Chesapeake Bay. It was listed as being one mile wide and two and a half miles long, but that didn't give the picture of the messy, undulating coastline, with fingers of land poking out into the bay, and inlets bursting with fish and water life. It had been a wonderland to Cody and his two foster brothers, all city boys, who'd spent their adolescence on the island.

Teaberry's business district, if it could be called that, consisted of two blocks of shops on High Street, and two cross streets: School Lane, where the island's small elementary school sat on a tiny rise of land, and Library Lane, where the post office and, of course, the library were located. At the intersection of High and School was a small park where the crab festival, the Teaberry Tune-Up folk music concert and other events took place in the summer.

But you didn't really need a park when you could walk

out in any direction and be surrounded by nature. Houses on the island weren't close together, even the ones that could make a claim to being downtown, and they got more widely spaced as the roads diverged from downtown and became more rugged, shell-strewn dirt paths.

During the warm months, there'd be a few of the island's friendly free-range dogs here and there, but he didn't see any now. He guessed that people had taken them in for the winter, as Ryan and Mellie had taken in Doughnut.

Along the east side of High Street were a couple of shops that were closed during the off-season. Next to them were the hardware store and a hair salon. Across the stream that bisected the island was a medical clinic that hadn't been there when Cody was a teenager; back then, everyone had taken their scrapes and colds and broken toes to the living room of a retired doctor who'd lived on the tip of one of the island's small peninsulas. Anything more serious, you'd had to travel by boat or, worst case, helicopter, to the mainland.

At the center of the business district, set off by a row of fig trees on one side and a small cemetery on the other, was the only church on the island. Directly across from the church was the market, owned by Betty. And sandwiched between the market and a ramshackle old Victorian house was Cody's destination, the Bluebird Bakery.

The bakery had a Closed sign on the door, and the Help Wanted sign was still in the window. But he'd seen Taylor go inside the building, still dressed in her church clothes, and now the lights came on in the bakery.

She was in there. Almost certainly working. According to Betty, who'd filled him in on Taylor and on the bakery, Taylor worked twelve-hour days and more, seven days a week.

The thought of that didn't shock him, not exactly. Taylor had always been the super-serious type. She'd gotten a summer job when she and Savannah had visited the island, even though they'd only been here for a couple of months. What teenager did that?

Taylor, that was who.

He tapped on the door. When she didn't answer, he waited a good three minutes and then knocked again.

No answer. He went around the building and found the back entrance. Next to it was a small window through which he could see a rack of baking trays.

He knocked on the window, a firm rap.

There she was, looking out, her expression annoyed. She pointed to the door. A moment later, she opened it.

She was already out of her church clothes and wearing faded jeans, a T-shirt and an apron, her hair tied back. "What?"

"Can I come in, or do you want to talk on the doorstep?" As if to accentuate his words, a gust of cold wind swept through, blowing leaves and a couple of crab carapaces along the street, whipping at Cody's hat.

Her eyes narrowed. "I don't *want* to talk to you at all. But come in." Leaving him standing in the doorway, she turned and walked away.

Once he'd taken off his hat and closed the door behind him, he sniffed appreciatively at the kitchen smells of cinnamon and nutmeg. She couldn't have put in anything to bake in the few minutes she'd been here, but the spices lingered. She'd definitely turned on the ovens, though; it was warm. Although the kitchen was small, every surface shone.

Her success was a little intimidating. Mostly, though, it made him want to be a part of it, to help her grow this place.

She wiped the spotless counter and then leaned back against it, arms crossed in front of her. "You had something to say?"

"I see you still have that opening posted." He gestured toward the front of the shop.

She nodded.

"I'd like to officially apply for it," he said. When she opened her mouth, he held up a hand to stop what was surely a turndown. "Just as a temporary measure. A trial run, maybe a month."

"Why?"

He straightened his shoulders as if she were his drill sergeant and put his cards on the table. "There are exactly two jobs available on the island. There's a nanny gig out on the tip of Oyster Point, some new rich guy with a daughter. And there's this one."

She lifted an eyebrow, a smile tugging at the corner of her mouth. "I can see you as a nanny."

Clearly she was joking, but Cody wouldn't have turned the job down. "I spoke to the man. He wants a female, because his daughter is thirteen and needs a woman's influence."

"So this job is your only possibility. Except it isn't, really. Why don't you move off-island?"

He couldn't do that, and he couldn't tell her why.

Couldn't even explain it to himself, not really. "Not an option right now. I could possibly get a job on an oil rig, but not yet." Which was almost saying too much. "So…would you consider hiring me? And renting your spare apartment to me?"

She didn't say no right away. That was a good thing. He restrained the urge to turn on the charm, to smile and joke with her. That wouldn't work on Taylor.

Instead, he started enumerating his qualifications. "I've baked all kinds of breads and rolls in the army, mostly large batches. Some desserts, not many, but I'm a fast learner. I'm reliable and I have nothing else on my schedule, so I can work overtime if you need. I'm a night owl."

Her eyes were exceptionally green, and her brows drew together. "I didn't exactly get the impression you were consistent and reliable when we knew each other as teenagers," she said in her blunt way.

Was she going to hold ancient history against him? Sure, he'd been a little wild, and he'd taken Savannah on a few dates to escape his growing feelings for Taylor, but she hadn't blinked an eye at the time. Hadn't even seemed to care.

"If you're talking about the way I ran around fifteen years ago, I'm not the same person. Stuff happened during my time overseas." Stuff that had destroyed his confidence and made him unsure of who he really was, how reliable and good a person. "I don't go out and party, and I don't date."

Curiosity flared in her very pretty eyes. Great. She probably thought he'd had a manhood-threatening injury. Oh, well, if it got him the job…

"How about a two-week trial, and you don't live in?" she asked.

He thought about it for a few seconds and then shook his head. "Two weeks is too short a time, and I need a place to stay."

She sucked in a breath and let it out in a sigh. Her eyes softened. "I *was* just at church hearing about forgiveness and renewal and fresh starts," she said slowly.

He wanted to pump his fist in the air, but that would make her mad. So he was silent, letting her think it through. Though he wanted the job, needed it, she had to decide for herself.

"Let me mull it over while I take you on a walk-through of the apartment," she said. "It needs some work. It might not be what you want."

Considering that his alternatives were horning in on the honeymoon phase of his brother's marriage or sleeping in the streets, he was pretty sure that it would be just fine.

She led him to the entryway and up a steep flight of inside stairs, and he made a heroic, nearly successful effort not to admire her shapely figure. At least, no more than any other guy would have done. He wasn't *gawking*.

At the top were two doors, one on either side.

"That's mine," she said, gesturing toward the door on the right. "And this would be yours. Or...whoever's that I hire."

"Right." He understood that she was still thinking about it. She was making that abundantly clear.

They walked into an apartment with scuffed wood floors and impressive woodwork. Front room, kitchen with a dining area behind that, bedroom and bath in the back. As she explained the layout, she accidentally brushed her hand against the overhead woodwork.

A big chunk of it cracked loose and started to fall on her.

He rushed forward and caught it, pushing her out of harm's way with a hip.

She staggered a little and so did he, and then he lowered the wood to the ground.

"Whoa," she said shakily. "Thank you. I didn't realize that was loose."

He studied the piece and then the arched doorway from which it had fallen. "I could fix that."

"You're a handyman too?"

"In my free time. I like to stay busy."

She came over and stood beside him, studying the wood and the place where it had broken off. "I'll need to get this place inspected for safety. I hope that's the only problem, but we can't feel one hundred percent sure."

"One hundred percent is for wimps." He smiled to let her know he was joking, that he took safety seriously. "All kidding aside, I can tell the structure is basically sound. This breakoff was probably a once-in-a-lifetime thing, but I can look over the woodwork for you."

"Why would you be willing to do that?"

"So I don't get beaned in the night?" He tried for a joking tone.

"Good point." She frowned. "It's got to be a safe place or no one can stay here."

"Show me the rest of it."

As they walked around, he looked at the various

views of the Chesapeake and felt something loosen inside him. Regardless of Taylor or the job, he'd have liked this apartment. It had the feel of being a lighthouse, up off the ground, windows all around. He had developed a dislike of closed-in dark places during that misty, confused time overseas.

And maybe he could help her fix things up. Staying busy, day and night, would help him make sure that his forgotten past stayed forgotten. Maybe even let him sleep. He didn't have many possessions, just whatever he'd been able to fit into the well-used car he'd bought as soon as he'd arrived back in the states. He'd have to borrow some furniture from Mellie and Ryan. Having seen Mellie's crowded basement, he figured that wouldn't be a problem.

He looked out the window that faced the old Victorian. "Do you own that place, too?"

"No." She looked a little wistful. "I'd like to buy it and fix it up to actually live in one day, if I ever…" She looked away with the slightest little sigh. "Well. I have plenty to focus on here in this building, as you've seen."

If she ever what? Married and started a family? Why hadn't she done that yet, anyway? He looked over at Taylor. "I like the place, and I can work on it, fix it up," he said.

She lifted her hands, palms up, and laughed a little. "You've given me so many reasons to hire you," she said.

"Then do it! As a trial."

"You'll live up to your responsibilities? Be flexible?"

He nodded, wondering. Did he have the job?

"Trial run it is," she said, and they shook on it.

Now to convince her to keep him on long enough to exorcise his demons and get back on his feet.

SAVANNAH SAT INSIDE the Bluebird Bakery, mostly hidden by a potted plant, watching her sister.

She wanted nothing more than to throw herself into Taylor's arms, but she held back. The years and what she'd been through had made her cautious.

Taylor was doing well, obviously. The bakery was darling, with its blue-checkered café curtains that let in the bright sunshine, the fragrance of bread and muffins, the little ceramic bluebirds on each table. The meaning of the bird motif wasn't lost on Savannah, but truthfully, she was surprised. Birdy, their mother, had abandoned them in the worst way possible. Why was Taylor honoring her in the name and decor of her bakery?

But she couldn't think about that just now. Now she had to see if her sister would accept her and give her a hand even after she'd fallen out of touch.

Taylor greeted each customer in a friendly way, got their food and took their money with scary efficiency, and moved them along. She had always been a good cook, and apparently, she was good at running a business, as well.

But she was tense. Savannah could tell that.

Was it because of how busy she was as a newish entrepreneur? Or was it chronic, just their childhood, the things that had made them both tense?

Whatever. It had made them resourceful, too. Savannah looked down at her trusty go-bag and ran her fingers through her hair, hoping the fact that she hadn't washed it for two days wasn't too apparent.

She wasn't up to Rupert's standards, but she'd pass for okay-looking on Teaberry Island.

She hadn't heard from Rupert during the short time her cell phone had worked. She'd known he would cut it off as soon as he thought of it, or worse, that he'd use the GPS to track her. When the phone had gone dark, she'd been relieved at the choice he'd apparently made to wash his hands of her. Once she was even a few blocks and a few hours away from him, she'd felt a sweet rush of relief, wind beneath her out-of-practice wings.

That had been followed by some exhausting resourcefulness, but she'd made it here.

The bakery rush seemed to have ended. The last customer walked out the door with a wave and a few friendly words. Taylor was going to notice Savannah in a moment, so she'd better take the initiative herself. She went to the counter. "Ma'am, I'd like to try one of those teaberry muffins," she said, her voice breaking just a little on the last word.

Taylor's head shot up, and their eyes locked. For a moment, Savannah felt stark terror in her heart. What if Taylor shunned her, held all those ignored phone calls and unanswered letters against her?

"It's you!" Taylor rushed around the counter and pulled her into a hug that felt like the best thing Savannah had ever experienced in her life.

She hugged her sister back. Sweet relief. Taylor still loved her. Taylor would help her find her way again.

"What have you been doing? How'd you get here?

Oh my goodness, sit down, sit down." Taylor let go of her and nudged her toward a table. She hurried to the door and flipped the sign to Closed, waving away the couple who were approaching. "Sorry, emergency," she said out the door.

The two turned away, looking disgruntled.

"You don't have to turn away business," Savannah protested.

"It's almost closing time. Let me get you something." Taylor bustled behind the counter, bringing out tea and a muffin, then a coffee for herself. Taylor still remembered that she liked her tea with cream, and for some reason, that made Savannah's eyes well up.

She wasn't too teary to eat the muffin, though. She devoured it in three bites and wiped her mouth.

Taylor sat back in her chair, sipping coffee and watching her. "You're not okay," she said.

"I've had a couple rough days, but I'm fine," she said.

"What do you mean? What happened?" Taylor frowned. "And why didn't you call? You know I would've come and gotten you."

"He cut off my phone." There was no need to name the "he." Taylor didn't know Rupert, but she knew the type of man Savannah hooked up with. "It's fine. I found places to stay."

"Safe places?"

Savannah nodded. "I stayed at a church shelter the first night. Then a little motel outside Wilmington. I did okay, but…" She didn't want to admit that she was almost broke. Nor that she'd chosen to spend her limited funds on a few more items of clothing rather than on food or decent shelter. "I would have figured out something else. I don't want to impose on you or mess up your life, but I felt like…" Her throat tightened until she couldn't get the words out.

Taylor was watching her quietly. "Like Mom?"

She nodded. "Like Mom."

"Then you were right to come. I'll—"

Loud banging on the door made them both jump. Savannah looked, and then stared out the door. "Is that…"

Taylor nodded, looking less than sure of herself for the first time. "Cody and Ryan," she said.

Savannah leaned back and stared as Taylor walked over to the door. She hadn't seen either of the foster brothers since that summer when they'd all been teenagers. Ryan had grown out of his awkwardness, gotten handsome. And Cody…

Cody had always been the best-looking boy on the island, and it seemed like he was now the best-looking man. She and Taylor had both fallen for him that summer they'd spent here, although of course, nothing had come of it.

Now there was something haunted in his expression, the way he carried himself, that struck a chord with Savannah.

Taylor opened the door. "You can take the back stairs," she said without holding it wide enough for them to come in.

"I'll pull the truck around." Ryan returned to the street and got in a small pickup.

"And I'll move my car." Cody glanced past Taylor

and saw Savannah. He did a double take. "Is that you, Savannah Harp?"

"Yeah." She stood and went to him, hugged him. She'd always liked Cody. She should have, considering the fact that he was such a decent guy. Better than most of the ones she'd met since.

But what was his connection to Taylor? She looked at her sister.

"He's moving in," Taylor said gruffly, then turned to Cody. "And you might want to get started."

"Sure." He gave Savannah a little wave. "Good to see you," he said and then strode away toward the side of the building.

Taylor watched him, her shoulders square.

Savannah hugged her sister from behind. "He's moving in with you? That's so cool!" Taylor was so independent that it was surprising to picture her as half of a couple. But then again, she didn't know Taylor that well anymore. "I'm happy for you."

"No, no, you've got it wrong. He's moving into the other apartment, upstairs. He's going to work for me. Looks like Ryan brought some furniture for him to use."

"Oh." That made more sense. Savannah nodded, swallowed. "So…can I stay with you? I know it's a lot to ask, but I was hoping for a little bit of refuge to try and put my life back together. I want to get strong for myself. Stay away from men."

"Good. And of course." Taylor hesitated. "You can, for a little while. But my apartment's tiny. And honestly…" She trailed off.

"What?"

"I'd worry about you and Cody, especially if you think you'd want to work here. You said you wanted to stay away from men."

"Oh, Taylor." Savannah sat back and tried to think of how to soothe Taylor's anger about the past. Savannah had bent the truth, trying to excuse herself for some seriously bad behavior. But she couldn't think of how to explain it in a way that would make sense to Taylor. In a way, her older sister was far more innocent than she was. "What happened wasn't Cody's fault, or not entirely. And it's over and done. I have no interest in him."

She could see Taylor wasn't buying it. How could Savannah explain the worlds she'd lived in, what second-rank beauty pageants and third-rate modeling had been like? How many men there'd been between a high school summer love and now?

She couldn't, so she didn't try. "Anyway, I'm not a cook. I wouldn't be much help around here. Know of any other jobs on the island?"

Savannah was seriously asking, but Taylor snorted. "You know how tiny it is. And how low the population is when it's not tourist season." And then her face brightened. "Although…wait a minute. I just might know of something. How are you with kids?"

"Inexperienced, but how hard can it be?" she asked, picturing a cute, cooing baby. Maybe working with a little one, or a roomful of them, would push back the darkness that kept trying to encroach on her.

Famous last words.

CHAPTER FOUR

AT 4:00 A.M., Taylor half walked, half stumbled out of her apartment. She and Savannah had stayed up past midnight, talking. Now she felt like her eyes were swollen shut.

A dark shape rose up on the stairs, and she shrieked.

The form backed away. "Sorry, sorry." It was Cody. "I didn't have a key to downstairs, so I waited here. Didn't mean to scare you."

"It's fine. Let's go." Taylor felt awkward and covered it with a brusque tone. "We have a lot to do before the bakery opens at six thirty."

She led the way down the stairwell, lit with a single dim light. Cold air blew in through the edges of the downstairs door, making it rattle. She unlocked the bakery door and flipped on the light.

She was sure she looked her absolute worst, on four hours of sleep and with no makeup. At her best, she was what people called *cute*. At 4:00 a.m., anyone who saw her might have other, less kind words to say. But working in a kitchen, there was no point in dolling yourself up. She usually slipped upstairs right before the bakery opened to wash her face, change her shirt and put on a little makeup. Terrifying the customers wasn't good for business.

Cody apparently woke up handsome. His hair was a little mussed, and he hadn't yet shaved, but the stubble just made him look like a movie star. It figured.

She pulled back her hair, put on a hairnet and handed him one, then turned to wash her hands. "Our most popular item is scones, so we'll start with that," she said. She showed him where flour, sugar, baking powder and salt were, and the proportions in which to toss them into the large mixer bowl. She pulled butter out of the freezer. "We freeze it and grate it, or the scones won't be the right texture," she explained, and showed him how. He mixed while she started batter for teaberry muffins.

"I think it's ready," he said a few minutes later.

She came over to check. "Perfect. Now, heavy cream." She pulled it out of the fridge. "Eggs, vanilla. We'll mix that up, and then do a couple different add-ins. Teaberries for one batch, and for the other..." She paused, thinking.

"Lemon," he suggested.

"Lemon poppy seed. People love that." The flavor decided, she showed him how to mix in the wet ingredients without overworking the batter, how to form the dough into disks and cut wedges. She explained the importance of refrigerating the formed scones for a bit before baking. "I usually do half an hour," she said, "but we're behind, so fifteen minutes will do."

"Sorry. I've held you back."

"You gotta learn. We'll put you behind the counter, and all the ladies will be fine with things being slow."

Her cheeks went hot as soon as she said it, and she looked at his face. "Sorry, that was objectifying you."

"It's okay."

She liked that he didn't pretend he didn't know what she meant. He was gorgeous and had probably benefitted from that all his life. Certainly, when they'd been teenagers, his looks had been one reason he and Savannah had been pushed together. Savannah was the female equivalent of him in terms of attractiveness, whereas Taylor was just...not.

A distant memory surfaced, more a feeling than an event: the day she'd realized he had switched his affections from her to her sister. Even then, she hadn't been shocked, but it had definitely hurt. She'd thought he was different.

She refocused on the task in front of them, showed him how to mix up muffins. When it was time, they brushed the scones with more heavy cream and slid them into the rotating rack oven alongside the muffins.

"And now we have twenty minutes to get presentable," she said. "People will be at the door at six thirty sharp, and we need everything ready to go by then." She forced a tired smile. "Eventually, once you've learned the ropes and the recipes, I'll leave you to the night and early morning baking, and I'll handle the daytime. For now, though, I'd like you to work some daytime hours, too, see how the business operates."

He nodded, and they both trotted upstairs. Taylor tiptoed past Savannah, who was sleeping on the couch, and made her way to her bedroom.

She could have taken a little extra care with her makeup, or put on a cuter-than-usual shirt, but she didn't. Her pride wouldn't allow it. On a small, gossipy island, people would notice and suspect the reason.

It wasn't that she *liked* Cody. But more that she didn't want to appear pathetically inadequate working beside him. However, if she primped and then he went for Savannah, it would be an echo of her teenage humiliation. No way was she going to do anything to bring that on.

When she came out of the shower, ready to go downstairs, Savannah stirred. "You need help?" she asked sleepily.

She looked stunning, even just getting out of bed. Hair tousled perfectly, skin flawless. No shadows under *her* eyes.

Some people just got extra doses of the genetic endowment of beauty, and Savannah was one of them. Taylor was used to that, resigned to it; she even saw where Savannah was sometimes at a disadvantage because all that people could see was her beauty.

"No, I'm fine. Go back to sleep. You need to rest up for your interview."

"Right." Savannah leaned back and watched Taylor. "Can't believe you get up this early every day."

"I love it," Taylor said simply. "And…" She consulted the clock on the wall. "I've got scones to get out of the oven before they burn."

"They smell fabulous. I'll be down soon to score a couple of them."

And as for Taylor, she was about to see how Cody did facing the public.

CODY HADN'T EXPECTED to be working the counter, but after just an hour in the bakery, he realized it was inevitable. Not because she thought he'd impress the ladies, though he did like the idea that Taylor found him good-looking. But because in a small business, everybody did everything.

They were too busy, and were working too closely together, to allow him to stay behind the scenes. Taylor would come in the kitchen or call back and ask him to help her carry something out, or to bring something. Then he'd end up answering a customer's question, or trying to. "Were these baked today?" was a common one, and he did know the answer to that.

And then Taylor had to run to check on something, because she truly was the skilled one in their team. And after a short lesson, he found he could ring things up pretty well.

Pretty well, that is, until a man he'd never expected to see again walked into the bakery.

"Heard you were back in town," Manson said. He gave a disgusted look around the bakery. "Bit of a comedown, from the 82nd Airborne to a shop cashier."

Manson wasn't wrong about the comedown, and Cody didn't fault him for the attitude, either. What Cody had done to him had been downright mean, and all out of his own cockiness. "We all do what we can to scratch out a living," he said. "This is what works for me now. Can I get you something?"

"Yeah, you can get me something," Manson said. "One of those cinnamon rolls. And this time, stay away from my woman."

Cody raised his hands like stop signs. "Never meant

to come close." He slid a cinnamon roll into a bakery bag, hoping Manson wanted his order to go.

"Well, you *are* close to her," Manson said. "A little too close."

At that moment Taylor came out of the back. "Oh, hey, Manson," she said, and came around the counter to give him a side hug and kiss his cheek. "How come you're not on the water?"

"Heard you had a new employee," he said. "Wanted to check him out."

"Oooohhhh." Taylor looked from Manson to Cody and back again. "You two know each other?"

"We've met," Cody said diplomatically. Apparently, Taylor hadn't realized that Manson had a jones for her sister that long-ago summer, but Cody had. It hadn't stopped him from moving in on her.

Now, with both Taylor and Manson living on the island, it looked like the two of them had hooked up. Cody didn't see it. Taylor was so cool, whereas Manson was a bit of a jerk.

He toyed with the idea of asking her later: What's a nice girl like you doing with a guy like him?

Manson put a possessive arm around her. "Am I going to see you tonight?"

She shook her head. "Too much going on. Besides, isn't it your poker night?"

Interesting. They knew each others' schedules. Did that mean they were serious about one another? Cody found he didn't like that idea.

"I'd skip it for you, babe." Manson gave her a hard

kiss on the mouth and then strode out, walking like an Old West gunslinger.

"You would not," Taylor said to his retreating back. Then she came toward Cody, rolling her eyes. "Guess he wanted to stake his claim on me in front of you."

"Does he *have* a claim?" Cody pretended not to be too interested in the answer to that question.

"Not a claim. We date some." Taylor knelt to move some cookies around in the bakery case. "Slim pickings on the island, and he's a nice guy."

"Is he, though?"

"Pretty nice," she said with a shrug.

Cody's shoulders relaxed, but not all the way. She didn't seem too attached to Manson, and that was good; on the other hand, she *did* date him, which could lead to something more serious.

But he had nothing better to offer her and no business interfering. He needed to drop the topic.

Just then two women walked in the door, probably a mother-daughter pair. "I brought Ruthie for her job," the older woman said.

"Oh, great. Hi, Ruthie. This is Cody. He's working here now."

"Hi." The thirtyish woman's flat-sounding voice made Cody suspect a cognitive impairment.

"You know where the broom is. I want you to sweep the whole floor, back and front," Taylor said.

The woman nodded and started to sweep. Taylor watched her for a moment, then stepped back to stand beside the mother. "She can work for a couple of hours today if that's okay with you," she said. "We need a good dose of Ruthie's sweeping. She's so careful. Have you met Cody Cunningham?" She started to introduce them.

But the woman waved the introduction away. "I've known this young man for years," she said. "I'm Peg, Betty's friend."

"Oh, hey!" Recognizing her now, he held out a hand to shake hers, and the handshake turned into a quick hug. "You're the one who's headed out to France with Betty."

"That's right." She frowned. "Ruthie's brother is coming to the island to take care of her. I'm hoping that will go okay."

"We'll all watch out for her," Taylor said. "There are so many people on the island who love Ruthie. She'll be fine. And you'll have a wonderful time."

"I hope so." Peg's worried gaze followed her daughter as she swept, back and forth, back and forth, intently focused on the job.

"It might even be good for her," Taylor continued. "I talked to Mellie, and between us, we're going to have Ruthie working every day for at least a couple of hours. That'll give Tom a break and keep Ruthie busy. And the bakery will benefit from the extra cleaning."

"You're a good person, honey, and I thank you," Peg said. "I'd better run and do my errands while I have a little time to myself."

After she left, Taylor met his eyes. "Peg hasn't had it easy," she said. "But speaking of easy, you're done for the day. The bakery's quiet in the afternoon."

Cody appreciated her thinking of him, but he also

saw the weary expression in her eyes. She'd be staying around, doing more baking, he suspected. Did she ever get time off? And was her only other help Ruthie, who would probably always require some amount of supervision?

He'd try to take some of the burden off her, he decided. He'd try to ensure that she got at least a little time off.

He'd like to see her old smile back in her eyes. Probably a misplaced desire, but he couldn't deny it.

CHAPTER FIVE

SAVANNAH WAS NERVOUS, applying for a job for which she had zero qualifications. But she was also desperate. She wanted, maybe even needed, to stay on the island, near Taylor. But she needed for it not to be *with* Taylor, in Taylor's tiny apartment. They loved each other, but they were no longer accustomed to each other. In fact, although they were sisters, they'd rarely lived together once Mom had died. They had some issues and needed space.

She called on her inner pageant queen as she disembarked from Digger's pedicab, paid and tipped him, and approached the front door of a big, sprawling house. It looked like something Frank Lloyd Wright might have designed, the way it blended into the landscape, all windows and low lines.

The red wooden front door opened, and rather than the housekeeper or servant she'd half expected, there was the man himself. She knew because she'd researched him online.

Hank Robertson had a friendly, intellectual look, with glasses and straight, slightly messy brown hair. He was bigger than you could notice in pictures. Forty-something, dressed in high-quality, L.L.Bean-type clothes. A very slight paunch.

He looked at her and his face fell.

That wasn't a reaction she was used to. She usually got double takes and smiles.

"Come in, come in." His voice was deep and hearty, and he'd quickly recovered from the apparently unpleasant shock of seeing her. "We'll talk in my study."

She introduced herself, gave him a firm handshake and then followed him through the house. It was nicer than Rupert's showpiece, because it looked like you could actually kick off your shoes and relax on the comfortable furniture or leave a paperback facedown on the coffee table, as someone had actually done in a room they breezed by.

She had a moment's misgiving as they got farther away from the escape hatch of the front door. She knew facts about him—he was an executive in the building industry, and active with a couple of charitable organizations—but what did she really know about his character? If he turned out to be a predator, she was out of luck.

You're fine, she reassured herself. In addition to researching him online, she'd gotten Taylor to ask around. At least three people who knew him said he was a good guy and could be trusted.

She shouldn't assume Hank shared the bad qualities of men in her past. "Did you build the house?" she asked.

"I did." He didn't volunteer any more information.

In his study, he gestured her to the chair in front of

the big desk while he sat behind it. He had her résumé pulled up on the computer that was off to the side.

"It looks like your professional experience is limited to modeling," he said.

"That's right. I've been around kids, though."

"In what capacity?"

She had practiced how to answer this. "I mentored the teenage models at my agency, helped them acclimate to the environment," she said. "And I babysat." She didn't add that she babysat only rarely, watching a friend's baby or toddler. "How old is the child in question?"

"She's thirteen."

Savannah tilted her head to one side. "And you work from home."

"Yes."

"Well then…why do you need a live-in if you work from home?"

He looked affronted that she'd ask that question. "Travel," he said. "I'm away a couple of times per month."

"But can't you get someone just for those times?"

He let out an exasperated-sounding sigh and leaned toward her. "It sounds like you don't actually want the job."

"No, I do, I do!" She straightened. "I just feel like I should understand the situation and your needs to see if we're a good fit."

He nodded. "Nadine needs consistency. Her mother was…inconsistent."

Was. "Is she…still living?"

"Yes." He glanced toward one of the bookcases, and

she saw a picture of a striking blonde with her arm around a young child.

"Is that her?"

He nodded.

Savannah leaned closer to study the picture. "She's beautiful. And Nadine is a real cutie."

"In my experience, good looks can be somewhat superficial. She hasn't visited Nadine in a year."

"Oh, no." Savannah's heart twisted with sympathy. Birdy had abandoned her and Taylor in a sense, but while she'd been living, she'd loved them fiercely. "Have you had other helpers, then?"

"A couple. They didn't work out."

He was clearly a man of few words. And might very well be difficult to work with, too. "Well, then, can you tell me what the job would involve?"

He nodded. "Cooking and light housekeeping, for starters."

"I can do that," she blurted, even though she'd barely done either one in her life.

"Good. We need to eat healthier food. The main thing, though, is to be a presence in Nadine's life. Help her with her homework, talk to her, take her to do things on the island. It seems like the moment she gets off the school boat, she's playing games on her phone, and that's about all she does. She's…" He frowned and looked at his hands. Large hands. "She's not doing well, and she's not always connecting with me. She needs a woman."

"Why a woman in particular?"

Hank lifted his hands, palms up. "She dyed her hair blue and then cried for hours because she didn't like how she looked. I just don't know what to do in that kind of situation."

Savannah almost smiled. "I can see why a woman would be helpful with that. When you say she's not doing well, what do you mean?"

He shook his head. "Friends, puberty, extracurriculars. She misses her old school and friends. She feels like she doesn't fit in."

Savannah couldn't tell if they were talking about a normal teen girl or a seriously troubled one. Then again, the line between the two was a thin one. Most troubles felt serious to a teen girl. "Seems like the island could be cliquish. I'm not from here, but I know a few people and might be able to figure out what there is for a young girl to do."

"That's where I'm not skilled," he admitted. "Also, she blames me for the move and for…everything else in her life."

Savannah thought back to how she'd acted out with Mrs. Williams. "It's not your fault, most likely," she said. "But an outsider can be helpful."

"That's what I'm hoping," he said. "Why do you want this job? You're…" He trailed off.

"I'm what?"

"So attractive, frankly. Why the career change?"

That he thought she was attractive gave her a little *thrum* in her belly. A lot of people thought she was attractive, but this man seemed like more of a challenge to win over.

"I need to get away from that world," she said firmly. No need to mention that she'd *been* away from it for a couple of years, except for the occasional isolated gig. By model standards, at age twenty-nine and weighing one hundred thirty pounds, she was old and fat.

He stood.

Uh-oh. She'd lost her chance.

"I would really like to give this a try," she said, trying not to sound as desperate as she felt. "I'd like a chance to make a difference in a young girl's life. My sister and I…we lost our mom at about that age, and I know how hard it can be."

His face softened a little. "I'm sorry to hear that."

"Thank you." She pinched the skin between her thumb and forefinger, her usual strategy for keeping her emotions inside herself, and looked away.

"Let me show you the quarters," he said, "see if you'd find them acceptable. While we talk a little more."

They walked through a state-of-the-art kitchen and into a suite of rooms that was basically its own apartment: sitting room, bedroom, bathroom. The views of the bay were spectacular. "I'd love to live here," she said. "This is amazing."

"I'm…glad you like it."

"Are you offering me the job?"

He looked out at the bay and then turned back to her. "If your references check out, yes. For a trial period. I have a trip in two weeks, and if you and Nadine and I are all comfortable with the arrangement by then, I'll leave her with you and we'll go forward. If not, I will take her with me and you can…move on."

That was blunt, but she liked that. "Sounds fair," she said. "When do you need me to start?"

"ASAP," he said. "Again, if your references check out. I'll tell Nadine about you tonight, and if you can move in tomorrow, you can meet her after school."

"Perfect," she said. She reached out and shook his hand again.

He held on to her hand and looked into her eyes. "She's my world," he said. "Don't damage her."

It was the most human he'd been. "I'll do my best with her," she promised, even as nerves squeezed her stomach.

It sounded like Nadine was really struggling. And Savannah would be in charge of her, even though she really had no idea what she was doing. Hopefully, this wouldn't be a disaster.

On Thursday, Taylor followed Savannah toward Hank's big, modernist home, her arms loaded with Savannah's things. More Taylor's than Savannah's, really; she'd given her sister a few things to personalize the apartment and a few items of clothing that might not swim too much on Savannah. "I'm glad you found a job," she said, "but it seems like you barely got here."

"I feel that way, too," Savannah said. "You should be glad, though. That apartment over the bakery is too small for both of us."

"*This* place is plenty big," Cody said. He was bringing up the rear, nodding toward Hank's mansion.

Something about the three of them together reminded Taylor of the summer they'd spent as teens. There had been that golden moment when Cody and Taylor were starting to fall in love, and Savannah had arrived, and Taylor had felt proud to show him off to her sister.

She hadn't even had time to tell her sister they were a couple before Cody had spun in Savannah's direction, dropping Taylor like she'd been a practice round before the real thing. For the sake of her pride, Taylor had hung around with the two of them some.

Now it was different...but not entirely.

Even though both Savannah and Taylor had told Cody there was no need for him to come along, he'd insisted. Which annoyed Taylor quite a bit. Why was Cody so interested in Savannah, after their summer romance had ended in a mixed-up fizzle?

But she knew why. Every man was interested in Savannah.

The wind whipped from across the bay, and Taylor let a box slide to the ground and clapped a hand to her head to keep her hat from blowing away. Her cheeks felt frozen. Ahead of her, Savannah turned and waited, shivering. "I didn't know it got so cold here."

"I thought you were a tough New Yorker." Cody's tone was teasing. He knelt and swept up the box Taylor had set down. "Seriously, we're supposed to get six to twelve inches of snow sometime in the next few days."

"I can handle a New York snowstorm," Savannah said, "because there's always something to do. But here? Do the ferries stop running?"

"They do." Was Savannah going to be a prima donna, complaining of boredom on Teaberry Island? The place was beautiful, but a little wild. You had to be resourceful to get through the cold part of winter, and the truth was, Savannah might not have it in her. "Aside from a helicopter to take out medical emergencies, we're stuck for a few stretches each winter. Let's go inside," she added.

"Sure." Savannah sounded reluctant. She seemed to be having second thoughts about this job and this place.

"You're sure you want to take this on?" Taylor tried to hide her panicky feeling. She'd just regained her sister again after a lot of years apart. "All kidding aside, I can try to make room for you in my place if you'd rather stay there."

"No, I won't do that to you," she said. "Let's go. He told me to use this entrance."

"Servants' entrance?" Cody muttered behind them.

"Shh," Savannah said as the door in question opened. Hank, a man Taylor had met once or twice, briefly, gestured them inside. A cell phone was pressed to his ear.

"This way." Savannah led them into a darling little apartment with windows looking out onto the snowy bay. Ice was starting to build up on the pilings, making a bleak but beautiful landscape.

It figured. Savannah, a newcomer with no money, had landed a cushy job and an apartment way nicer than Taylor's. She'd probably have her pick of men, too, with both Cody and Hank being part of the array of choices.

Whereas Taylor had Manson.

If that's how you feel, why are you even dating him? But she knew why. Manson was what she could get.

Scolding herself for her attitude, Taylor studied the sitting room. "Nice furniture," she said.

"It's basic, but it'll be a refuge from Nadine and

me." Hank had come back into the room. "You can do whatever you want to make it comfortable, Savannah. Hi, Taylor." He reached out and shook Cody's hand. "I don't think we've met."

"Cody Cunningham."

"Are you…" He gestured between Savannah and Cody.

"Just a friend of the family," Cody said.

Taylor turned away to conceal her eye roll. Did *everyone* have to automatically assume that Cody and Savannah were a couple?

Hank's phone buzzed, and he glanced at it. "Sorry, but I have to take this. Middle of a deal."

"By all means," Cody said in a slightly sarcastic tone.

Both Taylor and Savannah turned to him after Hank left the room.

"What's up with you?" Taylor asked.

He was looking after Hank. "Just wondering what line of work he's in."

"Something about business development and construction," Savannah said. She was moving boxes. "Lucky this is furnished. Since I basically have nothing."

"You let me know what you need." Taylor wanted to pursue Cody's emotions with him, to find out why he was copping an attitude, but now wasn't the time. "No kitchen?"

"I'll share it with the family. I'm doing some cooking for them."

"Do you know how?" Taylor asked. "It's not like we learned at our mother's knee."

Savannah snorted. "Come on. Birdy was a pro at boxed mac and cheese. Or actually, that was you. Birdy could burn water."

They exchanged wry glances. Taylor always felt guilty thinking unkind thoughts of her mother. Knowing Savannah had similar thoughts was a funny kind of comfort.

"Anyway, as for cooking, I'm as bad as she was," Savannah said, "but how hard can it be?"

That wasn't promising. "You can call me if you have any cooking questions," she said.

"I will."

Taylor glanced through the door of Savannah's new apartment, which was positioned off the kitchen. On the other side of that, she could see that Hank was winding up his call. "I'd like to talk to Hank for a minute," she said.

"You don't have to do the big sister thing." Savannah barely glanced up from the box she was unpacking. "I already vetted him online. And you told me everyone you asked vouched for him."

"Still, I want to. If you don't mind."

"I'd like to talk to him, too," Cody said.

They both turned to him. "Why?" Taylor asked.

"Just to make sure he's aware there's a man looking out for you," he said.

Taylor stared at him. The idea that he could take that kind of authority stunned her, and the fact that he'd want to filled her with a mix of annoyance and jealousy. She'd never in her life had a man try to take care of her and protect her.

Savannah propped a hand on her hip. "Look, my goal being here on Teaberry is to get confident and stay away from men. That means I'm here to do a job and nothing else. And I can handle whatever comes on my own, thank you very much."

Hank walked through the doorway. "What did I miss?"

Savannah spun to face him. "Nothing. These two are getting ready to leave."

"Uh…" Taylor realized she was being patronizing and that Savannah might not need any big-sistering, but come on. She'd taken care of her sister when they were young, and then that opportunity had been snatched away. No way was she leaving Savannah to the wolves again. "I'd like to talk to you for a moment. Alone," she added, glaring at Cody.

"Taylor…" Savannah sounded exasperated. "You don't have to do this. I'm fine."

"Of course," Hank said to Taylor. "My office is this way."

She followed him through the truly enviable kitchen, gleaming with brand-new appliances, a chef's six-burner stove with a built-in grill and a range hood, a stone chopping block, two sinks.

It would all be wasted on Savannah.

Why couldn't Taylor be a regular, unambitious person who could be content with a temporary, cushy job? Especially if it got her the opportunity to cook in a kitchen like this?

Unfortunately, she was ambitious in everything she did. She needed something to sink her teeth into, and for now, the Bluebird Bakery was that thing.

Hank's office was all tasteful mahogany. Books that looked like they'd actually been read lined the walls, and the desk was scattered with a few papers and a laptop. Clearly he worked from here. It wasn't just for show.

She sat in the chair he indicated, and he sat behind the desk.

"Listen," she said, "Savannah will do a great job for you, but I…" She hadn't really considered how to put this. "She hasn't always had the best luck with men. I want to make sure you're not expecting—"

"I'm not," he interrupted. "For one thing, I'm raising a teenage daughter, and I'm conscious of setting a good example for her. For another…" He glanced toward the apartment. "She's an extremely attractive woman, and I'm sure I'm not her type."

Taylor felt a little embarrassed for him. He wasn't bad-looking. He looked…nice. Tall, which was in his favor, and he had all his hair. Glasses that made him look studious, a nice smile, a slight gut, but not a big beer belly like Manson. Older, but not out of range for a woman of Savannah's age. At least, most men wouldn't think so.

He was the kind of guy a woman like her might aspire to. She was like the female version of him in terms of looks. Cute, but not pretty. In decent but not great shape. Always praised for her nice smile.

Taylor and Hank would match. Too bad she wasn't in the least attracted to him, nor did he seem attracted to her.

A door slammed somewhere in the house. "Dad!"

A moment later, a girl of twelve or thirteen burst

through the office door. Corkscrew curls tipped with a little blue dye frizzing their way out of a purple scrunchie, thick glasses and a skinny physique, half girl, half woman.

Taylor remembered that awkward phase, because she'd seemed to be in it forever. Unlike her sister, who'd never even had an awkward minute.

The teen skidded to a halt when she saw Taylor.

"Taylor, I'd like you to meet my daughter, Nadine."

The teenager gave a small wave. No smile.

"Nadine, this is Taylor. She's the sister of Savannah, the woman who's going to be staying here helping out."

Nadine pressed her lips together.

Taylor needed to get out of the middle of this. "Hi. Nice to meet you. I'd better check on my sister." As she left she heard Nadine say, "She's *here* already?"

"Come meet Savannah," Hank said, and their footsteps followed Taylor across the kitchen.

In the apartment, Cody was helping Savannah move a desk. They both looked up once it was in place, and seeing Hank and Nadine behind her, Savannah stood and pushed back her hair. "Hi, I'm Savannah," she said, striding across the floor and shaking Nadine's hand.

"Hi." Nadine looked to the side, obviously less than thrilled.

"I'm Cody." He gave Nadine a little wave. "And I'd like to talk to your father for a minute."

Hank nodded, and the two men walked out into the hall.

Savannah rolled her eyes, looking like a teen herself. Then she shook it off and smiled at Nadine.

"It's nice to meet you. I'm excited to be living here for a little while and—"

"It's just a trial," Nadine said flatly. "Dad told me you might not work out."

Savannah looked the slightest bit flustered. "Right. I'm hoping it will, though."

Nadine shrugged and pulled out her phone.

Savannah gave Taylor a *help* look.

"Were you glad school was canceled?" Taylor asked the girl, trying to make conversation with a topic of interest to her.

"Duh," Nadine said without looking at either of them.

Taylor spoke without thinking. "I can see why your dad thinks you need some extra support. Maybe with social skills?"

Nadine looked up quickly, eyebrows shooting up.

"Taylor...that's not helpful," Savannah said.

Nadine seemed about to make a snarky response, but her phone buzzed. She looked at it and her face lit up. "School's canceled tomorrow, too," she said.

Savannah looked like she'd just been sentenced to the lion's den. Taylor didn't envy her being stuck here all day with a sulky, unpleasant teen she'd just met.

Cody was still talking intently with Hank, just out of earshot.

"He's hot," Nadine commented, nodding toward Cody, and looked at Savannah. "Is he your boyfriend?"

Of course it hadn't occurred to the girl that Taylor and Cody were together. Cody and Savannah matched, both gorgeous.

"No, uh-uh. We're friends." Savannah was frowning

as if she didn't know how to deal with Nadine. Which, of course, she didn't. Maybe this job had been a bad idea. Maybe it wouldn't last beyond the trial period.

Taylor couldn't worry about that, not now. "Hey, Cody," she said loudly, "If you're through playing patriarch, we have baking to do."

Everyone looked at her like she'd been rude. Probably she had. Talk about a lack of social skills! She didn't know quite why she felt so out of sorts. She hugged her sister. "Good luck. Call me if you need me."

Savannah hugged her back, hard, and Taylor's heart melted a little. She and Savannah were rebuilding their relationship, and that was what mattered. Not men. Especially good-looking, annoying ones.

THE DAY AFTER moving into Hank and Nadine's place, Savannah sat on the buttery-soft leather couch in the den, alternately looking out at the ice-covered bay and through the hall to Nadine's closed door.

She wasn't yet clear on her role here. Should she be spending time out here in the main house, or should she hole up in her apartment? Honestly, she'd prefer the latter, since Nadine was sulky and Hank was a little awkward around her. She felt judged by both of them, and not positively.

Especially after cooking them lunch.

She'd figured grilled cheese sandwiches would be easy—she'd made them before—but on an unfamiliar and fancy stove, she'd managed to burn the sandwiches and to choose a type of cheese from the array in the fridge that neither of them liked.

"Why did you have it, then?" she'd ventured to ask as they'd picked at the sandwiches.

"Because Dad gets one of those meal delivery services and he doesn't have a clue about what to order."

"Because your tastes change every day," he'd said mildly. "This is fine for a first effort, Savannah." He'd been trying to be kind, but although he was a big man and probably had a hearty appetite, he'd eaten less than half of his sandwich. Now he'd gone out to the post office, claiming he wanted to beat the snow. She wouldn't be surprised if he stopped at the Bluebird Bakery and grabbed himself a second lunch, maybe some of Taylor's perfect crab pastries.

She stood up. Comparing herself with Taylor was never a good activity, mental-health-wise. She hesitated and then walked to Nadine's door and tapped on it.

"What." The voice was flat and sullen.

"It's Savannah. Do you need anything?"

"Go away."

Yes, the girl could certainly use some training in manners. At the same time, being the politeness police was no way to touch the girl's heart. She had a sudden flashback of being Nadine's age herself. Going from Birdy's care to Mrs. Williams's. From her mother, who cried when she acted bratty, to Mrs. Williams, who screamed at her.

Neither approach had worked. But now, looking at the situation from the adult point of view, she felt a little rush of sympathy for both women. She hadn't been an easy teen.

Nadine had gone from a neglectful, basically absent

mother to Savannah, a clueless stranger. No wonder she wasn't all sweet and social.

Savannah stepped back from the door and leaned against the wall, thinking. She had to find a way to connect with Nadine. She had to make this work, show Hank she wasn't incompetent and could stay past the brief trial period he'd suggested.

Because if she didn't make it here, what would she do?

She hadn't heard anything from Rupert, but then, he had no idea where she was. If she went back into his realm, he'd be able to find her, and he would not be happy. At a minimum, he'd have poisoned her reputation with anyone in their circle who might have considered hiring her or recommending her for a job.

There was a pounding on the front door, and she looked out the window to see a bundled-up person. Fear washed over her, but a closer look told her that this was a boy, not a man. Not Rupert. She hurried to answer it. "Yes? Can I help you?" she asked the boy. He was Nadine's age or a little older, with the faintest shadow of a mustache showing on his upper lip.

"Nadine here?" He shifted from one foot to the other, whether from the cold or from nerves, she couldn't tell.

"Are you a friend of hers? What's your name?"

"Sorry. I'm Kevin." The wind whipped behind him, tossing the tops of a row of pines.

Maybe a visit from a friend would improve Nadine's sour mood. "Come on in. I'll get her."

As she took his coat, he had the nerve to give her a not subtle once-over. *Really?*

But she was used to it, from all ages of males. She double-checked her outfit for appropriateness—yes, sweater and jeans, nothing revealing—and then directed the boy to a bench by the door while she went to check on Nadine.

"Hey," she said, tapping quietly.

"I said, go away."

"Kevin's here."

The door flew open, and Nadine looked out frantically. "What? Kevin Granger?"

"I guess? He just said his name was Kevin. He's a ginger. Tall and thin."

"That's him. I look awful." She rushed back to her dressing table and started brushing her hair frantically, making it look worse.

The floor of the room was strewn with clothes, and various bottles were open on Nadine's dressing table. She had her phone propped up, a makeup video still playing. Savannah looked at her more closely and saw that her eyes were heavily made up.

Was she allowed to wear that much makeup at thirteen? Was that appropriate?

Savannah had been allowed. Not only allowed, but she'd *had* to wear makeup for her pageants, at a way younger age than Nadine was.

Nadine was now scrubbing her face with a makeup removing wipe. "What does he want? He's one of the most popular boys at the middle school."

"Apparently he wants to see you." She approached Nadine and gently pushed her down onto the bench of her dressing table. "Here. Let me help you."

She surveyed Nadine's cosmetics, then selected concealer and tapped it on a mid-forehead pimple, blending it as she'd done for hundreds of other models and had done for herself, as well. She brushed a little blush onto Nadine's cheeks and pulled out a soft pink lip gloss. "Put this on," she ordered, "and I'll fix your hair."

"I still look bad," Nadine moaned, but she did as Savannah said.

"You look beautiful. But no one else will believe it unless you do," Savannah coached. "Look at this hair. So thick and wavy. People pay hundreds of dollars for hair just like this." As she spoke, she twisted the unruly sides and clipped them with barrettes, then fluffed up the back. She pulled a few strands out around Nadine's face. "There. You look pretty without trying too hard. I'll go tell him you'll be right out."

"Thank you," Nadine said from beneath the shirt she was changing.

"You're welcome." It was the most positive interaction they'd had yet.

But as she crossed the living room, she wondered: Why was she showing Nadine how to please some random boy who'd showed up on the brink of a storm?

Savannah tried and failed to make conversation with Kevin, who kept staring at her breasts. She should probably give him a pass, given that he was of an age to be at the mercy of his hormones, but *ugh*.

When Nadine came out, she did look sweet and pretty. Kevin gave her the once-over, too. Double *ugh*.

"Can we go to your room?" he asked Nadine immediately.

"No," Savannah said.

"Sure," Nadine said at the same time.

Nadine turned to her. "Dad always lets me," she said.

Kevin cleared his throat. "I just…need some help with homework."

"Does your dad really let you have boys in your room?" Savannah asked.

Nadine lifted her chin. "I said yes."

Savannah didn't want to destroy the slight rapport she'd built with the girl. "Okay, but leave the door open," she said.

"We will." The two of them rushed into Nadine's room.

Savannah then was faced with the question of where to be. She wanted to supervise, but she didn't want to spy. She should have just made them hang out in the den. There was no reason homework needed to be done in Nadine's room, and in any case, it was a mess.

She walked past and the two were bent over Nadine's laptop. So, okay, maybe her desk was where she studied and kept her books. That made sense.

She went out to the kitchen, opened the fridge and studied its contents. What should she make for dinner, when lunch had been such a failure?

She found frozen fillets of salmon as well as a head of broccoli. That would have been a perfect model's meal, but a teen and a man probably needed more. She rummaged around and found a box of rice. Wondered if she should call Hank and ask him to pick up bread at the bakery, but that sounded a little too domestic for the first day on the job. Maybe she'd make corn bread or biscuits, she thought, kneeling to check the cupboard for baking supplies.

Not finding any gave her the perfect excuse to check on Nadine.

When she walked back into the hallway, though, the door to Nadine's bedroom was closed and she could hear music inside. That little stinker. She raised her hand to knock.

The front door opened and Hank came in, his shoulders coated with snow that must have just started to fall. He was smiling, his friendly, open face and confident movements making it clear he was the man of the family and comfortable with the role. Just seeing him soothed a raw part of Savannah's psyche.

"Cold out there," he said. "Where's Nadine?"

Savannah suddenly felt nervous. "She's, uh, in her room," she said. "With Kevin."

His pleasant expression disappeared. "What?" He stomped across the floor in his snowy boots and pounded on the door, then flung it open.

Savannah couldn't see past him, so she didn't know what he'd caught the two of them doing, but whatever it was, it didn't make him happy. "We have a big house. There's absolutely no reason for you to have a boy in your bedroom."

"But Savannah said it was okay."

The traitor. Savannah opened her mouth to defend herself and then shut it again. She'd explain later.

"And you, young man, you should know better. I'm going to have to ask you to leave."

"Dad!" Nadine's voice quavered like she was about to break into sobs.

Kevin stalked out, muttering. "She said it was fine," he said, nodding at Savannah before shrugging into his coat, stepping into his boots and slamming out the door.

"Nadine," Hank said, "you know the rules. No matter what Savannah said, you shouldn't have broken them."

"I didn't—"

"You ruined everything!" Inexplicably, Nadine was yelling at Savannah. She stormed back into her room and slammed the door.

Hank yanked it open again. "I'll deal with you later," he said over his shoulder to Savannah, every bit as if she were a disobedient child.

The tone was way too much like the tone Rupert had used with her, and the lies the kids had told were too much like what other models had used against her in the mad fight to get to the top. Savannah didn't know how she could have replicated her past life so closely on a tiny island that was worlds removed from New York, in a polar opposite job, but somehow, she had.

Head down, she turned and skulked into her apartment, wondering if she should pack her bags.

Rather than making a good impression today, she'd screwed up. It had happened because she was trying so hard to do things right. What would happen on a day she didn't try so hard?

And when Hank had said he'd deal with her later, just what, exactly, had he meant?

CHAPTER SIX

TWO DAYS AFTER they'd moved Savannah into her new living situation, the predicted snowstorm had materialized. Fortunately, it was a Saturday, so those who worked on the mainland weren't forced into days off. Same with the kids, like Nadine, who attended the junior-senior high school on the mainland. Maybe fortunately—Cody wasn't sure—they all seemed to have decided to come to the bakery at once.

"Is it like this every Saturday?" he asked Taylor as he passed her, heading back to the kitchen to replenish the display. They'd planned for him to take over all the night baking soon, but it seemed to him that Taylor needed help during the days, too.

"Not this busy. Why? Too much for you?" Her tone wasn't joking, but challenging.

He rolled his eyes as he moved cookies from the cooling racks to his tray. He had no idea why she'd gone snarky on him, but it made him question whether the arrangement would work out.

He carried the tray out to the front. "I wasn't complaining," he murmured to Taylor between customers, his hands busy arranging cookies in the display case. The position required him to be very cozy with Taylor, so much so that he caught a whiff of the honeysuckle fragrance she wore.

It suited her, sweet and wholesome and summery.

"They're buying everything they need for the storm. I'm sure the market next door is just as busy," Taylor told him breathlessly during a two-minute break in the traffic. And then the door opened again, and three more people came inside.

Cody was getting into the rhythm of the work, despite his questions to Taylor. He liked being busy, liked making people happy. Not that he'd done any of the complicated baking, but the customers seemed pleased with the scones he'd put together at oh-dark-thirty this morning.

He wasn't sleeping much, still, so working some daytime hours in addition to the night baking didn't bother him.

Finally around noon the customers trickled to a halt, and Taylor locked the front door. "If you sweep, I'll clean out the case," she said. "I'm looking for a nap."

"Same." He grabbed the broom and started sweeping. Amazing the crumbs people could leave in just a few hours.

Amazing, too, that he'd gone from putting his life on the line for his country to sweeping a bakery's floor. It didn't make a whole lot of sense, but everything in his life seemed to be in flux.

If he moved on from here, where would he go? What would he do?

He was stuck like a crab in a trap, and it was nobody's fault but his own. A better man would have had a profession and options nailed down. Look at Ryan, who'd already earned a PhD and was doing important research about the Chesapeake Bay. Or Luis, who routinely made millions for the companies that hired him to turn them around.

Cody, on the other hand, could barely support himself as a low-level bakery employee.

Army counselors had warned him about the difficulties of reintegrating into civilian life, especially with the trauma and memory loss he'd experienced. They hadn't mentioned the hit to his self-esteem.

He realized he'd stopped sweeping and got back to work, reaching the broom under tables draped with blue-and-white-checked tablecloths, each topped with a different small statue in the shape of a bluebird. Taylor had definitely done a good job making the place homey.

His broom encountered an object, and a sharp cry rang out. Beneath the table he spotted movement. What on earth?

He lifted the edge of the tablecloth and knelt to look underneath.

A boy, maybe six or seven, was holding an even younger girl on his lap, arms wrapped around her. They looked bedraggled, and the girl's face was streaked with tears.

"Hey, Taylor, c'mere a minute," he called over his shoulder, figuring she'd know them. Then he addressed the kids. "What are you two doing here? Where's your mom?"

"She had to go 'way," the boy said.

"When will she get back?"

"She's not coming back," the boy said.

The girl, maybe three years old, started to cry.

"In a year she might come back," the boy said, patting the girl's shoulder. "We hafta be brave. That's what she said."

This was way above Cody's pay grade. Thankfully, Taylor came hurrying over. "What's going on? What are you two doing here?"

Her voice was sterner than Cody's had been, and tears rose to the boy's eyes. He hugged the girl tighter and shrank back against the wall.

"They said their mom left them here," Cody said. "I figured it was a small enough island that you'd know them."

She shook her head. "They're not from the island," she said, her tone softening. "Come on out, kids."

The boy said something into the girl's ear and then slowly scooted halfway out, still holding her tightly.

"Are there social services on the island?" Cody looked up at Taylor.

"Not officially." She knelt beside him. "There's the church."

"I guess…should we take them there?"

"Do you have coats?" Taylor asked the children.

The boy reached under the table and pulled out a backpack, then two jackets. They were sweatshirt weight, definitely not warm enough for today's winter storm.

Taylor was on her phone. "I'm texting the pastor," she said.

Cody settled himself cross-legged on the floor.

"Where'd Mom go?" he asked, deliberately keeping his voice calm and quiet and friendly.

"She left on a fast boat," the boy said. "With her new friend. She didn't have 'nuff money for us. For food and stuff. Right now."

Taylor had finished texting, and at the boy's words, she frowned. "When was the last time you ate?"

The boy reached into his backpack and pulled out a baggie that held crusts of bread. The remains of a peanut butter sandwich, from the look and smell of it. The girl reached out and started stuffing crusts in her mouth.

"We gotta save some," the boy said, pulling the bag back.

Cody felt awful he hadn't thought right away that they might be hungry. "Can we…"

But Taylor was already headed back to the kitchen. "She'll bring you a snack," he assured the kids. "Why don't you come wash your hands, and then you can sit at a table and eat it?"

They seemed to understand that. They got to their feet and followed him to the sink behind the counter, where he supervised their hand-washing.

"See?" the little boy said to his sister. "Mom told us he'd take care of us."

The little girl glanced over her shoulder at him, her face skeptical.

As he helped them dry their hands and then led them back to a table, and as Taylor served them crab rolls and cookies, which they ate voraciously, Cody processed what they'd said, and a horrible suspicion took hold of him.

Even though he hadn't spoken with her in years, Cody remembered all too well his mother's ability to absolve herself of responsibility and disappear. That was one reason Cody himself didn't do commitments. He'd grown up lacking in that department. Barely knew what a commitment looked like.

But surely she wouldn't have... No. No way. She didn't have children other than him.

Did she?

Once they'd slowed down to a normal pace of eating, Cody made himself ask the question, even though he had a sinking feeling he knew the answer. "How come your mom said I'd take care of you?" he asked.

Taylor tilted her head. "She said that?"

He nodded, waited.

The girl swallowed a large bite of cookie. "Because," she said, "you're our brudder!"

Cody sucked in a breath, blew it out and studied the grimy little kids, his chest going warm and tight at the same time. Nothing was proven, and yet he knew in his heart it was true. He'd never tried to keep track of his mother, but if she'd wanted to find him, it wouldn't be hard. He wasn't hiding. An internet search would do it.

What he didn't know was how he would take care of these kids, whom he couldn't quite think of as his siblings. He glanced over at Taylor's shocked face. "If she's right," he said, "I might need some help for a few days."

THAT NIGHT, Taylor settled Danny and Ava on her couch with a bowl of popcorn between them. She'd called around and gotten the loan of some pajamas and warm clothes for the kids. Now they were relatively calm and relaxed, for the evening at least.

Sleet beat against the windows outside, and the eaves

of the old building creaked. Still, the bakery—a stand-alone building, although close to the market on one side and the old Victorian on the other—was soundly built. Inside, it was warm, and Taylor thanked heaven for the builder who'd put a fireplace in each of the little apartments. Those, combined with the blue-painted shiplap walls and slanted ceilings crossed by sturdy rafters, made each apartment feel like a home.

It seemed to her that what these children needed right now was a home.

She'd talked to the pastor, or rather, his wife, Tiffany. Pastor David was knee-deep in sermon preparation, and discerning that the situation wasn't quite an emergency—and that public social services had already been contacted—Tiffany promised he would talk to them tomorrow after services.

The least Taylor could do was keep the children for one night.

Their little faces were clean, their eyes sleepy and glued to the kids' movie she'd found in a stack of old DVDs. Even in a storm, with the satellite TV service less than reliable, her ancient DVD player worked fine.

She glanced toward the kitchen, where Cody sat at the table, tapping on his phone. He'd said he was going to try to locate information on their mother so he could figure out what to do.

She couldn't fathom what he was feeling, discovering he had two siblings and having them dumped on him. It was even worse for the little ones, being left alone in a strange place with a brother they didn't know.

"I'll be in the kitchen with your brother," she said to

Danny and Ava. "You call out if you need us, or come right in."

Both kids nodded without looking at her. Their hands went from the bowl of popcorn to their mouths, steadily. They'd both eaten hamburgers for dinner, but they still seemed hungry.

She stood, walked into the kitchen and just looked at Cody for a moment.

That was *not* a hardship. Even with his hair practically on edge from him running his fingers through it, he was gorgeous.

His brow was wrinkled, though, and when he looked up, his eyes had shadows beneath. She felt a surge of sympathy.

She sank down into the chair catty-corner from him. "Did you find out anything?"

He shook his head. "I've searched her name and all kinds of variations. There's nothing, no record. She did put some abbreviated medical records in the backpack, which scares me."

It scared Taylor, too, because it made the woman's absence more likely to be long-term at best, permanent at worst. "No note?"

He shook his head.

"Are you thinking they're really your siblings?" You couldn't tell it from looking at them. They were cute kids, but Ava's blond coloring was distinctly different from Cody's brown hair and tanned skin. Danny's hair was brown, but his eyes were green. Of course, with the age difference, they were likely to have a different father.

Cody sucked in a breath and let it out in a sigh. "Yeah. I showed Danny a photo of my mom, and he started crying and patting it. He said that was their mama."

That pretty much clinched it. "When was the last time you saw her? The picture, was it old?"

"Very. I haven't seen her since I was…maybe ten? It was a picture from back then." He scrolled through his phone pictures and found one, blurry, obviously a snapshot of a crinkled and cracked photograph.

"Wow." She studied it and looked at him. "Wonder how she found you?"

He shrugged. "Military records? And there were a couple of news stories when I came home. They might have said where I was planning to live."

She tilted her head to one side. "News stories about your cooking show?"

A dull red flush stained his cheekbones. "Some BS about what I did over there, right before I came home." His voice was dismissive; he clearly didn't want to talk about it.

Fine, but Taylor promised herself she'd find the stories later. Knowing Cody, she was willing to bet they were full of praise that made him uncomfortable, something about his heroism or medals.

He was clearly upset and distracted, which wasn't surprising. His mother had placed him in foster care, and now she'd managed to locate him only when she wanted to dump her other kids on him. But you didn't criticize someone's mother to their face. Instead, she said, "I just don't get how you can have siblings that young."

He shrugged. "I'm twenty-nine. Mom had me when she was sixteen. So she must've had these two in her late thirties, early forties. Honestly, there could be more of us floating around. She seems to be pretty fertile."

He said it like he was talking about a stranger, and she studied him. "How are you doing?"

He looked up from the phone screen and met her eyes. "Honestly? I'm freaking out a bit."

The wind whistled around the old building, above the quiet sound of the TV from the other room. She'd dimmed the lights, and the kitchen was small and snug. It was like they were the only ones in the universe.

He glanced toward the living room and then back at Taylor. "I feel for them. I've been where they are. But I wasn't expecting this kind of responsibility. I'm not equipped for it."

"And you don't have to take it on," she said gently.

He looked at her like she was crazy. "If they're my brother and sister, and I'm their best option, I do."

His certainty startled her. In general, he seemed pretty carefree. "They're your half brother and sister, most likely, right? And you didn't know they existed until today. This kind of situation is what the foster care system is for."

"Well…" He shook his head. "I don't know. I've been there, done that. I had a good run in Betty's house, here on the island, but there were some rough years before that."

Taylor had heard as much, just from local gossip.

"I wonder if there are other relatives who'd consider doing kinship care."

He shook his head again. "That's who my rough years were spent with."

She winced. "The kids' fathers, maybe?"

"That's the next step. I can try to find out some information from the kids, although…" He shook his head. "If their fathers haven't been around so far, and according to Danny they haven't, I don't think it's likely they'll step up now."

"You're probably right." She thought. "Maybe Betty could take them in when she gets back from Paris. And there's at least one other certified foster family on the island. A gazillion more in Baltimore, I'm sure."

"The more we talk about it, the more I think…it's going to be me. Taking them in."

She studied him for a minute and then got up and pulled out two coffee cups, put coffee on to brew. "You're serious about this."

"I'm serious." He leaned back in his chair. "And I realize this throws a wrench in your plans for me, as your employee, but for my own finances I'll have to work as much as we discussed, if not more. I just need to find a new living situation, and a babysitter, and…" He let his head drop into his hands for just a minute, then looked up and met her eyes. "Well. I don't know exactly what I'll do, but I'll figure it out. It's not your problem."

For the moment, it was, though. They were in her apartment right now, because she'd had food and provisions for hot chocolate and a DVD player. She gestured toward the window. "This snow's going on for a while, and there will be small craft warnings even after it stops, and…basically, we're stuck here for the next little bit. Plus, tomorrow's Sunday, and the bakery is closed."

He blew out a breath. "Okay."

"That gives you time to figure things out." She brought his coffee over, along with a carton of milk, and slid the sugar a few inches toward him. Then she fetched her own coffee. "Everyone on the island will help, Cody. I'll help."

"Why?" he asked, looking blank.

She sipped coffee and shrugged. "You need help." She thought of Savannah, of that awful day when they'd lost both their mother and each other. "I know what it is to be torn away from your family. I have some sympathy."

A sound rose above the movie's lively music. Someone was crying. Taylor glanced at Cody, and they both stood and hurried into the living room.

Danny was trying to comfort Ava, but tears were running down his face, too.

Without words, Taylor went to Ava's side, and Cody went to Danny's. They each pulled a kid into their laps, cuddled them, said soothing things. The crying went on a little longer, and Taylor stood with Ava on her hip and grabbed a big box of tissues to put between them. She moved the popcorn bowl away and sat back down.

"Can we stay here?" Danny asked.

"For tonight, of course." Taylor was pretty sure she had enough blankets and pillows to set them up here on the couch. Or maybe she'd sleep on the couch and let them take her bed.

"There's a boy's side and a girl's side," Cody said unexpectedly.

What did *that* mean? Taylor stared at him for a moment, then looked at Danny and Ava, expecting them to start crying again.

But Danny just nodded, seemingly unsurprised.

"That's how shelters are run," Cody explained, his voice matter-of-fact. "They're probably used to it."

And Cody must know that because he'd experienced it, too. Wow.

"And speaking of that," Cody went on, "we men had better turn in. Bed or couch, my man?"

Danny actually smiled. "Bed," he said.

Taylor looked at the little girl in her lap. "How about you, Ava?" She was so small. "I think you'd better sleep in my bed. I can take the couch."

Ava clung to her more tightly. "Sleep with *you*," she said. Her weight felt good and right in Taylor's arms.

Taylor looked at Cody, who shrugged.

Ava started to cry again.

"I mean, I guess?" She wasn't even sure whether a three-year-old could safely stay in a bed alone. And what did it mean that Ava attached so easily to a complete stranger? Taylor had read somewhere that that was what kids who'd been neglected in overfull orphanages did. "Sure, honey," she said, patting the child's soft curls. "You can sleep with me in my bed on the girls' side."

She had the disturbing feeling that she and Cody had just become surrogate mother and father to these kids.

Which meant they'd be spending a whole lot more time together.

CHAPTER SEVEN

TAYLOR REALLY, really wanted to make a success of her bakery. She also really, really wanted to be the kind of woman who could do it all: run a thriving bakery *and* care for two traumatized kids *and* be a supportive friend to their incredibly hot half brother who'd spent all morning calling social services and making another effort to track down the kids' mother.

But today, a Monday, she'd had to handle the bakery mostly alone. Thank heavens she'd gotten an assist from Lolly, a retired seafood plant worker who sometimes filled in at the bakery. Lolly had taken the front counter while Taylor had caught up on the baking. But having Lolly at the counter created a whole other set of issues as Lolly cheerfully insulted customers, swore like a sailor, and otherwise stirred the waters of the normally peaceful and supportive Bluebird Bakery.

The kids, meanwhile, ran wild around the shop, having apparently lost their inhibitions after two good nights' sleep and plenty of reassurances from their newly discovered brother that he'd take care of them.

Yesterday's talk with Pastor David had helped, but just a little. In addition to talking to them about services they could access for the kids, he'd confirmed what she and Cody had already suspected: that the foster care system was overloaded, that January right after the holidays was a particularly busy time, and that it was possible the kids could be separated if they went into the system.

The pastor had also said that, regardless, it would take time for the children to be placed. Since they were staying with a relative, their needs would be considered less urgent than the needs of kids whose parents had gotten ill or been arrested or succumbed to a drug overdose.

That was only right. Taylor understood, of course. But it meant that the task before her grew in enormity.

No, Danny and Ava weren't her responsibility. Not technically.

But they'd been abandoned by their mother at *her* bakery. She felt like she had to see them through, at least until other arrangements could be made.

Cody had gotten angry with her for even asking the pastor about foster care, insisting that wasn't an option, but come on. He had no resources to deal with two kids, despite his insistence that he was going to take care of them. If something wasn't done, he'd end up having to quit the job for which she'd had no other applicants.

If he did that, how was she to fill all the orders she'd unexpectedly gotten, the orders that were going to catapult the Bluebird Bakery into major success?

And was she a terrible person for thinking about her business and its needs when two young kids were without a stable family?

"No, Ava, don't put your hands in there," she cried

now as Ava reached into the display case and fingered all the cookies before selecting the one she wanted.

Right in front of a customer.

Luckily, that customer was Taylor's friend Mellie, who laughed. "Grab me one of those, too, honey," she said, making Ava smile and finger the cookies all the more before selecting one to hand to Mellie.

As Ava continued to fumble through the pile of cookies, Taylor put her hands to her head. The mess meant more baking to do before tomorrow, and she didn't have time for what was already on her to-do list.

The thought of it all made tears rise to her eyes. She grabbed napkins and wiped her face, but the tears kept coming.

Of course, Mellie noticed right away. "Closing time," she said. She walked over to the bakery's door and turned the sign from Open to Closed.

Taylor blew her nose and tried to regain control of herself.

Cody had come in, phone pressed to his ear. He gave her an apologetic wave and sat down at one of the bakery tables.

Danny plopped down across from him, eating easily his eighth sugary snack. Then he looked at Taylor, did a double take and came over to study her, his face worried. "Are you okay, Miss Taylor?" he asked.

Ava, apparently alert to the distress in her brother's voice, looked up at her and then clung to her leg.

"I'm f-f-fine." *Not exactly convincing, Taylor. Good job, now you're upsetting the kids.*

"Kids," Mellie said, "I want you to take my phone

over to that table—" she pointed to an empty one in the corner "—and take turns playing games. Only appropriate ones," she added to Danny, who nodded as if he understood what that meant.

"Now come tell me what's got you so upset." Mellie dragged Taylor over to the table beside Cody's.

"I just don't know how to catch up on everything." Taylor grabbed more napkins from the silver dispenser on the table and wiped her eyes, feeling like a fool.

Cody finally looked up from his phone. "Hey, what's wrong?"

"She's been dealing with your kids, and she's frazzled," Mellie said.

Immediately, Cody pulled his chair to their table, shoving his phone into his back pocket. "I'm sorry I dumped them on you. They're not your problem, Taylor."

"But they showed up in *my* bakery. And I want to h-h-help." There was a good chance she wasn't going to have a family of her own, given that she'd committed to Teaberry Island, where prospects were so limited. But the other good thing about Teaberry was that so many people here had found alternative routes to biological families. She liked to envision herself as someone who opened her arms to kids in need, made them welcome, babysat them, cared for them.

And both yesterday and this morning, she'd awakened to find that the sleeping Ava had burrowed into her arms, smelling of baby shampoo, totally relaxed.

It was everything she'd ever wanted.

Except, apparently, she couldn't handle it. Tears overflowed again. Good heavens, it wasn't even her hormonal time of the month. What was wrong with her?

"Look," Mellie said, her voice firm, "you're all coming over for dinner tonight. Alfie will play with the kids, and Ryan and I will help you hammer out a plan."

"It's kind of you, Mellie, but it's not your problem, either," Cody said.

"Oh, really?" She raised an eyebrow. "Is that a little bit like how Alfie wasn't your problem when you found out he was actually your nephew? And if so, how come you and Luis jumped into the role of being his uncles without a second thought?"

"That's different," Cody said.

"No, it's not. If those kids are related to you, they're related to Ryan and Luis, as well. Maybe not by blood, but in every other way, because you're brothers." She stood up. "I'm going home to cook up…" She frowned. "Any idea of what Danny and Ava like to eat?"

"Anything," Taylor said.

"Everything," Cody said at the same time.

"Crab cakes it is," Mellie said, "and a heap of fried potatoes. Give those kids a nap and then come over around five."

Taylor let out a sigh, her shoulders relaxing for the first time all day. She saw a similar look of relief on Cody's face.

They weren't going to have to handle this alone.

The trouble was, that meant they'd handle it together. She and Cody. Starting with a family-like evening tonight.

THAT NIGHT, Cody pushed away his plate, turning down Mellie's offer of more crab cakes. He noticed with concern that Danny was wiping Ava's face and urging her to clean her plate. Parental tasks, and the child was only seven.

From his own background in the foster care system, he pulled out memories of sibling pairs who acted that way, one of them taking on a parent-type role. It almost always happened because their parents hadn't filled the role themselves. Kids like that were used to being left alone to fend for themselves.

It was admirable in Danny that he'd taken on the care of his sister, but it also made Cody livid. How had his mother left a seven-year-old to care for his baby sister? What had the kids been through? And how had she reconciled dumping them off on the faith that Cody would care for them? She didn't even know Cody anymore, and she hadn't bothered to say hello. Somehow, she'd found out about his location but hadn't even considered reconnecting.

No doubt she knew what a monumental favor she was asking, and didn't want him to have the option of refusing to take responsibility for Danny and Ava.

"More wine?" Ryan walked around the wood plank table, filling the adults' glasses as the dog, Doughnut, made fast work of cleaning the floor around the kids' seats.

When Ryan reached Cody's place, he put a hand on Cody's shoulder and squeezed, so quickly Cody wasn't sure he'd really felt it.

Ryan wasn't a toucher. It had taken him forever, as a teen, to accept Betty's hugs. Ryan, Cody and Luis had mostly interacted with each other by semi-friendly punches and insults.

He watched as Ryan knelt beside Alfie and whispered something to him, his arm unselfconsciously around his newly discovered son. Fatherhood was changing Ryan. Fatherhood and Mellie.

"Yeah!" Alfie said. He looked over at Danny and Ava. "You guys wanna come to my birthday party?"

They both nodded immediately. "I *love* birthday parties," Ava said.

Danny frowned at her. "Don't lie. You never went to one."

"Never?" Alfie sounded shocked.

Taylor and Mellie looked surprised, too.

"Nah," Danny said. He must have noticed everyone's reactions, because his cheeks reddened. "We got asked to one once, but we couldn't go. Mom had something else to do." He stared at the floor.

Cody felt like he was looking at his younger self, making excuses for why he couldn't accept the few invitations he'd received. The truth was, Mom was sensitive, and probably knew the dirty, bedraggled new kid in the class was only invited because the birthday child's parents had invited the whole class. Plus there was no extra money for gifts. Mimicking Ryan's fatherly behavior, he put an arm around Danny. "Hey, kiddo. I never went to a birthday party, either."

"Never?" Taylor blurted out. The rest of the room went silent.

Pity was worse than being left out of a common childhood tradition. Even at Cody's age, it stung. He kept an arm around Danny. "No big deal. I made up for it when I grew up."

Ryan broke the silence. "I remember a couple of blowout graduation parties. You definitely made up for lost time, party-wise."

Mellie seemed to realize the emotional minefield they were skirting. "Well, we'd love to have all of you come to Alfie's party," she said in a hearty voice. "It's in March, but we're already planning for it."

Danny looked at Cody. "Will we be here in March?"

Ava's gaze was glued to his face, too.

Cody felt like a deer in headlights. But these kids needed reassurance. "There are things we need to work out, so I can't promise, but I hope so." And how heart-breaking it was that these kids had so little stability in their lives that they took nothing for granted, not even having a home.

"Time for dessert," Mellie sang out, and she hurried to the kitchen and brought back a tray of brownies. Ryan whispered something to Mellie and then went to the kitchen himself, coming back with a big container of vanilla ice cream. Danny's and Ava's eyes grew round as they, along with Alfie, were served big plates of dessert.

Cody watched them eat, and then all the adults were watching because both Cody's siblings consumed the food so quickly. Ava put down her spoon on her empty plate and pressed her hands to the sides of her face. "My head hurts," she said.

"Brain freeze," Alfie informed her, his mouth full of his own dessert.

Cody wondered, but didn't want to ask: Had they never even eaten ice cream before?

The sun had set, but there was still a little aura of

light at the horizon, reflecting onto the bay. Looking down toward the dock behind Mellie and Ryan's place, Cody could see pillars and sculptures of ice, built up from the constant wave action. Beautiful, but cold.

Inside, all was warm. Golden lamplight, and comfortable chairs around a table laden with good food, and mellow guitar music playing in the background. The kids ran off to Alfie's room, using treats to lure Doughnut into following them, and the adults gave a mutual sigh of relief and shared smiles.

It was all warm and family-like, and Cody didn't take it for granted. Couldn't, not with his background.

"So let's talk about what you're going to do with those two little angels," Ryan said, nodding in the direction the kids had gone. "Your mom dropped them off and split?"

Cody nodded. "They were hiding under a table at the bakery when we closed down on Saturday. That's how Taylor ended up involved." He met her eyes directly. "I apologize for that. You've really stepped up, but I don't expect that to continue."

"I want to help," Taylor said. "It's just, there's a lot on my plate right now, with the bakery getting so many off-island orders."

Mellie lifted an eyebrow. "And with your new employee suddenly distracted."

Cody winced. He was failing, and he didn't like that. He wanted to do a good job, for the kids and for Taylor.

"What are your options?" Ryan asked. "Can your mom be held accountable? Would she come back if you found her?"

Cody spread his hands. "I've been looking for traces of her online, but no luck so far."

"She didn't leave a note, but she did leave the kids' medical records," Taylor chimed in. "Which makes it seem like she didn't plan to come back."

"And even if she could be made to, would that be best for Ava and Danny?" Cody ran a hand through his hair. "Having grown up during my younger years in her care, I don't think so." He had a fleeting memory of the two of them sleeping in a bus station, all of their belongings stacked around them. Mom had pegged it as an adventure, but he'd seen how eagerly she drank from her flask and chatted up any guy who walked by, until one of them took pity—or advantage—and drove them somewhere to stay for a few days.

"So, like Ryan asked, what are your options?" Mellie leaned forward and propped her crossed arms on the table.

Taylor spoke up. "I thought they might go into the foster care system—"

"No," Cody said.

"No," Ryan said at the same time.

Taylor looked stricken, as if she'd inadvertently said something awful, so Cody put a hand over hers. "Thanks for trying." Her hand was tiny and almost delicate, but a little rough-skinned. That was so *Taylor*, small but mighty, a worker.

He realized he'd let his hand linger and that Mellie, at least, had noticed. He pulled it away and looked at Ryan.

"It's not that the system is bad," his foster brother began.

"There are some great families. Like Betty's," Cody

added. "But siblings can get separated, and families get overfull and overburdened, and…no. Not if there's an alternative."

"Exactly," Ryan said. He'd had a few bad experiences in the system and in a group home before coming to Teaberry Island as a last resort.

They'd all three been considered lost causes, to tell the truth of it.

"Betty saved us," Cody said, "but there aren't too many Bettys in the world."

"So, no foster care," Mellie said, ticking off a finger. "And no sending them back to your mom, if she could even be found." She ticked off another finger.

"Right," Cody said. "So that leaves…me. I have a military pension. And a job, or—" He looked at Taylor. "I did. I haven't exactly been a stellar employee."

Taylor's forehead wrinkled. "No, you haven't. But you have a good reason. And you're doing your best."

He could hear the ambivalence in her voice. She wanted to help, but she also had a business to run. "I'll do my job well," he promised, "or I'll quit, and you can find someone else." He looked around at the three of them. "Honestly, quitting seems like the only option right now, but I still don't know what to do with the kids. How to manage their lives. I have zero experience, and they need extra help and skill, not barely adequate care."

Mellie and Ryan glanced at each other. "Don't worry," Mellie said, her voice firm. "We're going to help you figure out what to do."

"The boy needs to get enrolled in school," Ryan said. "Can't let his education fall by the wayside."

"There are great teachers at the island elementary school," Mellie said. "They were terrific with Alfie."

"Isn't there a Head Start program somewhere on the island?" Taylor looked a little more optimistic.

"Not officially, I don't think," Mellie said, "but if you could get Ava in with Arletta Lincoln, she'd get a whole lot of enrichment."

"Arletta! That's a great idea," Taylor said, and looked at Cody. "Want me to text her and ask?"

"Sure," Cody said. If both Taylor and Mellie were enthusiastic about this woman, she had to be good.

"There's a library program on Saturdays," Mellie said. "I think both kids could go. I know the bakery's busy on that day."

"I usually spend time with Alfie at the library on Saturdays," Ryan said. "I'd be glad to take your two, as well."

As everyone spoke, Cody felt a weight lifted off his shoulders. That was what was so great about Teaberry Island. It was what had saved him and his brothers. More recently, it was what had pulled Betty out of her doldrums after her husband had died. It was a community of good-hearted people, but more than that, they were practical and hardworking and self-sufficient. They had to be, living isolated as they did.

For the first time, he realized that his mother might have done something right, leaving Danny and Ava here. "If you guys can give me this kind of guidance, I won't have to put a burden on Taylor like I've been doing the past two days."

"I want to help, too," she said. "If they're staying with you, at your place, I can do some babysitting. And we can adjust the schedule for the baking, see what works with the kids."

He looked at her, tilting his head. "I get why Ryan's helping," he said, punching his foster brother lightly in the arm. "And Mellie's hitched to him now, so she feels duty-bound to help, too. But why would you want to be involved?"

"I just like kids." Her cheeks went a pretty shade of pink. There was something else going on there.

"Well," he said, "I appreciate it." He was having a hard time looking away from her open, friendly face and warm eyes. Her goodness drew him like a magnet.

When he finally did look away, he saw that Ryan and Mellie were both watching their interaction with interest.

Great. He'd shown them what he shouldn't have: that he was attracted to Taylor.

He could never be with her in a million years. She was the marrying kind, and he didn't do commitment. Never had. But it was worse now, after what had happened to him in those last days of combat. How could he commit to someone else when he didn't even know who he was, what he'd done?

He just had to be cautious and guarded as they continued to spend more and more time together, both at the bakery, and now, taking care of the kids.

SAVANNAH'S TRIP TO the market with Hank didn't go any better than the weekend had.

Savannah knew her cooking was bad, but she hadn't

realized just how bad until she'd tried to figure out a slate of meals an adult male and a teen would enjoy.

She'd subsisted on salads herself, in her modeling days. Rupert always had a cook.

But Hank, apparently, liked meat and potatoes. Nadine preferred pizza and pasta. None of it seemed too challenging when she looked up recipes online, but the results hadn't pleased her new clientele.

Thank heavens, thank *heavens* Nadine was back in school today. The snow days followed by the MLK holiday weekend had meant five days in the house with a kid who was not only a thirteen-year-old girl but also knew how to hold a grudge.

Nadine had spent the entire time in her room or bothering her dad. Somehow, though he'd been the one to lay down the law about her having a boy in her bedroom, all the ill feelings had fallen on Savannah.

So Savannah, at loose ends in her own little apartment, had gone online to look for additional ways to make money. She'd first thought about doing makeup videos, but the people who monetized those seemed to be ten years younger than she was and with thousands of followers. Next she'd researched several home marketing schemes, but when she'd asked Hank if she could host a candle party at his house, he'd flatly refused. "You have no friends on the island who would come," he'd said, "and besides, those pyramid marketing schemes are a racket. You'll just lose money."

She'd tried to show him the cars and vacations other salespeople had earned, but he'd snorted in exactly the way he snorted at Nadine's impulsive ideas.

Today, trying for a fresh start, she'd offered to go
to the market to get more foods of the type he and Nadine might enjoy. He'd agreed, but then he'd insisted
on coming along. Whether because he didn't trust her
food choices or he didn't want her using his credit card,
she didn't know. Probably both.

Now, as they roamed around the market, Savannah
realized she hadn't planned well. She'd intended to just
browse and look up recipes on her phone and figure
it all out as she went, but with Hank looking over her
shoulder in that disapproving way, she was too flustered
to think. Plus, she'd forgotten how limited the selections
were on an island of this size. There wasn't a whole lot
of fresh arugula or star fruit to be had. The aisles were
full of canned goods and hardware and even some really awful clothing items. There *was* a fresh food area,
but it was small.

Finally, she saw Mellie behind the deli counter and
rushed to her. They didn't know each other well, but
they'd met all those years ago, and she was pretty sure
Taylor had said she and Mellie were good friends. "Can
you help me?" she asked. "I'm Taylor's sister, and I'm
desperate."

"I can try." Mellie smiled good-humoredly. "What's
the problem?"

Savannah explained her cooking woes, keeping her
voice low, and Mellie nodded and laughed and didn't
seem to judge. "My husband likes basic food himself,"
she said, "and I have a preteen son, so I know what
you're up against. Have you ever made a meat loaf?"

"No. I'm not sure Nadine would like that."

"She will if you make a pizza-flavored one." Mellie paged through some recipe cards that looked like they were from a meat distributer. "Here," she said. "Bake potatoes in the oven with it, and the next day, you can make sandwiches with the leftovers." She slipped a jar of gravy into Savannah's basket. "Open-faced, with gravy on them. They won't notice it's not homemade." She tossed in some white bread.

"Oh…" Savannah said. "Not whole grain?"

"Not for your clientele, but for you—" She grabbed a loaf of multigrain. "This is from your sister's bakery, and it's to die for."

"You sell her stuff?"

"Just some basics." Mellie went on to suggest a prepared potato salad meal with grilled chicken.

"Grilled? At this time of year?"

"I've heard about his kitchen," Mellie said, nodding at Hank, who was studying the hardware. "There's an actual grill in it. The good thing is, you can make him do the honors. Here." She threw a jar of barbecue sauce into the cart. "Brush this on top of these chicken pieces," she said, adding a package to Savannah's cart. "Everyone likes that. If they don't turn out well, it'll be his fault. As a man, he has to be able to grill."

"If you say so." Savannah grabbed a couple of packages of lettuce and two tomatoes, determined to add at least something healthy into the mix.

Airily, she beckoned Hank over and checked out. That hadn't gone so badly, after all.

As they walked back out to Hank's jeep, the smells

from the Bluebird Bakery were amazing, a mix of bread and sweets and savory sandwiches.

And it was lunchtime.

They turned toward each other at the same moment. "Would you want to…" Savannah started.

"I'd like to take you to lunch," Hank said at the same time.

"I'd love that." The fact that he'd asked her that way made her nearly bounce with happiness. It wasn't that she wanted to date the man, of course; he was so much older and way too serious and nerdy for her. But it would be nice if he *wanted* to date her, like most other guys she encountered. The fact that he'd been so resistant to her feminine charms had rankled, she realized now that he seemed to have succumbed. She looked over at him and smiled, her face heating a little.

"I didn't mean like a date," he said hastily. "I'm sorry if I gave that impression. We need to talk."

Oh. "Great," she said, meaning anything but. Never in the history of the world had "we need to talk" meant a happy discussion of good things.

The bakery did smell amazing, though. No one could bake like Taylor, and as they walked inside, she felt proud of her sister's success.

Cody was at the counter, Taylor carrying something out from the kitchen. Savannah and Hank got into line with four people ahead of them, and since she felt worried about what Hank might want to say, she focused on watching Cody and her sister.

They worked together like they could read each other's minds, dodging past each other with inches to spare, passing each other needed items, handing orders to the correct people without having to direct one another. There was a subtle physical awareness between them, too. A sort of buzz or haze.

They were attracted to each other. Savannah could see it even if the two of them hadn't recognized it yet, and happiness bloomed inside her. Taylor was so hard-working and driven. It would be wonderful if she'd relax enough to fall in love.

Once they'd gotten their sandwiches—cheese with tomato pesto for her and a Reuben for him—he led the way to a table that was tucked in a corner. They both chowed down happily for a few minutes, and then he set the rest of his sandwich down and wiped his hands.

Here it came.

He opened his mouth, his expression serious, but a little girl came running over and barreled right into his leg. "Hey," he said, catching her, a smile breaking over his face.

To Savannah's surprise, it was Taylor who came running to collect the child. "Sorry to interrupt your lunch." She swung the little girl onto her hip.

"It's fine." Savannah smiled at the child, who was adorable. "Who's this?"

"Long story short," Taylor said, "I'm helping Cody take care of his half brother and sister. Hey, Hank."

"Good to see you," he said. "Great sandwich."

"Let's talk soon," Savannah said. She now saw why Taylor had responded to her phone calls with terse texts. Looked like she'd been busy. "I'll come over. Maybe tonight? Give you a hand if you need it."

"How will you get there?" Hank asked.

Savannah hadn't thought about it. "Probably Digger," she said. "Or I'll walk."

He shook his head, for all the world like a dad.

"We'll work it out," Taylor said as more people came into the bakery. "Got to go."

"She seems pretty efficient," Hank said, watching as Taylor spoke to customers and took orders, all with the little girl on her hip. His expression was puzzled.

Suddenly, Savannah understood why. "You're wondering why she's efficient and I'm sort of a disaster, aren't you?" she said. "Part of the reason is that we were separated into different households as teenagers and had different lives. Look, I know it's not going well, but I'll improve." She tapped the bag beside her chair. "I have the next couple of meals all planned out. You and Nadine will love them."

"Maybe we should cut our losses," he said.

"Should cut…" *Crap, crap, crap.* He was firing her.

Her shoulders slumped, and her heart seemed to freeze inside her, allowing her to take only short, shallow breaths. A cold, dark fog pushed at her.

She sucked in a breath, fixed her eyes on her busy, bustling sister and stiffened her spine. She couldn't sink into despair and helplessness. She turned back to face Hank. "But our trial was two weeks. It's not even one yet. Teenagers take a while to warm up."

"It's not working. But since I did promise you a two-week trial, I'm willing to pay you for both weeks."

"And still cut me loose?" That was tempting. She hated the feeling she was having around Hank now, that of being a disappointment, someone he didn't want there.

The little girl who'd come over before came running toward them again, full tilt. She started to skid on a slippery stretch of floor.

Savannah jumped to her feet, took a giant step and caught her before she went down. "Whoa there, sweetie. You need to walk, not run." Then, because the girl clung to her a little, Savannah stepped back to the table and sat down, perching the child on her lap.

Hank smiled. "You like the little ones."

"I like all kids, it's just…as I said, teens take a while."

He studied her. She could see in his eyes that he was wavering. But then he shook his head. "I'd like to settle up," he said. "I can send someone over with your things."

"Hey," Taylor said, coming over in a breathless rush. "Thanks for saving Ava. Whew." She pulled out a chair, sat down and ran the back of her hand over her forehead. "At least the rush is slowing down."

"Looks like I might be coming back to your place for a while." Savannah figured there was no point in hiding it.

Taylor frowned and looked from Savannah to Hank and back again. "It's not working out?"

"Not as quickly as Hank would like." Yeah, Savannah was twisting the knife a little, but for Pete's sake. He wasn't even giving her a chance. And just like always, being near Taylor made her feel stronger.

"It's been less than a week," Taylor observed.

Hank opened his mouth, started to speak, then

clearly changed his mind about what he wanted to say. "This is a discussion that needs to be between me and your sister," he said to Taylor.

"Fine, whatever." Taylor angled away from him and faced Savannah, the little girl perched on her lap and playing with her name tag. "The problem is, it's worked out that Ava, here, is staying with me and her brother with Cody. Space-wise and emotion-wise, I don't have a lot of extra room."

Savannah swallowed hard as that refuge closed to her. Unbidden, an image of Rupert came into her head, along with the refrain that had echoed ever since he'd last said it.

You're nothing. Beautiful, but nothing.

She guessed he'd had a point.

"Oh, this came for you." Taylor pulled a business letter from her pocket and pushed it toward her.

Savannah took one look at the return address and her hands involuntarily flew back from it. Had she conjured up Rupert by thinking about him and his harsh words?

"Something bad?" Taylor looked concerned, but then Ava slipped down from her lap and started tugging at her. The bakery's bells rang, indicating another customer. "We'll talk later," she said, and followed Ava, giving Savannah's shoulder a quick squeeze.

Savannah flipped over the envelope so she couldn't see the return address, but it seemed to glow on the table like something radioactive. Her mind raced. How had he found her address, or rather, Taylor's?

Then she realized that it probably hadn't been hard. She'd left in such a hurry, and now that she thought about it, there were several letters from Taylor that she'd kept but never answered. Instead, she'd stuffed them in a drawer, complete with envelopes and return addresses. Stupid of her.

Her stomach churned and her mind spun. She probably had options. There were always options, but right now, she couldn't think of a single one.

Deep breaths. In-hold-out-hold. She looked out the window at the island's main street. A few pedestrians walked along the sidewalks, a couple and two women solo. The two women encountered each other and stopped to chat. One of the island dogs trotted up to them, and they took turns petting its shaggy head.

There were a couple of boarded-up storefronts. Maybe there was a business she could start here. Or that Victorian next door. It needed a ton of work, but she could imagine it as a bed-and-breakfast.

But what was she thinking? She had no business skills. No money to invest in a new venture.

Too bad. She liked it here. Wished she could stay.

If wishes were horses, beggars would ride. That was what Mrs. Williams had told her when she'd expressed her desire for a different life. She didn't admire coldhearted Mrs. Williams. The woman had taken Savannah in, which couldn't have been easy, but she'd also done pretty well with Savannah's childhood modeling income. When the jobs had faded away and Savannah had turned eighteen, Mrs. Williams had politely shown her the door.

She'd been fending for herself since then, and she could do it again. When she'd pulled herself together, she scooted back her chair and forced a smile at Hank. "I'll get my things out myself, this afternoon."

"Where will you go?"

"Good question." But already, her mind was racing with ideas. "Taylor might know someone who'll rent me a room for a few days, just until I figure out what's next." As she reached for the shopping bags, she saw the envelope on the table and couldn't stop herself from grimacing.

"That letter. Seems like it's important to you. Should you open it?"

"It's not going to be good news." She started to stuff it in her purse, but he put a hand on her wrist.

"Better to face it, eh? Find out what you're really dealing with."

"Why do you care? You just fired me. I'm not your concern anymore."

"Nonetheless, I'm concerned," he said. "Why don't you open it?"

She glared at him a few seconds longer and then opened the envelope. Pulled out the one-page business letter.

Then she sat back down again. "Can he do that?"

Hank sat, too. "Do what?"

"The man I lived with before," she said slowly. "Can he charge me back rent? Demand that I return gifts he gave me?"

Hank's brows drew together. "Very doubtful that would hold up in court. How valuable were the gifts? And was it clear they *were* gifts?"

She shook her head, trying to clear it. "A necklace I

was wearing that night," she said. "Nothing expensive. Everything else I left. But the rent on that place would be astronomical."

"Did he say anything else?"

His voice was kind rather than judgmental, and her throat tightened. "He wants me to come back. If I do, he'll drop legal proceedings."

She let the letter slip from her fingers to the table.

"And if not?"

"I can either pay up, or he'll come and get me himself."

Hank made a disgusted sound. "Right there, that shows me this isn't a genuine legal document from a lawyer. He's just trying to scare you."

"Ri-i-ight." She drew out the word.

"Do you think he'll pursue it?"

"Fifty-fifty," she said slowly. "He's busy, and he could easily find someone else to fill my role. But he has a pretty strong sense of justice—"

"Justice?" Hank snorted.

"Well, I mean…he gets furious if he's cut off in traffic or someone outbids him for a business he wants. He kicked me out because I wouldn't…well." Looking at Hank's open face, she couldn't bear to admit that Rupert had tried to share her with a friend. "Not important. And not for you to worry about."

She looked around and stood again. "I need to get moving."

"I want you to stay on."

She frowned as she gathered the bags at her feet. "I'll help you carry these to the car. Then I'd better hang out in town and see if I can rustle up a place to live for a bit."

"I mean it. Stay on. I promised you two weeks, and I want to stick to that."

"Because you feel sorry for me."

"Because I…yes. Somewhat. And I like you. I certainly don't want to see you out in the cold with some sketchy character after you." He was ushering her out of the bakery, and the wind whipped past her, blowing her hair across her face, half blinding her.

Her hands were full, and he reached out and tucked her hair behind her ear. In a paternal way, probably, but the touch of his rough fingertips woke her up inside.

Given the context, though, she stepped back. "I don't… I won't…" She trailed off.

"I'm not asking you to do anything besides help out with cooking and Nadine." His face reddened. "I'm sorry. I promise to keep my distance. But do come and finish out your two weeks, and we'll see. You'll be safer with me than roaming from boarding house to hotel to your sister's doorstep."

"Way to make me feel pitiful," she said in what she hoped sounded like a joking tone. "But…I'll take you up on that very kind offer, and thank you." Her insides were in turmoil. Still, something about Hank's strength was reassuring in a most disturbing way.

CHAPTER EIGHT

ON WEDNESDAY, Taylor helped Ruthie finish up her cleaning and thanked her, then walked her outside to where Tom, her brother, was waiting. "She's doing a great job," she told him. "Make sure you tell her mom that, next time you talk to her."

Ruthie beamed.

"I will," Tom said. "Thanks, Taylor. You're a lifesaver."

"Ruthie's an important part of the Bluebird Bakery." She hugged the woman.

Ruthie hugged her back, hard. Probably missing her mom. "See you tomorrow," she said in her flat voice.

Taylor walked back in. She checked with Lolly, who liked to work the counter during the quiet hours of the workday, and headed for the kitchen. And there was Cody, waiting for her as if that were the most natural thing in the world. She had to marvel at how fast she, Cody and the kids had become something like a family.

Cody had enrolled Danny yesterday at the island elementary school. The child had been hesitant to go in, but he'd come home smiling last night, full of stories about his classmates and his wonderful new teacher. Today he'd gone to school eagerly.

Ava had spent a half day yesterday at Arletta's day care and had loved it, and she'd gone for a full day today.

They were resilient kids, and the only problem Taylor could see was getting too attached. The family-like situation they'd fallen into couldn't be permanent.

"We have a couple of hours until time to pick up the kids," Cody said. "Do you want to go for a walk?"

She glanced over at him, surprised. "Just for fun, or is there something you want to talk about?"

"For fun." Those penetrating eyes held hers for a second too long.

Her heart rate accelerated, and heat rose in her chest and face. Nervous, she grabbed a rag and started wiping things down.

His offer was tempting. Too tempting, and she briefly considered accepting it. But he was just being friendly, probably wanting to show her he appreciated her help.

Hanging out with him beyond what they were already doing would only take her in the direction of the growing mix of feelings she was trying to avoid. "No, thanks. I have to get going on birthday cakes. I have three to do."

"I thought we were doing those tomorrow."

"That was the plan, but I'd like to get a jump on it." And then she clapped a hand over her mouth. "Do you... Do birthday cakes make you sad, because, you know, you never went to a birthday party?"

He shook his head, laughing a little. "No. Believe me, that's easy to get over. I want to learn how to make birthday cakes. Just...not today. Today, I want to go for a walk." He put a hand on her shoulder as she scrubbed the counter. "With you."

Her rag slowing to a stop, she looked up and met his eyes.

Immediately, her heart went into conniptions. Of course it did. Those warm eyes, that beard stubble, the square jaw and strong shoulders… It didn't mean anything that she felt fluttery when she looked at him. She was willing to bet that three quarters of the women who came into the bakery, married or single, old or young, felt the same.

All the more reason to keep her distance.

She looked away and continued scrubbing. "You go. I'm not paying you enough to work 24/7, the way I do."

"No, that's true," he said. He wasn't backing off. "But it does affect me, and the kids, too, if you crash and burn. I've been here for almost two weeks, and I've never once seen you take a break."

"I'll sleep when I'm dead," she joked, and then saw his horrified look and waved her hand back and forth. "It's an old song. My aunt used to sing it. I didn't mean anything by it."

"We're going for a walk," he said firmly. "It's a warm day, at least for January, and sunny, and you need to get some fresh air."

"Bossy," she commented.

"So I've been told." He held her eyes steadily. "Come walk with me."

He wasn't going to back off. She could see that. A jazzy little streak of electricity flashed through her.

"Fine," she said, pretending to be grumpy about it. "Let me get my walking shoes."

Ten minutes later, they were strolling down the road toward the bay, and Taylor had worked hard to tamp down the jazzy feeling. The trouble was, the way she'd done it was to focus on her fears and anxieties.

She was worried about the kids, who were just starting in their new lives and surely would have an adjustment period as well as grief and loss to deal with. It could be argued that that wasn't her concern, but she couldn't help caring about them, more every day.

She also had the off-island bakery orders to worry about. Within the next twenty-four hours, in addition to the birthday cakes, she needed to make six dozen teaberry shortcake cookies and six dozen mini teaberry scones for a bride who'd visited in the summer and loved the teaberry taste. Taylor had offered a discount in exchange for a subtle label on the cookie tray giving their source as Bluebird Bakery, Teaberry Island.

She desperately wanted and needed to make a success of the place. Giving careful attention to wedding orders like this one would help that happen.

And then there was her sister. Savannah had postponed their get-together until tomorrow night, had said she and Hank had worked something out so she could stay there a bit longer, but Taylor knew her sister and could tell she was stressed out. In their family, that wasn't something to take lightly. Savannah had come to the island and Taylor because she'd felt herself sinking down into the kind of darkness that had taken their mother. And although they'd talked it through, and Savannah seemed better, Taylor remained concerned.

Still, as they reached the rocky beach, she felt her shoulders start to loosen. The sun warmed her cheeks, and the rhythmic sound of waves lapping the shore soothed her better than any meditation app could. Gulls swooped overhead, crying their concerns.

"So, what made you settle on Teaberry?" Cody asked. He seemed content to stroll slowly, which was Taylor's preference, as well. "You and your sister just spent a couple of months here as kids, right? If that."

"Yes, in high school, and I always remembered it," she said, looking at the expanse of the bay. "It's so beautiful. And I wanted a place where I could be the only bakery, where I could live close to it and build a community."

"Because you grew up in a city?"

She nodded. "When we were younger, Mom and Savannah and I moved around a lot, but after Mom passed, I lived with my aunt in Boston." She kind of hoped he'd skim over the fact of her mother dying. Most people did, when she treated it in a matter-of-fact way.

Not Cody. "Huh. I didn't realize you'd lost your mom at a young age."

"Yeah," she said. There was that little clutch she always felt when talking about her mother. She waited for him to ask what had happened to her, but he didn't. Paradoxically, that made her blurt out the truth. "She took her own life."

He made a little sound—it might have been a curse—

and slowed, glancing over at her. "I'm sorry. That must have been terrible."

"It was. Very hard on both of us, me and Savannah."

"Were you separated? You said you lived with your aunt, but what about your sister?"

He really listened. Not a common quality, especially in a man. "She mostly lived with a friend of my mom's. A woman involved in the pageant world. Aunt Katy made sure we got together some, like that time we spent here as teenagers."

"You seem close, for not being raised together."

Were they? Taylor didn't know anymore. "I'm glad she's staying here on the island. Who knows? Maybe she'll make it permanent."

"You'd like that?"

Slowly, she nodded. "I would. We're pretty different, and we had some conflicts when we were younger—" She broke off, realizing that she was walking alongside the source of one of them. Her face heated. "How about you, Cody? Do you think you'll stay on the island?"

He puffed out a breath. "No idea. I just had a major life change, and I'm… I'm dealing with some stuff from my time overseas. Mostly it's the kids, though," he added quickly. "Who knows how things will shake out with them? We'll see."

She admired that he'd assumed responsibility for his brother and sister. But telling him that would probably embarrass him.

She also noticed how he'd mentioned dealing with issues from his military time and then glossed right over it. She was curious, but it wasn't her right to probe.

So they simply walked, meandering down a path that ran between the shoreline grasses, stiff and brown for winter.

Here by the water, the breeze sharpened, chilling her cheeks. But the sun felt warm on her hair. The salt smell of the bay and the sound of the repeating waves soothed her, but all the same, being with Cody made her feel an edge of some dangerous possibility.

The way he listened, the way they'd been talking, wrapped invisible strings around them. They were getting closer.

"Quit worrying," he said, nudging her, and for a moment she thought he'd read her mind, that he knew she was thinking about them, together.

Of course he doesn't. He thinks you're worried about the bakery.

Either way, he was right; she needed to stop worrying and embrace this hour-long getaway from her cares.

With a man who was amazing and who, apparently, wanted to spend time with her.

They walked the bay path quietly, pointing something out occasionally, waving to a couple of intrepid January boaters and, by the time they finally turned around and walked back, Taylor felt refreshed and renewed.

They came to the little bridge that crossed over the stream, and as one, they leaned on the railing to survey the wild mix of vegetation and bay creatures and brackish water below them. "Thank you for this," she said. "You were so right. I needed to get away."

"I don't want to go back," he admitted. "I've enjoyed this time with you. It's good to be quiet together."

Taylor's breath was catching a little, and she was pretty sure it wasn't because of the exertion. She looked away from him.

She heard him chuckle and turned back. "What's funny?"

She couldn't help smiling.

"Do you know what this bridge is called?" he asked.

She looked around for a sign, didn't see one and shook her head.

"It's called the Kissing Bridge. On a romantic island, it's one of the most romantic places."

"Really?" Now she was having more trouble catching her breath.

"Really." His gaze flickered down to her lips.

Turn away, run away, one side of her urged.

Kiss him! said the other side.

She did neither. "So…like for wedding photos and such?" There, that was the ticket. Make it sound like she was just talking to a fellow professional. "How fun! We should do some photos for the bakery here."

He wasn't buying her act. "We could," he said. "Or… we could test it out." He moved marginally closer, a question in his eyes.

He was going to kiss her.

She wanted it more than anything.

And then an evil little voice spoke up in the back of her head. *Wonder how many girls he's kissed here?*

Probably a lot. Probably her own sister.

She took a big sidestep, putting enough distance between them that she could no longer feel his heat. That was one thing she didn't need to worry about. Making out with her new employee, the man with whom she was co-parenting—especially when he was just doing it for entertainment, since he'd never really want a woman like her—well, that would be a disaster. "We should get back," she said. "I should, anyway. Stay out here awhile, why don't you?"

"Is that what you want?" he asked, his eyes steady on hers.

No, screamed her heart. *No, I want you*.

Ruthlessly, she squelched her tender side. "Yes," she said, "it's what I want."

SAVANNAH EXPECTED TO beat Taylor to the Dockside Diner, but when she walked into the loud place on Thursday evening, Taylor was already at the bar. She headed toward her.

"He-e-ey," said some guy who was leaning against the wall, beer in hand.

She flashed him a noncommittal nod and kept going.

He followed her, and when she slid onto a bar stool beside Taylor, he sat on her other side. "Buy you ladies a drink?"

"No thanks, Barry," Taylor said. "The two of us are having a private talk."

Barry slid off the stool and tipped his fisherman's cap to Savannah. "Barry Montrose."

"Pleased to meet you," she said automatically. "I'm Savannah Harp."

"You sure I can't buy you a drink?"

Taylor made a brushing off motion with her hand. "Like I said, Barry, the two of us need to talk. Privately."

As the man walked away, Savannah raised an eyebrow at her sister. "That was harsh. He seemed nice."

"Do you want to date him?" Taylor asked.

"No! No way. I'm not looking to…" For some reason, the memory of Hank's roughened fingers flashed into her mind. "I'm not looking for any relationship right now, believe me."

"Then you don't want to encourage a guy like Barry." Taylor waved to the bartender.

The woman came over to them. "Ready for another?" she asked Taylor, whose glass was, indeed, almost empty.

"Sure."

"What'll you have, honey?" The woman studied Savannah, then looked at Taylor. "I didn't know you had a sister!"

"Uh-huh. Surprised you could tell." Taylor finished her beer in one long swig.

"I'm Beatriz," the woman said, smiling at Savannah.

"Savannah. Pleased to meet you. Do you have prosecco?"

Beatriz frowned. "We did in the summer, but… I don't think so, not now. Not something the locals have a taste for."

"Okay, any kind of white wine." She watched as Beatriz walked away, then glanced over at Taylor. "Prosecco is the lowest-calorie way to get drunk," she explained.

"How come you want to?" Taylor rolled her shoulders back like they hurt.

Taylor was probably working too hard, like always.

Automatically, Savannah slid off her stool and stood behind her sister, rubbing her shoulders. "You're tight."

"Yeah, but don't change the subject. What's up with you? You sounded upset when you called."

Their drinks came, and Savannah sat down and sipped hers. Sweet, something Rupert would probably sneer at, but she liked it fine. She'd never acquired his expensive tastes, which, considering how things had turned out, was probably for the best. "I need advice."

"I'm listening."

Savannah took in a deep breath. "You know that letter that came to the bakery for me?"

Taylor nodded.

"Well, it was from…Rupert, the guy I was living with. And don't judge," she said, raising a hand to forestall any scolding. Taylor had lived an upright life with a strong set of religious values and, though she'd never said it, probably considered Savannah a tramp. "We were engaged, or so I thought. And he was going to help me figure out acting school."

"What happened?"

Savannah did a mental run-through of the last few months with Rupert and decided they didn't hold a story worth telling. "It just didn't work out. We had a…disagreement."

"It's good you got away, then."

"Yeah, it is."

"But…" Taylor prompted.

"But now, he's threatening some stuff. That's not what I want advice about, though."

Taylor waved Beatriz over and ordered Savannah another glass of wine. "Tell me."

"It's Hank. Really, it's Nadine." Savannah stared at the nicked mahogany bar. "The honest truth is, I'm bad at this job. I don't know how strict to be, I don't know how to cook, I can't connect with a teenager. Hank was going to fire me, but when he heard about Rupert's threats, he said he'd keep me on another week." She looked up and met Taylor's eyes. "Basically, I'm a disaster."

Taylor didn't look away. "Savannah, you're not a disaster. How would you know those things? You didn't have a regular childhood with meals and rules and same-age friends. You were always with adults once you started doing pageants. Adults, and other isolated pageant or model wannabes."

She'd never thought about it like that, but it was true. She had some Hallmark Channel notion of what ordinary families acted like, but she'd never experienced the real thing. "What do I do, though? I can't go back and remake our childhood."

Taylor frowned. "Cooking, I can help you with. Getting along with a teenage girl… I don't know. From what I've heard, that's kind of hit-or-miss even for experienced parents."

"I think Hank wants me to solve all Nadine's problems. Apparently, her mom was flighty and irresponsible, and that's how Hank sees me, too."

"Of course he does. You see what you're looking for." Taylor frowned. "Can you get things out in the open with them? Talk over the rules and boundaries, what's your domain and what's her father's? Honestly, he should have already done that with you."

"He did, some. I can try to clarify things." But she didn't feel all that hopeful. "Even I know that teenagers balk at the idea of a serious talk with adults."

"Well then…" Taylor thought a minute. "Get Nadine to help you cook a meal. If she's invested, she'll feel good about it. Tell her dad how hard she worked. And then…" Taylor lifted her hands, palms up. "I don't know why I'm trying to tell you what to do. The truth is, my childhood wasn't any more normal than yours. I mean, Mom was messed up for years before she…"

"Died," Savannah said firmly. "I always just say that she died."

"Right. Anyway, she didn't exactly set boundaries."

"You set them for me. You'd be great at this job," Savannah said, feeling gloomy. "Whereas all I can do is look good for a camera."

Taylor rolled her eyes. "That's not nothing. How many women would kill to have your looks?"

"Would you, though?"

"No, because I know from you what it's like. But there's got to be a way you can use your looks to get work. Can't you model again? Or, like, charm some guy into giving you a job?" She wrinkled her nose. "Kidding, but not."

Savannah stared at her sister. "Hurtful!"

Taylor looked contrite. "I'm sorry. I didn't mean *charm* in a bad way. And just until you get back on your feet."

"No. I don't want to rely on my looks anymore. Everyone thinks that's all I am. Shoot, at times *I* think that's all I am. I want to find out what else is there, but so far, I'm coming up blank."

"I hear you," Taylor said. "I'll keep thinking about it. And honey, you know you'll never starve or be homeless. You can stay with me if you have to."

The offer was reluctantly given, and Savannah could understand that. "How's it going with the little ones and Cody?"

Taylor shrugged. "What can I say? I'm in over my head. Way over my head."

Something about the way Taylor said it… "What do you mean? Are you…*in* it with Cody?" She'd definitely gotten that vibe from them.

"No!" Taylor's cheeks went pink, a dead giveaway.

"You *are*!" Savannah clapped her hands. "I would *love* to see you two get together."

"Never going to happen." Taylor's shoulders slumped. "As long as you're around, no man ever sees me."

"That's not true! I heard you've been seeing that one guy, Manson." As soon as she said it, Savannah regretted it. Manson wasn't worth Taylor's time. Savannah had seen through his bluster as a teenager.

"Well, Manson."

"You can do so much better, Taylor."

"I can't. So let's don't talk about it." She pushed her glass away. "I really wish I could give you some financial help. That's why I'm working so hard at the bakery, to get us a nest egg so we're never struggling again. I'm just not there yet."

"You're the best." Savannah hugged her sister. "And

you don't have to do that. Build up savings for me, I mean."

Taylor shrugged.

"You're down about it."

"Yeah."

Savannah was used to battling the blues, but she got the sense that Taylor wasn't. "You're not...down like Mom, are you?"

Taylor shook her head. "No. You?"

"Not anymore." She grabbed Taylor's hand. "But look, we're both afraid we'll get depressed like she did, and we have to fight it. Let's try to walk together every day, or most days, while I'm here."

"I can't. I've got kids around."

"Bring 'em," Savannah said. "It's most important to get out into the sunshine for a little bit of time each day. Shoot, I might even bring Nadine."

Taylor smiled. "That would liven things up, for sure."

"It might." Savannah pondered the whole situation they were in. "You know, I wonder if Nadine would like to babysit Ava and Danny some? She needs something positive in her life, and when you're a teenager, making money is positive."

"Interesting idea," Taylor said. "But I'm not sure the kids can deal with a new caregiver right now. They've attached themselves to Cody and me."

Savannah still wasn't convinced that "Cody and me" wasn't a thing, but she pressed on. "How about a mother's helper kind of thing? Remember when that really old lady helped take care of us during Mom's bad spells? Mom was there, but Mrs...."

"Mrs. Drummond! She let us eat Nutella sandwiches for dinner!"

"Right." That had been in the wonderful days when Savannah could eat whatever sweets she wanted without worrying that she'd burst out of her pageant dress. "Anyway, Nadine could watch the kids, at home or at your place, while you and Cody... I don't know, bake? Figure out your business plan?"

"Both." Taylor was nodding. "That's not a bad idea. I'll run it by Cody." She pushed her credit card across the bar to Beatriz, and when Savannah reached into her purse, she shook her head. "No, this is on me. I wasn't much help to you, but you've figured out something that just might help me."

Savannah felt good, and not just due to the gentle wine buzz. She *had* helped Taylor, for once.

Things were looking up.

SATURDAY MORNING, Cody yawned and stretched and realized that he'd actually slept last night. The night before, too. Having the kids had apparently exhausted him enough to cure his insomnia.

He would have loved nothing more than to lie around in his sweats and watch cartoon TV with Danny. He had the feeling Danny would've loved that, too. But he'd committed to enriching the kids' lives in all the ways, and today was some library program. Unfortunately, that meant combing Danny's hair and brushing his teeth and finding him a decent outfit. Then doing the same for himself.

He drew the line at shaving, though. Not on a civilian Saturday.

Across the hall, he could hear Ava's voice, high-pitched and insistent, probably asking more of the million questions she had about everything. That, or saying "no," one of her favorite words.

No bath. No bed. No going to sleep at Cody's place. Once again last night, she'd insisted on staying with Taylor.

Which was complicated, because they'd planned for Taylor to do the night baking this weekend. She'd texted him that she'd borrowed a baby monitor and could keep track of Ava fine, but it wasn't ideal. Ava shouldn't be her responsibility.

The thought of that galvanized him into faster action, and he grabbed a couple of muffins for the kids to eat on the way. He needed to step up and give Taylor a break, though knowing her, she'd use it to do more baking or planning or paperwork. There was no doubt she was a workaholic.

Thing was, he admired that in her. Even in the military, where strong women had been plentiful, there hadn't been a lot of people driven by their own internal motivation. It had taken the command of a superior officer to goad everyone into action.

Taylor goaded herself.

He ushered Danny out onto the landing between the two apartments and tapped on Taylor's door. "It's Cody. Is Ava ready?"

"Just about." Taylor opened the door. "Come on in.

We're working on her tutu. She wants to wear it to the library."

"Tutu?" Cody was unable to do more than glance at Ava, because his eyes had stopped at Taylor. She must have gone back to sleep after completing the baking. Her hair was mussed, her eyes sleepy, and was that a little ridge on her cheek from a blanket?

His mind went places it definitely shouldn't go as he tried to imagine the sleep position that had put the line on her face and mussed her hair. "Come on, Ava," he said. "We need to leave."

"Liberry, liberry!" She danced and twirled, and Cody stopped gawking at Taylor to watch and smile. Ava had to be the cutest little girl in Maryland, and she was his sister.

Not that he was taking care of her, not as much as Taylor. So the least he could do was to give Taylor a break.

Ava danced out the door, and Taylor handed her jacket to Cody and started to close it.

At which point Ava realized Taylor wasn't coming and started to cry. She turned, pushed her way back into Taylor's apartment and attached herself to Taylor's flannel-clad leg like a small monkey.

"Come on, Ava," Cody said. "We'll see Taylor later. Come with Danny and me."

"No! Want Taylor!" Ava sobbed as if her heart were being torn in two.

Taylor looked at him helplessly. "I can go," she said.

"No. You don't have to."

She looked down at the squalling Ava. "I just might

have to. But it's fine. I love the library. And I have some extra counter help this morning. Lolly wanted the hours."

"Taylor come to liberry," Ava said, smiling up at them both, dimples appearing on her rosy cheeks.

Man, the girl was going to be a master manipulator by the time she turned five. Cody knew he shouldn't give into her whims, but the parenting blogs he'd been desperately scanning at night didn't tell you how to peel a child off a more-desired person and get her to the library on time and quiet.

"Just give me a minute to change," Taylor said. She squatted down. "Ava, if you want me to come, you need to be quiet and wait with Cody and Danny while I get dressed."

"Okay," Ava said as if she were the most reasonable child in the world.

Minutes later they were walking through the Saturday cold toward the library. Ahead of them, another family seemed to be doing the same, judging from the stack of picture books the father was carrying.

Cody decided he would get a card and check out books for the kids. Get them excited about reading early, before technology got its teeth into them.

Up ahead, the man put an arm around his wife, and Cody felt a twist in his gut.

He wanted what they had. Wanted to give it to Danny and Ava.

Wanted it and didn't have it.

He looked over at Taylor, so sexy and so unaware of

it. He sighed. If ever there were a woman to evoke his desire for commitment, it would be Taylor.

But Cody didn't commit, no way.

IN THE LIBRARY, Cody breathed in the smell of books and was taken straight back to his high school years. Betty had insisted that they get library cards almost immediately on arrival, which had been a revelation to Cody and his foster brother Luis. Ryan, it turned out, had been a library user throughout his chaotic life. Probably part of the reason he was so smart.

Betty had insisted they check out one book per week. At first, Cody had grabbed any old book, knowing he wouldn't read it. But seeing Ryan engrossed in a book, and soon Luis as well, had made him curious. Eventually, he'd figured out how to find military adventure books, and from then on he'd spent time reading. Not as much as his brothers, not at first. But the habit had grown on him.

When he'd been overseas, there were long stretches of boredom. He'd been more than happy to discover that US civilians put together boxes of used books for military personnel, and he'd gotten so into it that the postmaster gave him first shot when one arrived. He'd pretty much always had a book to read, and it had been a comfort.

Now he glanced over the new fiction on a display case near the front door and was tempted to grab one of the bestsellers, a thriller he'd been thinking about buying.

"Are you here for the Saturday Reading program?"

a teenage girl asked. She had a name tag around her neck. Maddie: Volunteer.

He tore himself away from the new books. "Yes. Yes, this is Danny. And this is Ava."

"We need to get you signed in." She beckoned them over to the circulation desk and made name tags for the kids, then pointed them toward a colorful room that held the sound of children's laughter. But Ava clung to Taylor's leg.

"Mom will come in just as soon as she's signed some paperwork," Maddie said. Then she did a double take. "Taylor? I didn't realize you…"

Taylor laughed. "No, I don't have a secret family. I'm just helping out. These two belong to Cody." She gestured toward him.

"Oh, okay. Dad, you'll have to fill stuff out, then." The girl shoved two forms across the desk toward him. "You can take it into the children's room if you want. That way the kids will get to hear the beginning of the story. Here, I'll get you a clipboard."

Thus equipped, they all headed into the children's room. The librarian—he could identify her because of her air of authority and her name tag—was talking to some of the other parents, but she broke away to come over. "Hi, Taylor," she said and then held out a hand to Cody. "I'm Linda Iglesias. I don't believe I've met you yet."

"Cody Cunningham. And this is Danny, and the ballerina is Ava."

"Lovely," she said. "Children, you can sit on a square of carpet while I talk to your father."

Ava looked uncertainly up at Taylor.

"Go ahead. Sit by…" She looked around. "Why don't you sit right there, by the girl with the unicorn stuffie? Danny will sit close to you. Right?"

Danny frowned, but when he realized there was a boy his age directly in front of the girl, he nodded. "Okay."

Taylor was a genius with these kids. She'd be a wonderful mother.

Which wasn't a thought he'd had before about a woman, ever. Danny and Ava had rocked his world in all kinds of ways.

"Cody lived with Betty while he was a teenager," Taylor was explaining to Linda.

"Oh! That's fine then. Fill out the paperwork whenever."

"Thanks." Cody had to smile. "Betty's the person to know on Teaberry Island, just like when I was living with her."

The librarian smiled back. "We love Betty around here. She's leading our book club this year."

"You should come!" Maddie, the volunteer desk assistant, had appeared in the doorway of the children's room where they were all standing. "It's focused on science fiction." She was looking at him eagerly.

What was that all about? "Thanks," he said, "but science fiction isn't really my thing."

"I'd better start before the natives get restless," Linda said. "You're welcome to browse or hang out on the sidelines and watch, whatever works. Maddie, you need to get back to the desk."

Cody glanced around and saw a couple of comfortable-looking chairs that were in the kids' line of sight. "We'll sit over there and keep an eye on things."

Mrs. Iglesias got started with a picture book that involved the kids making animal motions with their arms and hands. Ava and Danny were immediately enthralled, so Cody led the way over to the easy chairs.

"You were mean to her!" Taylor said.

He lifted his hands, puzzled. "To Mrs. Iglesias? What did I do wrong?"

"No, to Maddie, the volunteer. She had a crush on you."

"She did?" It was news to Cody.

"Yes! You should take her out on a date!"

He laughed at the idea. "She's, like, twelve!"

"She's nineteen or twenty, I think."

He shook his head. "Not interested in dating. I have plenty on my plate." Which was mostly true. The only woman he'd fantasized about dating recently was Taylor. Even just sitting beside her in the library, he was extraordinarily aware of the honeysuckle fragrance of her hair, the curve of her smile.

Trying to distract himself, he gestured toward the kids, still sitting alert, listening to the story. "And listen, I'm sorry I got you involved in all of this. You were supposed to have a Saturday to catch up. I'll find a way to make it up to you, but right now, I'm not full of ideas."

"Stuff happens." She shrugged. "Savannah and I did cook up an idea, though. She thinks Nadine, the teen girl she's helping with, could use a job. Savannah suggested that we could hire her to watch the kids and play with them here and there."

"That would be great."

She nodded. "It would give us time to do bakery work."

Cody's thoughts headed in another direction. Taylor worked all the time. Too much.

Was there any way he could use this potential baby-sitter's availability to make time for a date with Taylor?

CHAPTER NINE

WONDER OF WONDERS, Savannah thought, Nadine was in a good mood.

The teenager had just bounced out of her room with a huge smile on her face. She looked toward her father's closed study door and then spun toward Savannah. "I have something to do tonight! It's a Saturday and I have something to do! With *friends*."

Even though Nadine had been nothing but obnoxious to her, Savannah's shoulders relaxed. A thirteen-year-old girl needed friends so very much, and apparently, Nadine had been struggling to make some since she and her dad had arrived here two months ago. Savannah's suggestions of joining a school club or the church youth fellowship had fallen on deaf ears, and her offers of taking Nadine and a friend to shop over on the mainland had been scornfully rejected.

Savannah realized this was something Nadine had to work out for herself, and apparently, she'd done just that, or at least taken a step. "Terrific. Who are they?" Or was that too intrusive of a question to ask? Savannah turned the page of the magazine she'd been reading, trying not to show too much interest. Nadine was like a hummingbird, hovering close, but ready to dart away if you turned and focused on her.

Nadine hummed in closer. "Abby and Emily. They're really nice! Popular, but not snotty and mean."

Savannah looked up and let herself return Nadine's happy smile. "That's great. Are you doing something fun?"

Nadine shrugged. "Who cares? As long as I'm not sitting around with my *dad* and my…my *babysitter*."

Was that meant to be an insult? Savannah had been called worse. "What are you going to wear?"

Nadine paused mid-twirl. "I don't know. I don't have anything. My best jeans are dirty." Her face started to fall.

"Come on. I'll help you." Savannah stood quickly, wanting to avert an emotional meltdown, and headed toward Nadine's room. This was one problem she knew how to solve.

At the doorway, she waited. Nadine stood where she'd been in the living room, her face indecisive.

Savannah could read her hesitation. Nadine had used her as a scapegoat for her misery the entire time Savannah had been here. Savannah's mishandling of the boy-in-her-room situation and her poor cooking skills had done nothing to endear her to the child.

Although Savannah had worked hard on the cooking thing and had improved to the point where she was making edible meals, she'd made little to no progress connecting with Nadine.

She'd have said "give it time" if someone else had consulted her for a similar problem, but she didn't have

time. It had been four days since her come-to-Jesus talk
with Hank, and she'd basically resigned herself to finding another job and place to live.

Which meant moving back to the mainland. Which
meant dealing with Rupert.

Right now, though, she could at least help a young
girl through a clothing crisis. "Come on," she said,
beckoning to Nadine. "I used to model, remember? I
know clothes."

Nadine looked toward her father's study, and again,
Savannah could read the girl's thoughts: no help there.
Hank was a good guy, but he wore dad clothes.

"Okay," Nadine said, sounding grumpy, and then, as
she reached the doorway, her face went panicky and she
gripped Savannah's arm. "I don't know *what* to wear!
I don't know what we're doing, where we're going, but
I can't call them back to ask."

Savannah got that. Nadine was the new friend and
couldn't rock the boat. "What things *could* you be
doing? Nothing fancy, I'm guessing." There was exactly one fancy restaurant on the island. Beyond that,
there was the Dockside Diner where she'd met Taylor
on Thursday, but it had more of a bar atmosphere. She
hadn't seen kids there.

Nadine shrugged. "Hanging at someone's house or
walking around outside, probably. But I want to look
cute!"

"Show me what you've got," Savannah ordered. "Tops
and jeans."

Soon they were rummaging through Nadine's drawers together. The child sadly needed a shopping trip. She'd talk to Hank about it…if Hank kept her on.

"I hate these." Nadine threw one pair of jeans to the side and picked up the only other pair. "These don't fit. I could wear joggers, but… I don't know."

"You said your good pair of jeans was dirty?"

Nadine nodded. "I wore them all weekend and you haven't done laundry since then." Her tone rose at the end.

"No. Uh-uh." Savannah wasn't taking the blame for that. "You're supposed to put dirty clothes in the hamper by the washing machine if you want them washed, and it's empty." It wasn't like Savannah had much else to do, so she'd picked up on that bit of household routine and taken it over.

Nadine's pretty face twisted into a pout. Of course, she knew Savannah was right. Then her lip started to tremble. "What am I gonna do?"

Savannah relented. "I know a trick," she said. "Come on, I'll show you. Grab your dirty jeans."

A minute later, the jeans were spinning in the dryer with a damp washcloth sprayed with perfume. "This is strictly for emergencies," she felt obligated to say. "Normally, you should wear clean clothes, but in a pinch, this will freshen them up."

"Cool!"

By the time they'd picked out two tops to layer together or wear alone, depending on whether they were inside or outside, the jeans were ready. Free of laundry-basket wrinkles and smelling like flowers. "Don't wear any more perfume on top of these," Savannah instructed. "You don't want to make people pass out."

"Okay." Nadine was already shimmying into the jeans. She pulled on the tops they'd chosen, trying them both single and layered, pirouetting in front of the standalone full-length mirror that would be the envy of most teens.

Savannah envied it herself. "You look really cute," she said, meaning it.

"I kinda do." Nadine frowned. "I need more jeans, though."

"You do. Would you be interested in getting a job to help pay for them? I have a lead on a babysitting job, but we'll have to ask your dad about that."

Nadine rushed to the door and flung it open. "Dad!" she bellowed.

Savannah winced and waited for him to come rushing in, thinking there was some huge problem, but he sauntered in without panic. Apparently, he was more used to teen dramatics than Savannah was.

"What hurricane hit?" he asked, glancing around at the clothes strewn on the floor. He stepped in gingerly, looking big and out of place among the lavender curtains and puffy pillows.

"I have to ask you something," Nadine said to him and then turned to Savannah. "Can you help me with my makeup?"

"Sure. Sit down." She selected a cover-up pencil from the makeup strewn across the vanity and started applying it to a small breakout across Nadine's cheek. "Be sure to take this off at night, so your skin can breathe," she instructed.

Hank leaned against the wall, arms crossed in front of him. "This is a world I don't understand."

"Obviously, Dad." Nadine tilted her head upward, and Savannah brushed a little blush across her cheeks. "Savannah might have gotten me a babysitting job. Can I do it?"

His bushy eyebrows drew together. "Of course not. You're thirteen!"

Savannah glanced up at him, then started on Nadine's brows, which were heavy like her father's. A brush with a touch of Vaseline smoothed them down. "It's a mother's helper type of thing. The adult caregiver would be there, but working, and Nadine's job would be to play with the kids. Or the kids could be dropped off here, where you or I could supervise them."

"I need money for clothes," Nadine explained.

Hank opened his mouth, and Savannah looked at him and gave a tiny shake of her head. He was going to offer to take her shopping and buy her whatever she needed, but it would be so good for Nadine to make money on her own.

"I'm sure your dad pays for the basics," Savannah said, "but a little cash for extras would be fun."

Nadine straightened and frowned at her father in the mirror. "Abby, who I'm hanging out with tonight, works in her family's business. And Emily babysits."

"Wait. You're going out?"

"These girls are fine, Dad. You met Emily's mom at the open house. She's the one with red hair. And

Abby was helping with that boat cruise we did when we first came."

Savannah watched Hank process that and didn't envy him, single-parenting a teen girl in a new place where you didn't know many people.

"There," she said, smoothing out Nadine's cover-up makeup with a pinkie. "You look perfect."

Nadine studied herself in the mirror. "No eye makeup?"

Hank started to bluster, but Savannah held out a stop sign hand to him, low, and shook her head. "Not for a night out with the girls. You don't want to look like you're trying too hard."

"Okay." Nadine spun on her bench to face her father. "So can I do the babysitting job?"

"It's for Cody's little sister and brother," Savannah explained.

"As long as it's people we know and there's an adult you can call on. A female adult."

Nadine's eye roll was classic. "Dad. Men are not the enemy."

He winced, making Savannah wonder whether this was one of Nadine's mother's sayings.

His phone buzzed, and he glanced down at it. "Quick call," he said. "Don't go until I come back. I want to talk to your friends."

Nadine's head sank into her hands. "He's going to grill them."

Savannah restrained herself from saying what she felt inside: *You're lucky to have a father who cares.* "That's a dad thing. I'm sure your friends' fathers do the same."

The doorbell rang.

"They're here!" Nadine ran to open it.

Instead of girl chatter, Savannah heard a deep voice and quickly headed toward the entryway. There was Kevin, the boy from before. "Want to hang out?" he was asking.

Nadine looked torn, and Savannah got it. She herself had broken a few plans with girlfriends to get together with a man. But it was a bad practice.

Savannah looked toward Hank's closed study door. She had to deal with this herself, and quickly, before it descended into another disaster like last week's. She sucked in a breath. "Nadine, I need to see you in here," she called from the doorway of Nadine's room.

Nadine looked at her with mouth open and eyebrows raised, a classic expression of exaggerated disbelief.

Savannah knew she didn't have the authority to hustle the girl along, so she looked right back with her own eyebrows raised, and waited.

Nadine huffed out a groan. "I'll be right back," she said to Kevin and then stomped back to the bedroom. "What?"

Savannah closed the door partway to give them privacy. "You wanted to get together with your girlfriends. Tell him you have other plans."

"But he's cool," Nadine half said, half whined. "And he likes me."

"He'll like you more if you're not so easy to get," Savannah said, advice she wished she'd followed more often herself. "And your new girlfriends will like you better if you don't ditch them for a guy."

"But—"

"Tell him you have other plans, or that you're not allowed to hang out with him tonight," Savannah said. "You can blame me. Or your dad, because I'm sure he would agree with me."

"I hate you!" Nadine muttered. She stormed out, slamming the bedroom door behind her.

Savannah opened it and stood in the doorway to make sure her instructions were being followed. "They won't let me," she was saying.

"Fine." Kevin sounded as sulky as a ten-year-old.

"Plus," Nadine said, "I have other plans."

His hand on the doorknob, the boy turned back. "Maybe we can hang another time."

Score one for Nadine, Savannah thought. *And for me.*

She couldn't wait to brag to Hank about how she'd handled that situation.

LESS THAN FIVE minutes later, Savannah was back on the couch with her magazine, and Nadine was in her room, no doubt plotting revenge.

Hank emerged from his study. "Sorry about that," he said. "Did I hear doors slamming?"

"Yeah," Savannah said. "That guy who was over before came back, wanting to hang out with her. I suggested she stick to her girlfriend plans."

"Good."

"I actually invoked your authority, so I'm glad you agree."

Nadine came out of her room, managing to slam it open, probably chipping the pretty lavender paint on the wall behind it. "Fire her," she said, pointing at Savannah with a straight arm and surly frown.

Savannah almost laughed. But the trouble was, he might.

"Nadine," he said sharply. "Manners. You can't—"

The doorbell rang again, cutting off any fatherly wisdom he'd been about to impart. Nadine rushed to open it and two girls came in. Now, there was the high-pitched chatter Savannah had been expecting before.

"This place is so cool!" one of them said.

"Was that Kevin Granger who was leaving here?" the other asked.

"Yeah," Nadine said. "He wanted to hang out, but I told him I had other plans."

"Girl power! I knew you were cool." The taller girl high-fived Nadine.

"Besides," the other girl said, "he's sort of a skug."

"Come back to my room," Nadine invited them, and after a breathless "This is my dad, this is Savannah, this is Abby and Emily," the door closed behind them with a decisive click.

Hank looked at Savannah. "What's a skug?"

"It's not good, I don't think." An alarm on her phone rang. "I'm going to put in the meat loaf."

She hurried into the kitchen and realized she hadn't preheated the oven, which, according to Taylor, was super important. She switched it on now. When she pulled the meat loaf out of the fridge and turned, she realized Hank had followed her into the kitchen.

Something about that made Savannah feel flustered

and warm. "I didn't know Savannah's friends would be here this early," she said. "I'd have put this in earlier."

"Teenagers are unpredictable, I'm learning."

"We can ask them to stay for dinner, but I don't know how good it'll be." The preheating bell rang—a benefit of the fancy oven was that it heated so quickly—and she slid in the meat loaf and pulled out potatoes to scrub. "It'll be another hour at least."

The three girls burst into the kitchen. "We're leaving soon," Nadine said as she helped herself to a cookie and then held the jar out to the other girls. Thank heavens Savannah had stocked it with cookies from the bakery.

"Mmmm, these are good!" Emily bit into a snickerdoodle. "Did you make them?" she asked Savannah.

Nadine snorted.

"My sister," Savannah said. "She's Taylor, who runs the Bluebird Bakery."

"Love that place," Abby said.

The girls lounged around the big table in the center of the room, and Savannah felt the strangest surge of longing.

What would it have been like if she'd had a normal childhood and normal teen years, hanging around the house, knowing her father, having friends? What would it be like if she were the real mom here, rather than the babysitter? "You girls are welcome to stay for dinner," she said. "Fill up before you go out, so you don't have to spend money on food."

"Nah, we're going to this lock-in at the community center, and there's pizza." Emily licked her fingers. "It's not very exciting, but there's nothing else to do here."

"It's an overnight, Dad. Can I go?" Nadine was trying to sound cool, but Savannah could tell from her shining eyes that she was thrilled to be included. Savannah was thrilled herself, on Nadine's behalf. Getting involved with some nice girls was exactly what the child needed.

"Abby, you're Renate's daughter, right?"

"Yeah, you talked to my mom at the open house, I think. Or maybe church."

"Can I have her number? I'd just like to give her a call."

"Dad!"

Abby laughed. "Sure. Mom always does that, too. I'll text her that you're calling." She typed into her phone and then wrote down the number and handed it to Hank.

Savannah pulled lettuce and cucumbers and carrots from the fridge to make salad, but didn't get it started. She didn't know how much to make. If Nadine were going to start having friends over, which Savannah hoped was the case, she'd have to be sure there was extra food on hand.

She listened as Hank called the girl's mother. He was self-deprecating, humble and by the end of the short phone call he was laughing. He'd probably charmed the woman.

He was a charming man. And she did *not* need to be thinking that about her employer. About anyone. She was a disaster with men.

Hank wouldn't be the same kind of disaster that Rupert had been, but Hank wouldn't go for her, of course. She wasn't his type. She was too incompetent and, well, trashy. Used up. She was nothing, as Rupert had told her, and he wasn't the first.

She swallowed the lump that rose up in her throat.

Nadine and her friends started putting on their coats.

"Don't you have to get your things?" Savannah asked. "Makeup remover, toothbrush?"

Nadine grinned, revealing her absurdly cute dimple. "I figured Dad would say yes, so I went ahead and packed." She grabbed a bag from beside the kitchen door.

"Do you girls want a ride to the community center?" Hank was already getting out his car keys.

Nadine looked at the others.

"No, we'll walk," Emily said, and the others quickly agreed.

Hank gave them a stern mock-glare and put his hands on his hips. "No shenanigans. You know I'll hear about it if you don't go directly to the center."

"Da-a-a-ad!" But Nadine didn't sound all that upset. The other girls laughed and promised to behave. It was clear that Hank had charmed them, too, in an every-dad sort of way.

A minute later they were out the door. Hank saw them out and came back into the kitchen.

The kitchen was warm and bright, and the food was starting to smell good. It was just her, and Hank, and a meat loaf. And a house that now lacked a teenage chaperone. Which she definitely had no business thinking about. "Do you still want dinner?" she asked. "I can save it for tomorrow if—"

"I still want dinner," he interrupted. "And I hope you'll sit down with me. We need to talk."

Great, Savannah thought as she glumly started cutting up the vegetables for salad. Why did they need to talk *again*?

TAYLOR WALKED THROUGH the door of the church, Mellie beside her, and put a hand on Mellie's arm. "I can't believe that sorting stuff for a rummage sale seems like a fun Saturday night."

"Welcome to motherhood," Mellie said.

The words gave Taylor a funny feeling. She *wasn't* a mother, had no formal connection to Ava and Danny, and yet she was already deeply involved in their lives. The feeling she had for them was definitely motherly. And she loved it.

The basement of the church was a work in progress. Half the room contained semi-neat piles of items, atop tables labeled with Boys' Clothing, Small Appliances and Craft Supplies.

The other half of the room held boxes full of colorful toys and clothing. Three other women were already working, going through the boxes, chatting as they went.

"More help! Thank you!" Linda Iglesias, the librarian, approached them. "Somehow, I'm in charge this year. What do you girls want to work on?"

"Can we sort out the toys? Over there, if possible." Taylor pointed toward the far corner of the room. "We have things to discuss."

Mellie raised an eyebrow. "We do?"

"We do," Taylor said firmly. She needed to work through all the confusing events and issues of her life right now, or at least vent about them. Mellie had done the same with her many times in the past. Taylor figured that Mellie owed her, plus Mellie was discreet.

Mellie and Ryan had also been incredibly helpful with the kids, giving Taylor and Cody a crash course in available activities, the health clinic on the island and doctors to use off-island, and child food preferences. Right now, Cody and Ryan and the kids were hanging out at Mellie and Ryan's place, eating popcorn and watching movies and, no doubt, playing with Alfie's light sabers and generally making a big mess.

Together with Linda Iglesias and a man Taylor didn't know, they carried boxes of toys to a table at the far side of the room. "You'll have some privacy here, but I wouldn't suggest revealing state secrets," she said after the man walked back to the sorting tables, with an exaggerated expression of caution. She nodded sideways toward the man. "He's new to the island, but he's very, um, interested in the town gossip and full of opinions," Linda said. "On the plus side, he's strong."

"Duly noted," Taylor said.

They quickly got organized, deciding to sort the toys by age and then subcategory if there were a lot of them. "Not by gender," Mellie said firmly. "If a girl wants to play with a truck, or a boy with a doll, I want them to go for it."

"Good. I agree." Her own words surprised Taylor. Her and Savannah's toys had been firmly in the "girl" category. When had she developed the opinion that kids should be raised to play with all toys?

They sorted in silence for a few minutes, quickly realizing they needed another section for toys too broken or dirty to be set out. "We'll wash them if we have time," Mellie said. "But who would donate a doll with no head?"

"Wait a sec." Taylor bent over another box. "Think I found it." She pulled out a doll's head, but it was blonde and pale, while the doll's body was dark-skinned. "Put them aside. We might find their mates."

"So how are things at the bakery?" Mellie asked.

"Crazy." Taylor pushed back her hair. "I can't bake fast enough for all the off-island orders that are coming in. I took down all my ads, but I'm still getting new customers every day."

"Word of mouth. That's fantastic." Mellie pulled a dump truck from a box, made sure it worked and put it into the toddlers' stack.

"It is. I'm counting my blessings, believe me. Except I can barely keep my head above water."

"Is Cody one of your blessings?"

Taylor laughed ruefully. "He's good at the job. He learns fast. Starts when he says he will, early even, and is glad to work overtime. But he's also the reason Danny and Ava are on the island, and those kids are a serious distraction from work, for both of us."

"I'm sure." Mellie glanced over at her. "You guys seem like a family, you know that?"

Taylor had felt the same thing, but hearing it articulated by her friend made her uncomfortable. "It's a temporary arrangement."

"Sure it is. But is there any chance of it becoming more permanent?"

"What do you mean?" Taylor got very busy carrying an armful of action figures to the school-age table. "Danny and Ava are his siblings. I don't know how long they'll be with him, but that's not my problem. Not my business."

"Isn't there something between the two of you?" Mellie tilted her head to one side, studying Taylor. "If there's not, there should be. You'd be great together."

Mellie's words made Taylor flush from her hair to the soles of her feet. "There's nothing between us," she scoffed. "I mean, look at him and look at me."

"I *have* been," Mellie said mildly. "Things get a little more electric when the two of you are in the same room."

They do? Certainly, Taylor felt a spark whenever Cody was around, but was it mutual? How could it be? "Not gonna happen."

"But it *did* happen, didn't it, when you and Savannah stayed that one summer?"

Disconcerted, Taylor headed back to where the others were sorting, grabbed a big container of disinfectant wipes and started walking back, her pace slow. She needed to cool down. This wasn't where she'd wanted the conversation to go.

Only maybe she *had* wanted to discuss the situation with her friend. Cody and the kids and the bakery were all tied up in her head, along with the longing she'd been trying without success to deny: the desire to start a family.

Wouldn't a bakery be a fantastic place for kids to grow up? They could remake the two apartments into a family home, the kids could run up and down the stairs all day and she and Cody could take turns caring for them, like…

Like they were doing now. Only they were doing it by circumstance and coincidence, not because they had made a commitment to each other.

She got back to the sorting table and started scrubbing down a particularly grimy set of plastic blocks, using the new container of disinfectant wipes. When she glanced up, she realized that Mellie was standing with her arms crossed, looking at Taylor expectantly. "What?" Taylor asked.

"I know you haven't forgotten my question, but I'll repeat it. What *did* happen when you knew Cody that summer?"

Taylor considered pushing the question aside as intrusive—which it was—but what was new? Everyone on this island tended to intrude in everyone else's life, usually out of kindness rather than simple nosiness. That was the case here. Mellie only wanted the best for her. "What happened is no surprise," she said. "Cody and I were getting to know each other, and then Savannah arrived. Cody took one look at her and never glanced back my way."

Mellie frowned.

Taylor went back to wiping off blocks.

"Do you think you gave up too quickly?" Mellie asked.

"What do you mean? There was nothing to give up on."

Mellie pushed herself up to perch on a table, no longer even pretending to work. "It just seems to me, looking at the three of you now, that you're much more Cody's type than Savannah is."

The words made hope bloom in Taylor's chest. If only they were true. But Mellie wasn't being realistic; she was being kind. "Savannah is every man's type."

"Savannah's gorgeous," Mellie admitted. "Probably there aren't that many men who don't take a second look at her. I know Ryan did."

"He *did*? When?"

"When he first saw her that summer," Mellie said. "And when he saw her last week."

Taylor's jaw dropped. "I'm so sorry. I thought you and Ryan had the perfect marriage."

Mellie tilted her head to one side, seeming puzzled. "We *do* have a great marriage. But that doesn't mean Ryan lost his vision. Honestly, I don't think there's a man on the island who doesn't pay at least some attention to Savannah."

Taylor laughed a little in disbelief. "I just don't see how you can be so calm about it."

"Um, because it's normal? Because I'm secure in my husband's love?" Mellie smiled and then shrugged. "I mean, *I* took a second glance at Cody when he showed up in his Santa suit, and that was my wedding day. Pretty is pretty."

Taylor remembered that day, when Cody had returned to the island by helicopter, making a showy entrance that had thrilled the kids. "Cody *is* good to look at, isn't he?"

"Yep. And there probably aren't many women on the island who don't notice him. But that doesn't mean they want to toss aside their perfectly good husbands or boyfriends and take up with him. I certainly don't. I'm crazy about Ryan."

"And he's crazy about you." That was obvious.

"Thanks. He is." Mellie's simple confidence made Taylor's stomach twist with envy. "I think you and Cody could end up crazy about each other, too."

Hope flashed through Taylor's chest, trying to take up residence in her heart. What would that be like, being crazy about Cody and knowing those feelings were reflected back at her?

But what were the odds of that happening? A lifetime of experience being herself told her: not a chance.

"I like him," she said, vastly understating the case. "But he'd never go for someone like me."

Mellie shrugged. "I think, if Cody went for anyone, it would be a person like you," she said. "But there *is* a problem."

Of course there was. "What is it?"

"Cody and commitment don't go together," Mellie said. "At least, that's what Ryan told me. Something happened to him overseas, and when you put that together with his childhood…whoever does fall in love with him is going to have a few barriers to overcome."

Taylor looked down at the box of toys and realized

she'd been wiping off the same plastic blocks for the past five minutes. They weren't going to get any cleaner. She scooped them into their container and carried them over to the toddlers' stack, picturing a young child's delight when they were brought home from the rummage sale.

Hopefully, they'd go to a family who'd really appreciate the toys, maybe to a kid who didn't have much to play with.

Just like Cody probably hadn't had much to play with as a child. She didn't know details about his childhood, but she'd gotten the outline of its difficulties, including from Mellie just now.

Cody had never even attended a birthday party.

When she knew of a child who lacked something, she wanted to provide it. When Ava cried due to missing her mother, Taylor didn't hesitate to pick her up and comfort her.

The thought of Cody having a deprived childhood brought out a similar instinct, only you couldn't pick up a grown man and comfort him. Cody had developed layers of protection to cover up his hurt.

Getting through to his actual heart would be a challenge, akin to breaking through the ice on one of the heavily frozen inlets on the island.

She shouldn't even think about trying. She was just ordinary Taylor, not sexy Savannah. There was every chance that if his heart opened up, it would react to her sister or another beautiful woman, not to her.

Besides, was it her business to try and reach him emotionally? Maybe he was closed off for a very good reason. A less nosy and intrusive person would leave him alone.

But Taylor had grown up thinking other people's emotions were her own responsibility, starting with her deeply troubled mother and extending to her sister, who'd needed nurturing their mother couldn't provide. Could she help it if she felt the same impulse toward a man who'd been disadvantaged through no fault of his own, in childhood, and then gone on to incur further damage in the name of serving his country?

Plus, he's got gorgeous shoulders and amazing eyes.

Mellie was talking about Cody again. "I'm hoping he can work through whatever happened to him in wartime. If he does that, maybe he can commit. He'll be a great dad, for sure, and now he has these kids."

"He's good with them," Taylor said, and a wave of longing washed over her.

Could she take the challenge, help him heal, and maybe even draw him to herself?

Immediately, self-doubt washed over her. She wasn't the kind of woman who attracted a man like Cody. She attracted men like Manson, men who sort of liked her, but would never put her first.

Men she didn't even find very interesting, she realized suddenly. She and Manson had little in common, except for being single and of similar ages.

Mellie looked at her phone. "Ryan just texted. He says he sent Cody over to walk us home."

The thought of seeing Cody made Taylor's heart dance. "What about the kids?"

"Asleep in front of the TV." The deep male voice

from behind her made Taylor's skin warm. "Ryan thinks if we wait until later and pick them up in the car, we can get them home and put them straight to bed."

"He's right." Mellie was slipping into her coat. "Tell you what. I'm going to let you two walk me home, and then you can go on and do whatever."

What did *that* mean?

"Knowing my boss," Cody said, eyes full of laughter as he looked at Taylor, "the *whatever* is getting started on baking for tomorrow."

Did he see her that way, as a no-fun boss? Probably so, because that was what she was.

"Don't do that," Mellie said. "Go look at the moon. Have a drink. Do *something* fun."

Cody glanced at Taylor and shrugged.

She shrugged back. "I don't feel up to working more tonight, that's for sure."

"Then I think we should do what Taylor said. Do something fun."

Taylor's heart began a mad dance in her chest. "All right. I'm game."

CHAPTER TEN

SAVANNAH HAD MANAGED to keep the dinnertime conversation going without Hank getting into his "we need to talk" topic. And the cleanup, which they'd done together. Hank had seemed content to dodge a serious conversation, too.

But now there was no more avoiding it. "You wanted to talk to me about whether to let Nadine stay here with me while you travel," she said as she put away the last pan.

"Yes. Come on out to the living room. I'm going to make a fire, and we can talk a bit."

Savannah was surely wrong to notice that his offer sounded romantic.

Why would she even think that? Hank was years older and eons more respectable than Savannah was. He mostly found her annoying. For that matter, she found him annoying, too, sometimes. But he could also be funny and urbane, as he'd been during dinner, telling her about his travels and about funny incidents when Nadine was a little girl.

He knelt before the already-laid fire and lit a long match. Without looking at her, he said, "I was all ready to let you go."

Savannah seized on the "was." It meant there was still hope she could stay.

She *really* wanted to stay. It was a place to land while she got herself organized for independence. The money was good, and with living expenses paid, she could save.

Plus, she was growing more fond of Nadine. She wanted to help the girl navigate the treacherous landscape of middle school.

You're growing more fond of Hank, too.

She shoved the thought away, impatient with herself.

"Did something change your mind?" she asked. "I would really like to stay. I think I could be good for Nadine."

"The two of you seemed to get on well tonight," he said. "I could see it working. I'm torn."

Savannah held her breath, not sure whether to argue her case or let him talk it through.

The fire caught, and he poked at a couple of logs, then glanced over his shoulder at her. "Do you think you can be responsible and stern enough with her? Keep her eating well and doing her homework and staying out of trouble?"

Honesty and humility would work better with Hank than false reassurances or bragging. "All I can do is my best," she said. "I doubt I'll do everything perfectly. But…"

"But what?"

She hesitated and then dove in. "Is it going to be all that much better to pull her out of school and take her on a business trip with you?"

He nudged at another log, then set the poker in its stand and moved to the chair across from her. "I don't know," he admitted. "I quit traveling for the past year, since leaving her with her mother stopped being an option."

Savannah was dying to ask why, what had happened with Nadine's mom, what she was like. *Stay focused*, she told herself. "I suppose it could be enriching for her, but won't you be in meetings all day? Where's your trip, anyway?"

"New York," he said.

She must have made some kind of sound, because he looked at her harder. "What?"

She shook her head back and forth rapidly. "Nothing. Nothing. I just... I used to live there, and I had a bad experience." More than one, actually. "I'm sure you know it's not a safe place for a young girl. Not unless you can supervise her all the time."

"That's just it. I'll be busy," he said.

She let out a breath and leaned back in her chair. "So you have to choose the lesser of two evils. Me, or New York."

"You're not an *evil*, Savannah. You're just not quite... what I had in mind."

An edge of darkness pushed at her chest. She wasn't quite what anyone had in mind, never had been.

Stop it. Make your case.

"Look," she said, "I came here with very little experience and...and yes." *Keep going.* "There's been a learning curve. Surely that happens in your line of work, too."

"Of course, but—"

"I'm trying, and I'm improving based on feedback. You let me know I messed up with that boy who came over, and I did better today."

"You weren't exactly stern."

"No," she said, "but I did get her to do the right thing. There's more than one way."

He nodded slowly. "You're right. And maybe yelling doesn't work for a sensitive teenage girl."

"Do you think?" She softened the words with a smile. "Anyway, I also got feedback that my cooking was terrible, which was true. So I'm working on it."

"Tonight's meal was good," he admitted.

Was she actually getting somewhere? Savannah felt a little flame of hope flicker to life.

He scratched his chin, looking uncomfortable. "There's something else that concerns me."

She opened her mouth to ask what and then closed it again. Had he somehow found out about her less than chaste past?

He was so wholesome, and also such a dad. He wouldn't understand the choices she'd made. She took responsibility for the fact that she'd hooked up with men to support herself. In a way, Rupert's efforts to prostitute her were a natural outcome of that.

Self-loathing coated her like an oil spill on a seabird. Would she ever feel clean?

Hank tilted his head to one side. "Did you hear that?"

"What?" Any change of subject would be welcome.

He walked toward the front door and listened again. "I heard something out here."

"Oh, my gosh, is it Nadine?" All the horror stories she'd ever heard about kids being hurt rose up inside her. She rushed ahead of him to the door and threw it open.

There was no one there. "Check in with Nadine, or I will," she ordered, her heart still pounding hard.

Hank raised an eyebrow. "Okay?" He sent off a quick text and then came to stand beside her at the door.

Almost immediately, an answer buzzed in. He read it and then showed it to Savannah.

I'm at the community center and they're going to take away our phones for the night. I'm fine.

There was a sound, not just the wind. A cry. "I heard it that time!"

"Stay here. I'll go check around."

She wasn't about to argue with that. She watched as he grabbed his coat from a hook and a flashlight from the shelf above it, and something inside her relaxed.

Wouldn't it have been nice to have a man, a partner, so competent, so quick to take responsibility?

He walked around, shining the light, while she leaned out the door and shivered. Then he beckoned to her from the corner of the house. "Come out. You've got to see this."

She stepped out.

He held up a hand. "Get your coat."

"Okay, Dad." She reached back into the house, plucked her coat from a hook and headed toward him.

The wind whipped her hair as she reached him. "What did you find?"

He gestured. "Take a look."

She leaned closer and gasped. There, between a dryer duct and a bush, a mother cat lay on her side. There were four small kittens in various stages of trying to nurse. "They can't be more than a couple weeks old."

"No, and it's cold." He nudged one of the kittens with the toe of his boot. "That one doesn't seem to be doing very well."

She knelt and studied it. "It's alive. I can see it's breathing," she said. "Can we take them inside? Will that make her reject them?"

"And will she let us?"

They both pulled out their phones and started searching online.

Savannah was shivering so hard she could barely touch the right line on her screen, but finally she got to a decent article. "Here it says that you can move them if they're unsafe. It's a myth that she'll reject them."

"Yeah," he said, "but what if she's feral?"

"She doesn't seem that afraid of us." She looked up at him, pulling her coat tighter. "We can't leave them here."

He put an arm around her and tugged her against his side. "You're freezing."

"Yeah." She welcomed the closeness, and not just because he was big and warm. It wasn't the raw sexual attraction she'd felt with Rupert initially, either.

Being close to Hank felt like returning to a safe,

happy home. Only it wasn't returning; it was for the first time.

And it *wasn't* safe. He was threatening to fire her. She pulled away and knelt beside the mama cat, her heart pounding. She reached out and stroked the soft fur, matted and wet in places. "Go get a couple of towels and a box if you can find one," she ordered.

He knelt beside her, still close, still big, still full of that protective appeal. "Do we want to take this on?"

"Do we want to be the kind of people who leave her here?" She was better at standing up for a needy animal than standing up for herself.

He held her gaze for a moment. Another.

Savannah's breathing quickened.

Abruptly he stood. "Be right back," he said, and he strode into the house.

Savannah sank into a sitting position on the cold ground and put a hand out to the cat again, stroking its soft head. When the cat butted against her, she knew it was domesticated. "Don't worry, Mama," she said, "with Hank on your side, you'll be fine."

Moments later he returned with a cardboard box and a stack of rags and towels. They lined the box with a couple of the towels and then used a third to lift the mother cat into the box. She hissed and struggled at being taken away from her kittens, but quickly they placed each one inside the box with her, and she relaxed. Savannah put the smallest one, the one that Hank had said didn't seem to be doing well, closest to the mama's face, and she licked it a couple of times. Then Hank carried the box into the house, with Savannah hurrying ahead to open the door for him.

Inside, he looked around. "Kitchen?" he asked.

"That's where they always put the mama cat in books." She was thinking of some story where a family put cats beside a stove to be warm.

Hank's house was warm everywhere, though. "Maybe the den," she said, "close to the fireplace. Nadine will love playing with them, and it's more comfortable there."

So he settled the box beside the fireplace, and they both sank down to the thick rug to watch them. The mother cat looked around a little, seemed to decide this place was fine, and started licking and washing the kittens.

Here, in the better light, the animals' coloring was visible. The mama and two of the kittens were gray-and-tan tabbies. Another was entirely tan, and the runt was a tuxedo, black and white. Their eyes were a beautiful soft blue color. "They're so adorable!" Savannah lay down on her side and propped herself on one elbow, watching them. "Which is your favorite?"

"The black-and-white one."

"Me, too!" She adjusted the towels. "We have cans of tuna we can give her for now, but tomorrow, we'll have to get some cat food. And a litter box. In fact, we probably better rig something up now for that. Do you have another box?"

He nodded. "You really do have a soft heart, don't you?"

"Yeah," she admitted. "I bet we can rip up newspaper and use that until we get cat litter." She grinned at him. "Since you're old-fashioned enough to still get a newspaper."

"I knew that would come in handy sometime. I'll shred some." He studied her. "This is a commitment, you know. We can't leave the cat and kittens alone now."

"You mean leave them out here? I think they'll be okay."

"I mean we can't leave them alone in the house for any period of time," he said slowly. "If Nadine and I go to New York, and you…take off for wherever you'd go. We can't do that."

She hadn't realized that taking in the kittens could work in her favor until just this moment. "Nadine and I could stay here and take care of them," she said, feeling suddenly a bit breathless.

He nodded slowly. "You could."

Was he offering to let her stay? The idea of this becoming a more permanent refuge made relief wash over her. A roof over her head, a job, an income. And at least to some degree, protection from Rupert.

But that was being too reliant on a man. And besides, she couldn't let herself hope, could she? That usually led to disappointment. "You said there was something else. When we were talking before about whether I could stay on."

He looked uncomfortable. "It was nothing. As long as you keep trying to get things right, and as long as you and Nadine are getting along okay, you can stay."

"You mean for the week, while you're on your trip?" Hope was blooming in her, but she didn't want to let it grow if this were just another temporary stay of execution.

"I mean for the foreseeable future."

"Oh, Hank, that would be wonderful!" She gave in to the impulse to hug him.

The moment her arms wrapped around him, everything changed. It felt intoxicating and sinful, like digging into a hidden stash of dark chocolate. Touching him, holding him, was wrong and dangerous. A better woman wouldn't have done it in the first place.

But she'd been gleaning comfort from men for most of her adult life, and Hank was such a steady, safe man. She clung on a little, feeling the scratchiness of his practical dad-style jacket against her cheek. It wasn't just comfort, either; it was more. The kind of more that made her inhale the skin of his neck and reach up to touch his hair.

He went still and then pulled away. "I'll…right. Okay. I have a few things yet to do tonight. Can you… watch over them?"

"Sure," she said easily. Inside, her mind was racing.

She'd wanted to watch over the kittens with Hank, but that apparently wasn't an option. He definitely seemed uncomfortable. Was he feeling the same kind of weird vibes she was feeling? Had hugging him been a mistake?

In her old world, she'd have pushed it further, tried to see if there was potential with a new man. Mostly, the answer had been yes. At least on the surface; at least temporarily.

Hank was a different kind of man, different in a good

way. The question wasn't just whether her mojo would work with a man like Hank. It was whether, if it did, that would be a good thing or a disaster.

She was just as glad he'd pulled away. She wasn't quite ready to know the answer.

CODY STOOD BESIDE TAYLOR, watching Mellie head into her house.

A moment later, Mellie stuck her head back out. "Still asleep," she called quietly. "That gives you a couple of hours until you need to come get them and take them home."

The point was clear. Mellie wasn't inviting them inside, probably because she was seizing the opportunity for a little alone time with Ryan while the kids slept. Anyway, he and Taylor had agreed to go have fun.

But watching the wind lift a strand of Taylor's hair and blow it across her face, Cody practically had to shackle one hand with the other to keep from moving closer to brush it back.

That wasn't all he wanted to do. But he had to follow his nobler instincts and keep things cool. They'd been thrown together tonight, and it felt like a date, possibly the start of something. But while the ladies had been working for the church, Cody had looked around at Ryan's super domesticated life, and it had felt like a prison.

Yeah, Ryan was ecstatically happy, but Ryan was Ryan. Cody wasn't made for that sort of thing. He'd screw it up. He didn't want it.

So what was he supposed to do with this pretty lady

who drew him like a magnet, but who was clearly a marriage type, not a strings-free hookup type?

And then it hit him. "I know what we can do," he said. "But it's outside. So first, we have to go put on more clothes. And...you don't happen to have ice skates, do you?"

As it turned out, she did. So he borrowed Ryan's, and they went home and gathered warm clothes and her skates. Moments later, they were walking toward the old barn at the edge of town.

There was a bonfire, and several people were there, probably about eight. All adults at this time of night. Four of them skating, and another four tending the fire, talking and laughing and drinking something from a flask.

"Well, if it ain't our very own hero," Weed Michaelson said. He sounded a bit slurry, which was often the case, but people gave him a pass because he'd been disabled in Vietnam.

"Hi, Weed," Cody said. Weed had been a fixture during Cody's adolescence, but they hadn't seen each other since Cody had returned.

"Drink?" Weed asked, holding out a flask. "This'll warm you up."

He took one, just to be companionable. He offered it to Taylor, and to his surprise, she took a swig too and didn't choke on the Fireball Cinnamon Whisky.

"Whyn't you tell us the story of how you chased down the enemy with a spatula?" Weed said, chortling.

Cody flushed, not for the reason people probably thought. He wasn't ashamed of defending his staff, and he'd done it with more than a spatula. What gave him pause was the fact that it had resulted in him being captured.

"Can it, Weed." Jimmy from Jimmy's Junk Joint clearly didn't mind getting into it with Weed. "He saved lives. What does it matter what kind of weapon he used?"

"I'll tell the story another time," Cody said to Weed. He hoped that was true. Hoped that someday, he'd remember the chain of events after he'd been captured. Hoped it wouldn't be too shameful, that he hadn't betrayed the trust his superiors had placed in him. "We're here to skate, though. Thanks for the drink."

There was a makeshift bench made of a split log, and Taylor was already sitting on it, lacing up her skates. "Better hurry up or I'll beat you in our first race," she said.

"Oh, so that's how it is?" He was happy to be distracted, happy he'd brought her. It was good to see her fun side. She was like a guy, competitive.

Then again, she was nothing like a guy.

They struck out across the ice, both of them getting their bearings. The wind had died down and the clouds were clearing, with stars visible in parts of the sky. The world seemed silent except for the brush of their skates and the laughter of the people around the fire.

True to what she'd said, she challenged him to a race.

Before he could answer, she yelled, "Ready, set, go!" and skated off.

"Game is *on*," he called, grinning. Arms and legs pumping, he skated after her.

His breath came in clouds and his muscles worked hard. He closed the distance between them, but she remained just out of his reach. The truth was, he stopped trying when he got close, content to stay at her shoulder and watch her move.

Economical grace. She had it in the bakery when she deftly rolled out dough or sliced pound cake. She had it when she dressed both kids faster than he could get an outfit onto one of them.

And she had it skating, clearly. She moved like a dancer or a gymnast, strong and coordinated. What an athlete she would have been if she'd decided to go in that direction.

She glanced back, and her determined expression and pink cheeks brought an even bigger smile to his face and propelled hot blood through his body. Lord, this woman got to him in every way a woman could get to a man. She was passionate and energetic and pretty, competitive and smart.

He wanted her.

He sped up to skate beside her, and they raced neck and neck. At the last minute, he slowed his pace just a little, and she reached the end of the pond before he did.

"You let me win," she accused him.

"Nah," he said, though he had. But she'd given him a good run for his money. She might not have his speed, but she was a skillful skater.

She glared at him, her expression indignant. "Don't do that. Don't treat me differently because I'm a woman."

"Really? No special favors?"

"Of course not!" She propped a hand on her hip, obviously ready to argue.

"Ready, set, go!" he yelled, and took off, laughing when he heard her surprised shout behind him.

He beat her that time, fair and square, and then of course they had to have a tiebreaker. He debated whether to let her win.

No, because she'd call him out.

Taylor would always call him out. He loved that about her.

His thoughts stole his focus. He hit a rough patch and was on his back on the ice almost instantly, gasping for air. When he caught his breath, he sat up and watched her skate on to victory, pump her fist in the air and then glide back to check on him.

She held out a hand, and he let her help him to his feet. Then he found he didn't want to let go. "Pair skate?" he asked her.

Her eyes sparkled. "Sure."

So he took hold of her and started, with her going backward and him forward. "Faster," she said once they'd gotten their rhythm.

"Can't, it's too bumpy."

"Scared?" she teased him.

He tilted his head and looked at her laughing eyes, and a strong urge came to him. He wanted to pull her into his arms. Kiss her silly.

It's Taylor. Don't start something. She was his boss, and she was the marrying kind. Only a fool would push that situation in a romantic direction.

Instead, he started them skating again and increased

the speed, just a little. Her skills were definitely up for the task.

Skating together wasn't much safer than kissing. It was intoxicating, guiding her in his arms, gradually speeding up until it felt like they were flying together. She let out a whoop at one point, but neither of them could talk. They both had to stay focused.

Cody experienced the same kind of exhilaration he'd felt jumping out of an airplane. Could hanging out skating with a woman seriously provide him with the risk and excitement he craved?

Could *being* with a woman provide that, if that woman was Taylor?

They rounded a bend too fast. There was an ice clump, and he accidentally skated her right into it. A millisecond later, they were both on the ground, him on top of her.

He scrambled to prop himself on his arms, looking down at her. "Are you okay?"

She made a tiny sound in her throat.

He scooted to the side. "I'm sorry. I crushed you." His weight was off of her now, but his leg was still over hers. He couldn't make himself move it.

She wiggled a little, and it was almost the undoing of him. "I'm fine," she said. "I think I'm fine."

He was leaning over her, and she was looking up at him, her lips parted. He sucked in a breath, and his heart pounded. He felt like a teenage boy.

He grasped at the remnants of his self control and rolled the rest of the way off her and to his feet, reeling a little on his skates, which he'd barely remembered he was wearing. He held out a hand to her. She let him help her up, looking dazed.

He put his hands on her shoulders. "How do you feel?"

She shook her head a little. "I'm fine."

"You didn't hit your head?"

"No."

"I didn't crush you?"

She laughed. "No. I'm not that fragile. Come on, let's skate."

So they did, but not as a pair, not touching each other. Soon enough, she went off separately to talk to Linda the librarian and another woman, and the three of them skated together slowly, yakking in that way that only women friends could do. So Cody stood by the fire with Weed for a little while, warming up and keeping the older man company. Trying to forget how it had felt to be sprawled on the ice with Taylor.

Most of the others who'd been here had left. When Weed held out the flask again, Cody took a tiny sip. No need to lose his head any more than he already had. Man, he'd come close to kissing Taylor.

"You come back okay?" Weed lit a cigarette.

The question startled him. "From Afghanistan?"

"Where else?"

Cody shrugged. He didn't know Weed that well, but he had the feeling the man would get it more than most people. "I had a memory lapse. There's three days missing, and something happened."

"Taken prisoner?"

Cody's gut tightened. "Yeah, from what I've put to-gether since. Don't really know what happened."

Weed exhaled a lungful of smoke. "Blocking it."

"Uh-huh." There was no use denying it. The army shrink had said the same when recommending an hon-orable discharge.

And he didn't want to think about that. "You were a POW, weren't you?"

Weed shrugged. "Captured twice, got away both times, went back to my unit to serve."

Cody lifted the flask in a salute. "More than I could do." He knew enough military history to imagine what Weed's captivity had been like: starvation, isolation and torture. His own three days, whatever they'd held, couldn't compare.

"Messes with you," Weed said. "I was no good to the marines after the second time. Got a bad paper dis-charge."

Cody winced. An other-than-honorable discharge meant that Weed hadn't qualified for VA benefits, most likely. Cody felt bad for the way he'd laughed with the other kids when they'd seen Weed stumbling through town, flat-out drunk. "They're changing some of the rules about that. You ever talk to anyone?"

Weed snorted. "They tried to get me to do a coun-seling group at the VA over in Pleasant Shores. I'd have had to take a ferry and then a taxi to get there. That wasn't happening."

Cody nodded. That would've been an expense, and while Weed crewed on some of the boats informally

and washed dishes at the local restaurants, he couldn't
have money for extras.

Especially when he spent most of what he did have
on alcohol.

"They tried to get me to join a group, too," Cody
said, "but…" He shrugged. What was there to talk about
when you didn't remember what had happened to you?
When your strongest memories of the military were
about being in a cooking-related reality TV show?

"Come down to the Floating Fisherman anytime,"
Weed said. "We can share our feelings." He guffawed.

Cody laughed, too, but he was glad of the invitation
to the informal bar-on-a-boat he'd heard about but never
visited. "I just might do that."

"You guys are having too much fun over here." It
was Taylor coming up behind them, and her voice sent
magic fingers up and down his spine.

A minute later, Linda and the other woman they'd
been skating with joined them. "We're taking off," the
librarian said. "Can you make sure the fire's out okay?"
She glanced from Weed to Cody, and Cody got the
message: don't leave Weed to do that part alone. "Sure
thing," he said.

Taylor sat down on the bench and pulled off her
skates. After a minute, Cody did too.

Weed threw another log on the fire before Cody
could stop him and then ambled off after the others
with a wink at Cody. "Have fun."

"Thanks." Weed was obviously trying to do him a
favor, ensuring that the fire would keep burning awhile.
This way, he'd have more time with Taylor.

The moon came out from behind a cloud, casting a glow over the now-empty pond. It was so quiet. Like they were the only people on Teaberry Island.

And Cody's desire to kiss her was back again in force.

"Did you have a good talk with Weed?" she asked unexpectedly.

He nodded. "We have some things in common, believe it or not."

"He's an okay guy," she said, to Cody's surprise. "He does repair work for me sometimes. You just have to catch him at the right time of day." She gave a wry grin.

"Before he starts drinking."

"Exactly." She frowned. "Seems like he could use a hand, only I don't know what to offer or how he'd take it."

"Hiring him to do a little work for you is a start," Cody said. "I bet there are a few vets on the island who could use a hand. Someone to talk to. Myself included," he added. "No civilian can understand."

He looked at her quickly. Had he insulted her?

But she was nodding. "If you get a group together, you're welcome to use the bakery to gather. Afternoons, once we've closed. I'll contribute baked goods."

"Nice of you, but why would you do that?"

She lifted her hands, palms up. "You've all fought for our country, and I know it leaves scars. There's not much I can do to help, but if getting together at the bakery would be a good thing, and if I can make you some scones or cookies to help out... I'll do what I can."

He appreciated what she'd said. "It's true I have some

scars. Not everyone gets that, especially when they're not visible."

"Do you want to talk about it?" The question was quiet. "Totally okay if you don't. No pressure."

He still *felt* pressure, though. "I'd hate to ruin a moonlit night with a pretty lady."

She flushed. "Don't do that."

"What?"

"Deflect to romance just because it's easier. I'd like to know the real Cody better. Not just suave, hot Cody."

That sent emotions pinging in all directions. She thought he was hot?

Even more surprising: She wanted to know the real Cody?

"Nobody knows all of it." He grabbed a stick and poked at the fire, making embers shoot high. "Not even me."

When he glanced at her, he saw that she was paying attention. She didn't look judgmental, or morbidly curious the way some people got. Just accepting.

"I was found wandering in the desert, three days after a big attack."

"The one that got you all the medals?"

He nodded. "I was...naked. Naked, and dehydrated. No memory of what had happened to me during those days. A few more hours out in the sun and I would've died."

"Wow." She frowned. "What do you *think* happened? Or do you not want to think about it?"

"I don't like to think about it. I had some injuries that suggested torture." And it haunted him, thinking of what might have happened, what he might have revealed under abuse. "As far as I know, I didn't reveal any state secrets." He tried smiling, wanting to make light of it.

She didn't bite. "That must be hard to deal with," she said.

"Yeah." He stood and poked at the fire some more. "But my experience was just once, for a few days. Weed was captured twice and still went back to serve."

"Just because someone else had a worse experience, that doesn't mean your experience wasn't bad." She reached out and squeezed his forearm, just for a second. "I'm sorry that happened to you. It must make it difficult to leave it behind and go forward, make plans."

"I think I want to stay here." He blurted it out and then realized it was true. "I feel like the island is a good place to be, to recover. And who knows? Maybe my idea about the vet group will work out."

"You could probably get funding from the VA for that, couldn't you?"

He shrugged. "Never thought about it." But hope grew inside him. If he could use what had happened to him to help others—and, who was he kidding, help himself in the process—then maybe he could get past some of the things that screwed him up.

The warmth in her eyes made him giddy, and he was suddenly aware of how close they were standing. It was easy to reach out a hand and touch her shoulder. "Thanks for listening."

He pulled her to him, meaning—truly—to hug her, as a friend. But what started out that way ignited quickly, the same way the fire beside them had.

Her hair distracted him with its softness as it brushed his fingertips. A faint fragrance of honeysuckle drifted up from it, making him think of longer days and sunshine. Her skin felt heated, warmer than his own.

Her steady gaze seemed to see past the joking and flirting shell he usually wore around women, to see through it to the real, flawed human inside.

He brushed back her hair and looked at those pretty lips and simply couldn't resist. Tried, but couldn't.

He looked into her eyes and saw an answering desire there, and that sealed it. He kissed her.

CHAPTER ELEVEN

IN CODY'S ARMS, Taylor felt the sparks that had been dancing between them grow into a flame. Not just a flash, either, but deeply warming, like the long-burning fire beside them.

His kiss was tender and hungry all at the same time, just as she'd known it would be. But it was more, too. The feelings he evoked came from the deepest, most secret part of her heart, the part she shared with no one.

Eagerly, she kissed him back, letting her hands splay across his hair, exploring the soft-yet-wiry feel of it. His mouth moved on hers in a way that felt completely different from the boys she'd kissed before. They'd all been boys—not that there had been that many of them—compared to the man that Cody was.

Experienced. He was experienced. He knew what he was doing, kissing her.

That's because he's kissed so many other women, including your sister.

She loosened her hold on him and started to pull away, but he frowned against her mouth and tugged her back to him. His fingers tangled in her hair, stroking the length of it.

Finally he lifted his head and she opened her eyes.

He was right there, his gaze on her in what she could only describe as a loving way. It was more than physical. He was looking into her soul.

Joy and delight and longing pushed her misgivings away. She pulled him back to her, kissing his cheeks and chin, delighting even in the beard stubble that scratched her face. He was into it, too, murmuring words of praise for how pretty she was, his quickened breathing telling her how much he wanted her. Even through their coats, she felt his warmth and pressed closer.

He growled into her hair. "I could lay you down right here and now and…" His words trailed off, but their meaning was clear.

Joy washed over her, as hard and fast as a sudden Chesapeake storm. She shouldn't feel so happy that a man wanted her physically. She should be remembering her values, the things Aunt Katy had taught her about waiting, preferably for marriage, or at least until a heartfelt relationship was assured.

But there had been so little passion in Taylor's life. She'd always been the wholesome, levelheaded, reliable one, the confidante for friends both male and female, consoling them for difficulties in their relationships even though she'd had limited experience of her own.

She'd wished to be the target of someone else's intense desire, but it had never happened before. Not, at least, with someone who mattered to her.

Precisely because it mattered, though, she didn't want to play this hand wrong.

The moon went behind the clouds again, dimming the sparkle around them, reminding her that even the most gorgeous moments had to end. Reality had to be faced.

She tugged away, and with obvious reluctance, he let her go.

"I might be in over my head," she told him. As much as she wanted him, and as much as she wanted to be spontaneous and fiery and passionate, she just wasn't someone who could dive into the physical and consider the consequences later.

No, that's Savannah.

"I don't mean it, what I said about laying you down here," he said quickly. His chest was rising and falling, his voice a tone deeper than usual. "That's disrespectful. I would never do that to you."

The way he said *you* seemed to make a subtle distinction between her and other women, and it bothered her. Didn't he want her, then, in the way he'd wanted the many other women in his life? Was he only kissing her because she was available and there was no one else around?

"Don't overthink it." He pulled her to him and kissed her, long and slow. And she was right back in the mindless pleasure of his mouth on hers, his strong arms holding her, this time with a little more tenderness.

He let out a little groan, started to say something, stopped. Kissed her some more.

Now it was her who wanted him, who was having thoughts of going way beyond this kiss. What if they could get closer, gradually, in every way? What if they could bring this romance to fruition? What if this could work?

The ringtone she heard wasn't hers, but it corresponded with a vibration in her back pocket. He pulled away to look at his phone as she reached for hers. She read the text from Mellie as he answered the call, putting the phone on Speaker.

"Where are you guys?" It was Mellie's voice. In the background, Ava was wailing.

Cody let out an exclamation. "Sorry, Mel. We'll be right there."

He ended the call and grabbed the bucket someone had been sitting on, throwing snow on the fire to douse it. After she'd caught her breath, Taylor helped him, scooping snow with her mittens.

Within five minutes, the fire was out, not even smoldering. Cody gave it one last stomp with a booted foot and then they headed away. He walked so quickly she had to run a little to keep up.

"I should never have let it get out of control," he said, the self-recrimination evident in his voice. "It was my fault."

"It's okay. The kids are safe. Mellie said—"

"It's not okay." He sped up again.

Taylor knew the kids would be fine. Mellie had said as much in her text, not that Cody was giving her a chance to communicate that.

He knew it, too, which meant that his upset had to do with the kiss they'd shared.

Every doubt she'd had about him multiplied. His interest had flagged so quickly! That couldn't be normal, could it?

As they passed through town, both half jogging now, he glanced over at her. "Look, that was a mistake," he said. "I hope it didn't wreck anything." He gestured at the bakery as they passed it. "Work-wise, I mean. I'm sorry."

Work. He didn't want to wreck their work arrangement. Of course. "You didn't wreck anything," she said.

Unless you counted her heart.

"I LOVE THEM so much." Nadine lay on the living room floor in front of the fireplace, watching the kittens as they slept.

Hank had left this morning, headed out for his week-long business trip. Savannah was thrilled that he'd agreed to go and to leave Nadine with her.

Whenever she thought about how it had felt to hug him, her stomach did a funny little flip. He was strong and reliable, not at all her usual type, but she'd felt the strangest urge to push closer and kiss him, to see where it would go, to destabilize that conservative, traditional persona and see what kind of passion lay underneath.

Thank heavens, she hadn't given in to that urge. As a result, she was here, with a good job that would allow her to get back on her feet. And to do it as an independent woman, not as some guy's girlfriend, subject to his changeable feelings and whims.

She hadn't expected it, but she was actually enjoying the chance to nurture and mentor Nadine.

One of the kittens stretched and yawned. "He's so adorable!" Nadine cried.

"Watch." Savannah touched the little guy and he made a tiny, hissing sound.

"Aw! He thinks he's tough!"

"Yeah. They slept most of the day, but they crawled around some." Savannah had spent a ridiculous amount of time watching the kittens, in between cleaning the house, playing around in the kitchen and surfing online to figure out what to do with her life.

She wanted to stay here, wanted to make it work. Besides the fact that she needed the income and housing, she genuinely liked Nadine.

But she couldn't just be a nanny to a thirteen-year-old girl. She'd realized that more than ever, now that she'd settled in and, hopefully, secured the job.

Since Hank was paying her a generous wage, and she had a place to live for now, she knew she needed to take advantage of the breathing room. She was looking into online degree and certificate programs, trying to see what she might want to do professionally.

Nothing had clicked so far, but at least she was trying.

"I love how they sleep in a pile, all snuggled together." Nadine looked up at Savannah. "I'm hungry."

"I made cookies. Come get some." Savannah rose to her feet and held out a hand, and after a moment's hesitation, Nadine accepted the help.

As they walked to the kitchen, honesty compelled Savannah to add, "I'm not sure how good they are, but I tried."

Nadine snickered as they walked into the kitchen. "They can't be as bad as your last batch. I thought Dad was going to break a tooth."

"And he was so polite about it," Savannah said,

laughing. She shoved the plastic-wrap-covered plate toward Nadine. "Try them. Want some milk?"

"Tea," Nadine said.

Savannah futzed around the kitchen, not sure whether to join Nadine at the table or not. They had reached a tentative peace, and Nadine definitely seemed glad her father had allowed her to stay at home rather than dragging her along on a business trip. But it wasn't like she and Savannah were best buddies.

Nadine pulled out her phone, and Savannah opened the refrigerator and studied the contents. She still wasn't used to cooking meals every night. Should she serve up the leftover mac and cheese from last night, or make something new? What did ordinary people do for dinner?

She'd better figure that much out if she wanted Nadine to give her father a positive report.

"What do you want to eat tonight?" she asked. "Any particular favorites?"

Nadine looked up from her phone. "Um… Yeah!" She brightened. "Do you know how to make chicken and dumplings?"

"I've never even *had* chicken and dumplings." Did people really eat that kind of thing anymore? Still, her job was to make Nadine happy. She opened the freezer. "We have a package of chicken pieces here. Do you know how to make dumplings? Or can you find a recipe?"

"I think I can." Nadine's fingers flew over the phone. "Here. It's my mom's recipe."

"Oh! Uh…" Savannah crossed the room and studied the photograph of a handwritten recipe as curiosity put a choke hold on her. Nadine's mom was supposed to be evil, or so she'd assumed from the little she had heard. But would a monster mother handwrite a recipe for chicken and dumplings?

"I miss it," Nadine said. "But Dad can't deal with anything to do with Mom."

That comment electrified Savannah's curiosity. What had happened between Hank and his ex, that he was hostile and Nadine was nostalgic? "I'll try to make it if you'll help me," she said, "but no guarantees."

Besides, maybe cooking her mother's recipe would help Nadine process the divorce and her mother's subsequent behavior a little bit.

So they put out the chicken to thaw, microwaving it a bit to get it started, yanking it out of the microwave when they started to smell cooked chicken. They mixed up a dough that looked like nothing to Savannah—just flour, water and salt, practically Play-Doh—rolled it out, getting flour everywhere, and cut it into triangles.

"This always happens to Mom, too," Nadine said, gesturing to her dark-colored shirt, now white with flour.

"Do you get to see her much?" Savannah asked, keeping her tone casual. She knew she was being nosy, and part of it was her impossible interest in Hank. But part of it was concern for Nadine. Hank had said she hadn't seen her mother for a year, but had she been sneaking out somehow?

"Never," Nadine said, matter-of-factly. "She got a

job with some screenwriters' association, and I haven't seen her since."

Interesting. "Is she far away?"

"California. We text and email some. I might be able to go see her in the summer, but..." Nadine shrugged elaborately. "I might not even go. I want to stay with my friends."

This from a girl who'd barely had a friend a couple of weeks ago. It didn't ring true.

The water was boiling, so they put in the chicken with plenty of salt and pepper, per the recipe. "Now we have to let it cook for, let's see. Thirty minutes? Forty if it's frozen."

"It's half frozen, so thirty-five?"

"Sounds good." Nadine hesitated. "Will you teach me to do makeup better while we wait?"

"Sure!"

So they checked on the kittens—all sleeping including Mama—and then went into Nadine's bedroom. As the pleasing smell of chicken wafted in from the kitchen, Savannah showed Nadine how to do a modified smoky eye and a lighter daytime application of eye makeup. Truthfully, Savannah found it soothing. She'd always enjoyed teaching the younger, newer models how to do makeup.

"You must have had a lot of boyfriends," Nadine said suddenly.

Savannah jerked, drawing a line of eye makeup across Nadine's temple. She wiped off the mistake with a tissue. "I have," she said, "but you shouldn't."

"Why?"

"You need to define yourself apart from men. I didn't, and now I'm playing catch-up." She didn't want to delve into the details. "What's going on with you and boys? Any more attention from that one guy who visited here? Kevin?"

"Who you made me kick out?" But Nadine didn't sound truly upset. "He hangs around me some at school."

"Do you like him?"

Nadine shrugged. "Not really, but he's the only one who likes me, so…"

"You have to wait for the right one," Savannah said, tracing feathery pencil strokes over Nadine's eyebrows. "Just think if a really great guy came along and you were dating Kevin."

"True." Nadine was watching Savannah's actions closely, and now she did the same, less expertly, on her other eyebrow. "Dad likes you, you know."

Savannah's face heated, and her heart jumped with hope. "I'm glad, since I'm working for him." Surely a friendly kind of liking was all that Nadine meant. Savannah didn't need to get all excited.

"No, I mean he *like* likes you."

She shouldn't react, but she couldn't help it. "He *does*?"

Nadine nodded. "I can tell. I mean, why wouldn't he? You're gorgeous."

Despair washed over Savannah like an icy Chesapeake wave.

She should be glad, shouldn't she? She was drawn to Hank in so many ways, and if he was drawn to her, even for a superficial reason, he was at least likely to keep her on. And she could work to deepen his feelings if things went well. She didn't have to accept that he cared for her only because of her looks, a kind of liking that would fade.

But she'd tried it before, tried to deepen a relationship that started with physical attraction—which was basically all of them—and it never worked. Rupert was the last in a long line of men who'd been excited to date a model at first, but who'd quickly gotten bored with her supposed stupidity and emptiness.

She looked at the makeup, looked at the intensity with which Nadine was now following her instructions for applying mascara for the most natural look. Why was she helping Nadine focus on something so destructive?

"Looks aren't what it's all about," she said, sweeping the makeup bottles and tubes aside with her forearm. "There are so many more important things to focus on."

Nadine snorted. "Looks *are* what it's all about. The pretty girls get all the perks." She pulled bronzer from the pile Savannah had pushed aside. "I wouldn't mind if you and Dad got together," she said, applying the stuff with way too heavy a hand. "You could help me be prettier."

"Not like that." Impatient with Nadine and with herself—maybe with the whole world—Savannah pulled the bronzer out of the girl's hands and wiped off the streak she'd applied with a too-rough swoop of a makeup wipe. "You want to put some in the palm of your hand and mix it with a light moisturizer. Then rub your hands together and put it over your face, real light." She demonstrated on her own face, then held out the products to Nadine. "We really should've done bronzer first, before the eyes. Be careful not to smear them."

"Right." Nadine painstakingly did what Savannah said.

"Let's go check on the chicken."

"Could you do it? I want to practice my makeup."

Great. "Sure," Savannah said.

As she walked out of the room, Nadine called, "Thanks, Savannah. You're the best."

And that left Savannah with extremely mixed feelings. She was starting to get fond of Nadine and was glad to make her happy. It made it feel possible that she could keep the job.

On the other hand, Nadine liked her for all the wrong reasons. Savannah was contributing to her becoming a looks-focused American teenager. Something that definitely wouldn't lead to happiness.

If Nadine was to be believed, Hank was getting interested in Savannah, too…for all the wrong reasons. And that was a one-way ticket to disaster.

CHAPTER TWELVE

CODY STROLLED ALONG the sidewalk with Taylor and the kids, the sport coat he'd borrowed from Ryan making his neck itch. The breeze felt balmy, a prelude of spring even though it was the end of January and snow was predicted for next week.

It felt ridiculously like being a family.

Taylor bent over to wipe a few crumbs from Ava's face. Taylor wore black slacks and boots and a sweater that showed off her stellar figure, and Cody's throat went dry every time he looked at her. That tender expression, that gorgeous body…it filled him with memories of how it had felt to kiss her.

He'd tried hard to avoid those memories during the week since that had happened. Had tried to get things onto some kind of professional level with her. Ava was sleeping at his place now most nights, since he'd rigged up screens and curtains to divide the bedroom into separate areas for each of them. He'd handled the visit from the social worker alone, even though Taylor had offered to sit in.

The social worker's visit was why they were headed to church, actually. A businesslike woman in her sixties, Mrs. Croft had questioned him about what he was doing for the kids' socialization beyond school. He'd stuttered out something about Mellie and Ryan and Alfie, and story time at the library, but he'd been informed that he needed to do more.

That was the only reason he'd approached Taylor about church services. He'd just meant to ask her the time, but somehow, that had morphed into them all going together.

Other dressed-up families were headed for church, walking, enjoying the sunny, breezy air. A crowd of people gathered outside, the kids running around. He tried to stop Danny and Ava from joining in, wanting them to keep their new dress-up clothes clean, but quickly saw it was a futile effort and gave up. He wanted them to fit in, to feel a part of things.

He didn't fit in. He felt like a loser and an outsider. Although Betty and Wayne had made their foster sons attend church when they were teenagers, that was the last time he'd darkened the door of a place of worship. Lots might have changed in the years since he'd last attended.

When the bells started ringing and people started going inside, he and the kids were swept along.

"Class for the younger kids is this way," a pleasant-looking woman he didn't know said, beckoning. Cody saw her name tag and realized she was the pastor's wife.

"Do you want me to come?" Taylor asked Cody, her voice low.

"No. No, you go on with your regular routine. You've done enough for us."

Her face twisted a little, almost like he'd hurt her

feelings, but that couldn't be, could it? He watched as she caught up with some others headed into the sanctuary, her face open and friendly.

She was everything he wanted and couldn't have.

He needed to keep things on a professional level with her. He couldn't give in to this misplaced longing to try to build something with her, because she deserved better than an attempt that would surely fail. Annoying old Manson reached out and gave her a hug, and she hugged him back, way too warmly in Cody's opinion.

But then Manson beckoned her to follow him, and she shook her head, patted his arm, and headed into the sanctuary with a couple of other people. Manson rolled his eyes and turned away, not even looking that upset.

The idiot. If *he'd* had a chance with Taylor, he wouldn't have blown it.

He had to remember that he didn't have a chance. He turned, resolute, and strode after the kids.

When he'd gotten them checked in, Ava clung to him. "Stay," she commanded.

He started to scold her for being bossy, but then he saw the tears in her eyes.

"Okay if I hang around?" he asked the teacher, and she nodded.

"Of course. I can always use an extra hand."

It was just as well. Nursery school was about his level, religion-wise. He needed the kid edition.

So he sat at a way-too-small table with Ava and three other little girls. Danny was at a table with some older kids, one of whom he seemed to know from school. The lesson was about forgiveness, and they all had to name someone they had gotten mad at and what it was like to forgive them.

Danny said he was mad at his mom, and when the teacher asked about forgiving her, he pressed his lips tightly together and didn't say any more. Then Ava piped up, out of turn. "He's mad our mommy left us here. I'm glad 'cause of Cody." She climbed off her chair and into his lap and popped her thumb into her mouth.

Well. Okay. His heart warm from Ava's trust and affection, he fielded the meaningful, questioning look from the teacher with a little nod, meaning he'd take care of this situation. Though truthfully, he had no idea how. As the other kids went around expressing that they'd gotten mad at a friend, or a little brother, or a teacher, Cody thought about his own heart.

He'd always carried anger toward his mother, who'd left him to the foster care system when he wasn't much older than Danny. That anger had doubled when his mother had dumped Danny and Ava on him. Not that he didn't want to know them, and not that he was unwilling to care for them, but Mom had gone about it in the wrong way.

The same way she did everything else. Deep inside, he feared she'd passed that particular tendency along to him.

"Jesus forgave everybody, even the people who nailed him to a cross," the teacher said, and Cody's eyes widened. These were little kids. Surely there was a softer way to present *that* story. "So if we want to be like Jesus, we have to forgive everyone."

To his surprise, the kids seemed to take it all in

stride. "Can we do our craft now?" a little girl from Cody's table asked.

"After we sing a song." The teacher led the kids in a peppy song about forgiveness. Then she passed out cut-out paper dolls and giant hearts to paste on them, and the kids were allowed to decorate them however they wanted.

Cody helped the kids with paste, its smell reminding him of his own primary school days. He'd attended five or six different schools in those first few years, but every one of them had included the same kind of white paste and the same blunt-edged scissors that Cody could never manage well. Finally, when he'd gone to a new second grade in Hagerstown, a teacher had introduced him to the scissors with green handles, for lefties. The world of cutting with scissors had opened up to him.

He'd cried when he'd had to leave that school just a few weeks later, but he'd remembered to ask for the lefty scissors after that.

The older kids had been given traced-out hearts and paper dolls to cut themselves. When Cody went over to check on Danny, he saw that the boy was using a pair of green-handled scissors.

He wondered when Danny had learned about those. Had their mother thought of it after all these years, remembered to mention his left-handedness to a teacher due to Cody's experience?

Soon the class was over, and parents started coming in to pick up their kids. As Cody helped Ava into her jacket, he covertly watched the other families.

He wanted that. He wanted to make a good family.

Unfortunately, he was starting to want to make it with Taylor, just because of the way they were spending all this time together.

Okay, not *just* for that reason. Also because Taylor was so competent and cute and appealing.

Also because he'd really like to kiss her again.

But he couldn't do that. He had to keep things on a professional level. He was no good at commitment, and Taylor deserved nothing less.

As they walked out of the classroom, Taylor was there, waiting. Ava ran to her and showed her the craft she'd made.

Taylor knelt down right away and admired it. Then she looked up, beckoned to Danny and got him to show her his craft, too.

Ava pushed past Danny and into Taylor's arms. "Hungry," she said.

Ava was acting for all the world as if Taylor were her mother. But Taylor hadn't signed up for this and had no obligation. Beyond that, Cody needed to put a halt to all this family-feeling business or he'd push his way into Taylor's arms, too.

That wouldn't be acceptable.

"Come on, Ava," he said, kneeling and attempting to unwind her arms from Taylor's neck. "Taylor doesn't cook for us. I'll make lunch."

Identical frowns crossed both Danny's and Ava's faces. "Yuck," Danny said.

A smile tugged at the corners of Taylor's mouth. "Let me talk to your big brother," she said to Ava and Danny, and rose gracefully to her feet.

So gracefully. So strong and fit and comfortable in her own body.

And he had no business noticing that.

She stood close to speak to him without the kids hearing. He caught a whiff of her hair, honeysuckle mixed with that slight cinnamon and vanilla fragrance that always floated around her. "It's true that I wasn't planning to cook," she said. "But the singles group from church is going to brunch. There will be at least two other kids. Do you and the kids want to join us?"

AN HOUR LATER, Taylor wiped her mouth and looked around at the so-called singles group, studiously avoiding Cody's gaze.

Besides Cody, there was Linda Iglesias, Missy Hanks, who taught at the elementary school, and her friend Jody Peters, an aspiring author who seemed to be independently wealthy. Missy's little boy was three, Ava's age. Her daughter, Catherine, was just a year older than Danny, and a take-charge type of kid. Catherine had suggested a kids' table with herself as the boss of it. All the kids had gone for that, even Ava. There had been very few squabbles, so the adults had actually had time to enjoy their brunch.

The café was warm, with brick walls and big windows that faced the street. Diner smells, bacon and coffee, filled the air, and the clatter of forks and low murmur of voices made for a friendly environment, punctuated by laughter.

"I'm so glad this place opened up," Missy said, looking around the café. "We needed a place downtown that served breakfast."

"Taylor's bakery serves breakfast," Linda pointed out.

Missy's hand flew to her mouth. "Of course it does. I'm sorry, Taylor. I meant no offense to the Bluebird Bakery. Do you feel like the café is competition?"

Taylor wiped grease off her hands. "Nope. Totally different kind of food." She gestured toward the toast, dripping with butter. "As a matter of fact, we're talking about me supplying them with bread. We just have to work out the details."

"And find the time," Cody reminded her. "You've already taken on a lot."

"Including a groovy helper," Jody said, winking at Cody. "If it weren't for you coming today, we wouldn't even be a singles group. We'd be an old hens group."

"Hey, hey now." Linda pointed at Jody with a piece of biscuit she'd had in her hand. "I object to the label 'old.' I'm only fifty-two."

"You're as young as you feel," Missy said. "You have tons more energy than I do."

Taylor looked at Cody, wondering if he felt out of place. Besides being the only guy, he was super attractive, to the point where a couple of sixtysomething women in a booth kept glancing over at him.

"I'm glad to be here," Cody said in his simple way. "It's nice to have kids for Danny and Ava to play with. And it's nice to have a meal that's not cooked by me or Taylor."

All three of the women's heads turned, as one, to Taylor.

"Something you want to tell us?" Missy asked, eyebrows raised. "Are you guys living together?"

"No! We're not *living* together." They weren't, but they were such close neighbors that the kids ran back and forth between their apartments a thousand times a day.

Should she add that they weren't involved? Well, they weren't, except for that one night, that one kiss she couldn't stop thinking about.

Forgetting their kiss didn't seem to be a problem for Cody.

"We're not involved," she said firmly. "We just got swept into caring for the kids together, sometimes."

"And working together," Cody said. "Taylor has to be sick of me. I'm surprised she let me tag along to your group."

Cody's self-deprecation had them eating out of his hands, and the women started to reassure him immediately. They were glad he was here. He should come to church every week. He should arrange a playdate with Missy. He should stop in to the library more often.

When the conversation turned to the lack of suitable and available men on the island, Taylor spoke up. "There are other single men in town, you know. A lot of them."

"Fishermen." Jody wrinkled her nose. "Besides the smell, they have to get up at all hours to do their job, and from what I hear, they come home too tired to have any fun."

Missy and Linda and Taylor all stared at their breakfasts. Disrespecting the fishing industry on Teaberry Island was practically a mortal sin.

Cody wasn't reduced to silence as the women were. "Taylor likes fishermen," he said, and turned to her. "Isn't that what your…special friend, what's his name? What he does."

Taylor glared at him. "Manson's not my special friend. He's just…well, a friend, I guess. And yes, he is an oysterman."

The waitress arrived in time to hear that last remark. As she refilled everyone's coffee cups, she raised an eyebrow. "Manson is a dreamboat. Are you still seeing him, Taylor?"

This was when being on a small island was not a good thing. Gossip. She needed to nip gossip about her and Manson in the bud. He wasn't right for her, and she wasn't going to play at dating with someone who wasn't right. Not anymore. "No, I'm not seeing him," she said. "I'm not seeing anyone. So if you want to ask Manson out, feel free."

The waitress smiled. "Thanks! Maybe I'll do that." She shot Jody a glance. "I don't mind early hours. I come to work early myself. Unlike *some* people."

Apparently, she'd heard Jody's disparaging remark about fishermen.

"Most people who work do get up early, here on the island." That was Linda the librarian. She frowned at Jody.

Jody looked from one woman to the next, her forehead wrinkling. She must have realized she'd done or said something wrong.

"Jody works," Missy said, patting the woman's hand. "She just works from home. And she's new. She doesn't know how important fishing is to the island."

"I'd like to learn, though." Jody looked contrite. "Maybe I'll put a fisherman in one of my books. Who knows?"

As the conversation went on to Jody's writing career, Taylor's mind drifted. Her eyes didn't, though. They stayed firmly on Cody.

He'd gotten up to wipe Ava's face, and as he picked her up and brought her back to the table to sit in his lap, she thought she'd never seen anyone so appealing. He was strong, and masculine, but yet still humble. He'd taken on his siblings as soon as he'd realized he was their best option, and he was learning more every day about how to care for them.

He had so many fine qualities, but the one that was keeping her awake at night was his kissing ability. Wow. She hadn't known a kiss could even be like that. It had rocked her world. She'd kept reliving it, over and over, to the point that sometimes she found herself touching her own lips as if she couldn't believe what had happened.

It would be easy not to believe it, because afterwards, he'd backed clean away. He'd kept a very professional distance between them at work, and mostly at home, too.

Not that she was surprised. She had always known her level, in terms of men. There was a certain range that was interested in her. Of men her own age, she attracted the lower half in terms of attractiveness and personality and success. Go up ten years, and they got more attractive and successful, and were happy to have a younger woman on their arms, even if she wasn't the most beautiful. Edge it up to fifteen years older than her, and she'd been asked out by some amazing men.

Romance was a marketplace, and Taylor understood markets.

Cody was at a level high above hers. Jody, who kept "accidentally" touching him as she talked and brushing back her hair and giggling, was almost at his level, but not quite, in terms of looks.

Savannah was the one. She and Cody were a perfect match.

Cody had issues, of course. Men were judged on their jobs and financial success, and there, Cody was a bit behind the curve. But there were also his good personality and his status as a war hero working in his favor.

He smiled at her. "You look like you're thinking hard."

Her cheeks reddened because she'd been thinking about him.

"It's the bakery, right?" he asked. He was cuddling Ava against his chest as her eyes drooped, nearly closed.

Linda smiled. "That's always on Taylor's mind. We're proud of her. She's going to put Teaberry Island on the map."

"I hope so. I just need to fill all the early off-island orders to perfection so that the bakery's reputation keeps growing."

"We'll do it," Cody said.

Taylor got a strange little shiver. That "we" was way too appealing.

"You should do live video," Jody suggested. "That's the best way to share your story."

"She's right, you should," the librarian said. "We've been upping our social media presence at the library. I don't think the Bluebird Bakery is even online, is it?"

"We have a website and a couple of social accounts," Taylor said. "I just don't have time to share anything."

"Live video is where it's at," Jody insisted. "And you two would be fabulous. You're so girl-next-door, and Cody's this hot returning veteran…"

As Jody went on talking, buoyed by the interest of the others, Taylor tried to explain Jody's words another way than how they'd sounded, in her own mind.

But there wasn't another way.

You're so girl-next-door and Cody's hot.

There you had it, in a nutshell.

She knew she shouldn't mind. Looks weren't the only thing, not even the main thing. Plenty of times she'd pitied Savannah for the lifestyle that had run her ragged, the pressure of living up to everyone's impossible expectations of a pageant winner and model.

A better person would concede gracefully. A guy as hot as Cody wasn't for her, but there were plenty of staunch, strong, steady men who would love to build a family with her. Well, maybe not plenty, but some. If they didn't fall head over heels like men did for Savannah, they'd see her as a solid partner. That would be better in the long run.

Yet she couldn't help but be hurt about it. Their mother had made no secret of favoring Savannah. Other children did the same: anytime the sisters had been around kids their age, everyone had gravitated to Savannah. Taylor had grown beyond it, at least partly, but the scar still hurt when you pressed on it.

She watched Cody lean back in his chair, oblivious to the admiring gazes around him. When you'd been in that kind of sunshine your whole life, you didn't even know what cold shade felt like.

Not that Cody had had it easy, any more than Savannah had. But in every arena of life, looks made for an easier journey.

Cody's looks meant that he was out of her league. The sooner she accepted that, the better.

They should never have kissed. That was what had thrown her into a tailspin, made her ten times more aware of him, awakened her old jealousies and feelings of inadequacy.

And she was about done watching him charm the singles group along with every female customer and employee in the café. "You guys, I'm going to take off," she said. "Lots to do."

Cody made a mild protest and then waved her off. "Go. Get some time to yourself. The kids and I won't bother you."

She would normally have said *It's not a bother*, because it wasn't. Truthfully, having Cody and the kids around took the loneliness out of Sunday.

But she couldn't let herself get used to that, because it wasn't destined to be. She would soon lose him to someone else, someone more at his target range. If not here on the island, then somewhere else.

No more kissing, she told herself sternly.

Not that Cody was likely to want to.

She gathered her things and left him to the café full of female wolves.

CHAPTER THIRTEEN

ON WEDNESDAY EVENING, Cody looked around his empty apartment and listened to the sleet beating against his window. He pushed away his half-eaten plate of left-over spaghetti and tried to ignore the occasional sound from Taylor's apartment next door.

The kids were off having dinner with Missy and her kids. Just as the social worker had predicted, getting to know other families outside of school was great for them. It should be great for him, too, to have a night off from caregiving, but he was bored and at loose ends.

Now that he'd wrecked everything by kissing Taylor, and then telling her that it had been a mistake, the two of them weren't spending much time together anymore. As a result, life on Teaberry had lost some of its color for him.

He thought about calling Ryan or hitting the Dockside Diner for a beer. But he didn't feel social. He hadn't slept well last night. His insomnia was back, not as bad as before, but bad enough. He'd finished a novel between the hours of one and three, and then there was no point in going back to sleep when he just had to get up and start baking at four.

He and Taylor had split that up now. They were each

taking three early shifts per week. She was kind enough to keep watch over the sleeping kids while he worked, and then when she came down to start her day, he'd run back up and get them ready for school.

It was a workable routine, and he was more than grateful to her for doing it. But there was something disturbing about seeing her stumble over half asleep on the mornings he worked and crash on his couch. Something intimate about seeing her that way.

At least, he experienced it as intimate. She didn't seem to notice. Sometimes it seemed like she barely looked at him.

And he needed to stop thinking about it. He checked the library hours on his phone and found out that Wednesdays were their late nights. He'd take back the book he'd finished and find another, just in case tonight turned into another sleepless one.

After a chilly dash through dark, rainy, empty streets, he was glad to enter the warm library. It was small, with just one main room and then a children's room off to the side, from which he heard distinctly non-childlike laughter. There seemed to be some kind of meeting going on there.

Just outside the kids' room was a display featuring books about Groundhog Day. Right, that was today. And although it was cloudy here, apparently Punxsutawney Phil had seen his shadow. Six more weeks of this ugly weather.

He had to shake off his mood. What he needed was a good escape novel. Some kind of adventure book, preferably set in a tropical climate, with a fearless main character winning out over the bad guys. And hot babes who weren't as complicated as those in real life.

He wandered through the stacks, pulling out books and putting them back. In a chair off to the side of the room, he saw Weed reading a fat hardcover.

Weed spotted him at the same time and raised a lazy hand. "Didn't expect to see you here."

"Likewise." He slid into the chair across from the older man. "Weather stinks. It's a night to stay home."

"Not much on TV tonight. Plus, I'm trying to stay off the sauce."

"I hear ya." Good for Weed, trying to cut down on his drinking.

"There's another reason I'm here." Weed nodded toward the back room. "I'm real interested in the librarian, Linda," he said. "But I can't seem to get her attention."

"What's the group back there?"

"Book group."

"Why not join?" Cody might, himself, except that he didn't think he should take on a new commitment when he'd just acquired two kids to care for. Missy had taken them tonight, but that wasn't going to happen often.

"Nah." Weed's mouth twisted. "Never finished high school. I'd look like an idiot with all those smart folks."

Cody gestured toward the book Weed was holding. "Doesn't look like something an idiot would be reading."

Weed colored slightly and held up the book: *A History of Western Philosophy*. Bertrand Russell was the author. "Just tryin' to understand life better."

"I'm impressed." They sat companionably for a few

minutes, chatting a little about books and the weather and Weed's tours in Vietnam.

"Screwed me up, man," he said. "You ever think about startin' up a veterans' group on the island, count me in."

Weed seemed to have gone from making jokes about sharing his feelings to actually wanting to do it. "Actually, I *have* thought of it," Cody said. "Just not sure I'm the right guy for the job."

"Who else will do it? Me?" Weed let out a laugh that turned into a cough. He swigged water from a bottle in his pack. "I'm too old and run down. But I was talking to a couple of guys at the Floating Fisherman. They said they'd go."

"Really?" Cody felt a flicker of interest. "We could meet at the Dockside, I guess, but…"

"Not a great idea to meet in a bar, for me, anyway."

And then he remembered Taylor's offer. "We could meet at the bakery. Taylor might even give us some refreshments."

"If it's free baked goods from the Bluebird, I'm there." Weed leaned back in his chair and studied Cody from hooded eyes. "You seeing her? You seemed pretty close the other night."

He opened his mouth to say *I wish* and then didn't. "I'm not much for commitment."

"And Taylor's the commitment type." Weed tilted his head to one side. "In fact, there's a few guys around here would like to make a commitment with her. If you have any thoughts of changing your mind, you'd best get on it."

People started coming out of the other room, talking and laughing. Linda waved to them. "Leftover refreshments in the Children's Room. Help yourselves."

Cody caught sight of a big cookie someone was munching on and his stomach growled. He rose to his feet, then held out a hand to help Weed hoist himself out of the easy chair. The older man pushed back his long hair and straightened before walking in Linda's direction.

More power to him, Cody thought. Maybe at least one of them would make progress with a good woman.

It wasn't going to be him.

He couldn't commit to a relationship. Wasn't cut out for it. Hadn't learned how. He'd left enough women crying in enough apartments and hotel rooms across the globe to know he needed to exercise extreme caution, especially when it came to a woman like Taylor, whom he liked as a person, depended on as a boss and knew was far less experienced than he was.

If he had a commitment bone in his body, it had to be devoted to his younger brother and sister. Speaking of which, he couldn't saddle a woman with the two of them. Taylor was the type of kind person who would take it on, but it just wasn't fair.

He checked the time and swore. Not only was he bad at big-picture commitment, he was bad at the little stuff, like showing up on time to pick up the kids.

So why was he even considering starting something with a bunch of veterans who deserved commitment as much as anyone?

He met Weed at the refreshment table and snagged

a couple of cookies, hoping they'd smooth things out with the kids and Missy when he showed up late. "I don't think it'll work with the veterans' group, man," he said. "Sorry. I gotta go."

He turned away when he saw the disappointment on Weed's face and hurried out of the library, without having even checked out a book.

SAVANNAH PULLED BACK her hair into a messy bun and checked the pot of chili cooking on the stove. Then she hurried out to the fireplace room.

She wanted everything to be perfect for Hank's arrival home tomorrow, so that he'd be glad he'd kept her on. *And so he'll like you.* Yeah, okay, and like her.

She and Nadine had had fun for the past few days, and the results showed up in the messy stacks of papers and magazines, the blankets and pillows strewn over the floor, the bowls containing last night's popcorn. She'd give the place a quick straighten before Nadine got home and then enlist the girl in helping her vacuum. Savannah had never learned much about housecleaning, since Taylor had picked up the slack their mom had left. Mrs. Williams had used a cleaning service.

But she'd watched some videos about cleaning. How hard could it be?

She'd carried the bowls and empty soda cans to the kitchen when she heard the doorbell ring. She frowned. It was time for Nadine to come home from school, but she always just walked in. It was her house, after all.

When the bell rang again, she put everything down on the kitchen counter and hurried to open it, annoyed.

Nadine probably had her hands full and didn't want to put everything down to open the door herself. "I was actually doing something, Miss…" She trailed off.

Rupert was on the other side of the door.

Savannah's stomach dropped. She clutched the side of the door frame as emotions swirled inside her. She should be angry, and she was. But after all, she'd cared for him deeply no matter what his feelings. And he didn't look good.

Beneath her confusion, another note rose: fear. She hated that. "What do you want?"

"I'm here to give you one last chance," he said, and shivered. His designer coat and Italian leather shoes were useless in this weather, and he couldn't keep his teeth from chattering.

"How did you find me?"

He snorted. "Podunk place like this, a beautiful woman stands out. The ferryman knew exactly where you were living."

His eyes were bloodshot, and she couldn't believe it was just from the wind. "What happened?" she asked, noting that his collar was buttoned down on one side but not the other. He never let himself look disheveled.

"I made a mistake," he said. "I shouldn't have let you go."

She studied him, skeptical. "And what else happened?"

He let out a sigh. "I've been subpoenaed. I was hoping I could lay low around here for a while. Maybe you could help me find a place."

Her eyes widened. She'd guessed he was doing something illegal, but she hadn't known for sure. "So you want me to help harbor a criminal? And you think you can really evade the authorities? We're isolated, but we're a part of the USA."

"Can I come in?" He was shivering hard now.

"No. No way."

"Just for a minute, while we talk. Then I'll leave."

She shouldn't allow it, but she didn't want him to die of exposure. And she also didn't want to enrage him. She knew his temper all too well. "Come in for a minute, as long as you leave when I tell you to."

"Thanks, babe." He came inside and leaned toward her like he was going to kiss her.

She took a giant step back and started to close the door.

"Wait a minute, we're coming!" Nadine's voice blew in on the wind, and then she and Kevin were in the entryway, too, stamping the snow and ice off their boots.

Worry twisted Savannah's stomach into an even tighter knot. She had Nadine to watch out for, and she didn't fully trust Rupert.

But after all, he wasn't the kind of crook who was violent. He'd been a functional member of the business and social world in New York. It wasn't as if he'd hurt a teenager.

She tried to carry on as if she were just doing her regular job of caring for Nadine. Which, right now, meant scolding her. "Nadine, you're not supposed to have company while your dad's away," Savannah reminded her.

When Rupert flashed her a sudden speculative look, she could have kicked herself. Until now, he hadn't known the owner of the home was away.

"Are *you*?" Nadine gave Rupert a look of appraisal. "Supposed to have company, I mean?"

"Okay, look," she said, because she felt like she couldn't be a hypocrite, letting Rupert in but not Kevin. "You fellas can both come in for half an hour. No closed doors. In fact, Rupert and I will be in the kitchen and you two can be here, by the fire." She glared at Kevin. "And I'll have my eye on you."

"Yes, ma'am," he said.

Maybe it wouldn't be bad to have another male in the house while Rupert was here. Maybe Kevin and Rupert would police each other.

She found herself longing for Hank's reassuring presence, but she squared her shoulders and shoved the feeling aside. Hank *wasn't* here. He'd left her in charge, and she had to deal with all of it.

She pointed to the kittens. "Be on the lookout," she said to Nadine. "They're getting more adventurous." Then she led Rupert back to the kitchen. "So talk," she said, pointing to a chair at the big kitchen table.

"You look good." He strolled around the kitchen rather than sitting down. "And that smells good."

She checked the chili and lowered the heat. It *did* smell good. She'd make some corn bread after Rupert and Kevin left, enough for her and Nadine to have tonight, and for Hank to have left over tomorrow. Nothing was homier than corn bread.

"I didn't know what I had." Rupert sounded sincere, even though Savannah knew he couldn't be. He looked around the kitchen. "This place is dripping with money. What kind of a job is this?"

"I'm a babysitter. A companion."

"Right. You pretended to be insulted when I wanted you to spend time with my friends, but it looks like you were just holding out for a better offer."

Sudden rage heated her cheeks. Hank would never pay for sexual benefits. Nor would he take advantage of a woman he'd hired to do a job for him. The implied insult to Hank rankled more than the insult to her.

Rupert sat down in Hank's chair and tipped it back, surveying the room—and her—with a cocky air.

What was she doing, letting this man who'd tried to pimp her sit in Hank's kitchen? "You need to leave," she said. "Now."

"You said half an hour," he reminded her.

"I changed my mind."

He didn't stand. "I know too much about you and your past, babe. You need to be a little nicer to me." He stared right into her eyes and called her an ugly name.

Nadine was suddenly in the doorway. "Don't talk to Savannah that way," she said.

The girl's words both strengthened and worried her. "Thanks, Nadine, but I can handle this." She glared at Rupert. "Leave. Now."

Rupert didn't move. Except his lips, which curled into a sneer.

Kevin had come up behind Nadine. He wasn't offering to help, more just watching it unfold. In a pinch, though, he'd be on Nadine's side. He was an islander, after all.

But Savannah was the grown-up, and fixing this was up to her.

"Nadine," she said, "go into the front room and call 911 if he's not gone in two minutes." Did they even *have* 911 here? Come to think of it, she'd never seen a police officer.

"On it." Nadine's words sounded confident.

Rupert started to rise, glaring at her. "You wouldn't."

She heard the front door open. What now?

"Hey, everybody, I'm home early!" The voice was familiar, welcoming, comforting. And terrifying.

Hank was home.

CHAPTER FOURTEEN

SAVANNAH GOT TO the front room just in time to see Hank's expression change from happy to concerned, then angry. "What on earth is going on?" he asked, dropping his suitcase to the floor.

He was looking behind her.

Rupert.

Rupert had the nerve to put his hands on her shoulders in a possessive way. "Just paying a visit to my sweetheart," he said.

She spun away, shoving at him. "No, you were actually leaving. Nadine, that 911 request still holds."

"And I'm still ready. He has…" Nadine looked at her phone "…fifteen seconds to take off."

"He has less than that." Still in his overcoat, Hank strode toward Rupert. "Get out of my house."

Rupert sneered. "Nobody likes to catch their woman in the act."

Hank did something with his hand and Rupert's shoulder, a move too quick for Savannah to follow, and then Rupert was sprawled on the floor, propped on one elbow, grimacing. "Go. Now."

"Dad!" Nadine's voice was a mixture of exasperation and pride. "You might have really hurt him!"

"And your friend will be next if he doesn't leave right behind this piece of dirt." Hank sounded firm and authoritative, and Savannah was so relieved he was here.

At the same time, she was horrified. Hank could find out about her past. That was problem one. Worse, Hank had no idea what kind of a man Rupert was and what kind of revenge he was capable of.

Rupert was getting slowly to his feet, moving oddly. "If you injured me, you have a lawsuit coming," he said.

"Right behind your home invasion suit." Hank walked over to the door, nudged his suitcase away with his foot, and held it open. "Gentlemen?"

Kevin practically ran out, and Rupert slunk behind him. Savannah felt a flash of old, misplaced worry. How would he get back to the boat docks? What would happen to him if the authorities were on his tail?

And then, like a wisp of old smoke, her concern for Rupert vanished. He didn't deserve it. She didn't have to waste another moment on a man who'd treated her so poorly. A man who, despite his wealth and power in the city, was no competition and no threat to a man like Hank.

Hank turned to her, his expression thunderous. "I come home to find each of you entertaining men? Is this what's been going on in my absence?"

Savannah was struck dumb in the face of his anger.

"Oh, Dad," Nadine said. "You make it sound like we've turned the house into a brothel. Savannah let both of them come in because it was freezing outside. She told them they could stay for half an hour. And then her, um, her guy, was rude, and she kicked him out early."

Thank you, Nadine.

Hank ran a hand through his hair, looking suddenly tired and every year of his age. "Lock the door and don't let anyone else in. I'm going to get cleaned up. We'll talk in an hour."

Savannah watched him walk away and then sank into a chair.

Nadine flopped down in front of the fire, on her back, stroking the mama cat. "He sounded mad," she said doubtfully. "Are you gonna get fired?"

"I don't know. Probably." The implications of what had just happened were beginning to sink in. *Would* Hank fire her?

Most likely. No matter how well the preceding week had gone, Hank had walked into a damning situation upon his return. How else could he interpret it than that she'd failed miserably and put his daughter at risk? And how could she explain away evidence he'd seen with his own eyes?

She leaned back and stared up at the ceiling, overwhelmed. She could crash at Taylor's for a few days, maybe even help out at the bakery a little now that she'd learned to cook. Hank wasn't the type to withhold her pay, so she'd at least be better off than she'd been when she came here.

But she didn't *want* to leave. She wanted to stay here.

Pain and panic threatened, and she took deep breaths, let them out slowly. *Think.*

She could maybe get a job on the mainland, as a housecleaner or caregiver. It wouldn't be long before some guy came along who wanted to rescue her from it all.

Slick self-loathing filled her. She wanted to escape that life. She wanted to figure out her actual talents beyond standing around showing her pretty face. Ultimately, she wanted the love and the family she hadn't had as a kid.

Starting with staying here on the island, where she could be with her only family, Taylor. And with the family that was starting to wrap itself around her heart, Hank and Nadine.

But was it possible for someone like her to have love and a family?

Trying to get out of her own head, she looked over at Nadine. "You okay, kiddo?"

"Yeah," Nadine said. "I didn't really want to hang out with Kevin, anyway. He's boring."

That revelation on Nadine's part sparked a tiny flame of happiness in her. Nadine was starting to see the light about Kevin, and that was so much better than being forbidden to see him by an adult. "You can meet someone a lot more interesting than that," she told Nadine. "Or you can hang out with your girlfriends, who are way, way more interesting."

"I know," Nadine said. Then she grabbed one of the kittens, scooted over and handed it to Savannah. Leaning against Savannah's chair, she looked up at her. "I hope Dad lets you stay."

Savannah reached down and tucked back a flyaway strand of Nadine's hair. "Me too, honey. Me, too."

TAYLOR WAS PACKING up the last of a big order of teaberry scones when Savannah tapped on the bakery's locked door. It was Friday afternoon, three o'clock, and Cody had agreed to run the order down to the mail boat.

And then she was taking the evening off. Or sort of. It still felt stressful because she was going out to dinner with Cody to celebrate.

But really, to work out their differences, or at least discuss them. The past week had been awkward, and the tenth time they'd inched past each other in the kitchen, carefully avoiding contact, they'd looked at each other and said, at the same time, "We need to talk."

So that was tonight. Yeah, no stress there.

As she let Savannah in the front door, Cody came out of the kitchen, dusting his hands on his apron. "Hey, Savannah. Everything ready, Taylor?"

"Here you go. Let's load it up."

"You ladies relax. I'll do the loading." And he grabbed a big stack of bakery boxes and headed to his car, parked in front.

"So you got your orders done?" Savannah leaned on the counter on her elbows.

"Yes, and I'm beat." She squinted at Savannah. Were those dark circles under her eyes? And come to think of it, she'd sounded a little raspy on the phone earlier. "Are you okay?"

"I'm fine." Savannah waved a dismissive hand. "That's great you're making it happen with all these off-island orders. I'm so proud of you." Savannah sounded sincere, and her words felt good. "*And* I'm proud of you for letting me do a makeover on you. You're going out tonight, right?"

Taylor nodded, looking away. "To the Dockside."

"With girlfriends?" Savannah persisted as she followed Taylor up the stairs to her apartment.

"Uh, no." Taylor ushered her through the door and closed it behind them. "With Cody."

"He asked you *out*?" Savannah's voice rose to a shriek. "Oh my gosh, Taylor, that's so great!"

"Shh." Taylor beckoned Savannah away from the door and the echoey hallway, then went to the window. Thankfully, Cody had loaded the last set of boxes in and was pulling away.

"You guys are so perfect together, and now you can explore it!" She clapped her hands. "And I brought *all* my makeup and some of Nadine's."

There was so much wrong with Savannah's statement. She and Cody *weren't* perfect together. Quite the opposite. Tonight, they needed to get back on a professional footing. To forget about that kiss, which had probably meant nothing to him except to make him feel a little awkward with her.

It wasn't a date, but she didn't feel like pounding that point home with Savannah right at the moment.

So Taylor lifted the bag she'd held back and shook it enticingly in front of her sister. "And I brought us teaberry scones," she said.

"First things first. Gimme."

In times past, Savannah wouldn't have indulged. Now she took a big bite, pointed to the remaining scone in her hand, and nodded. "Delicious."

Taylor was glad to see that Savannah wasn't restricting her food intake anymore. She actually looked like she'd put on a few pounds, which, in Taylor's opinion, she'd sorely needed to do.

She herself was a different story. She took a big bite of scone, anyway. "See?" she said when she'd swallowed it. "This is why I'm fat."

"You're not fat." Savannah frowned at her. "You're perfect."

"And why my cheeks are so full."

"Stop it. You're totally cute."

Taylor rolled her eyes and took another bite. Everyone said she was cute. "Cute isn't so cute at my age."

Savannah had finished her scone and was picking up crumbs from the plate. "I mean, no offense, but look at you. You're wearing mom jeans and a blue checkered blouse, which I get matches the bakery, but it's not exactly sophisticated. It's *cute*. And that ponytail…" She shook her head. "We're going to make you glamorous."

"I agreed to a makeover, but I don't want to be glamorous. I'd look weird wearing heavy makeup to the Dockside." Not to mention that all her friends would see that she was trying to glam herself up to Cody's level, which was never going to work. She'd seem pathetic.

Savannah got on her phone and started texting. When she looked up, she had a devilish grin. "You're not going to the Dockside."

"What?"

"You're going to the Rockfish Grill. I just texted Cody and told him, and he said okay."

"Savannah!" Taylor's cheeks heated. "He'll think I put you up to that!"

"Probably not, but so what if he does? It lets him know you're interested. Which you aren't the best at showing."

Against her will, the thought of his kiss pushed into her mind. He'd been so amazing. If getting glammed up and going to the Rockfish Grill would make that happen again, she had to admit she'd be thrilled.

On the other hand...no. Just no. This was a business dinner, basically, to talk about how to proceed with their non-relationship. "It won't work between me and Cody," she said flatly. "So there's no point in dolling me up."

"First of all," Savannah said, "there's *always* a point in getting dolled up. It makes you feel better. Look good, feel good."

"Maybe." Taylor wasn't going to acknowledge whether that was true. She didn't know, honestly. She so rarely got dressed up.

"And second of all, there's no reason it couldn't work between you and Cody. Why wouldn't it work? You two would be great together."

"He was with *you*," Taylor said. "He likes women like you. He's way, way out of my league." And she couldn't let herself dream otherwise. She had to protect her heart and focus on her other, more attainable dreams.

"That's ridiculous. I think you're still messed up from what Mom did. Makes you think you don't deserve good things."

Taylor stared at Savannah. "What?"

"Uh-huh. I'm the same. It just looks different on me. Now, sit down and take off your shirt. Or nix that. Leave it on, because we'll have you put on a dress later."

"A *dress*?" Taylor hadn't worn a dress in a year.

"Do you own one? Because I brought one of mine."

"Which wouldn't fit me in a million years. Yes, I own a dress. I own *two*."

"Let me guess. They're checkered, with full skirts."

"No way!" Taylor thought. "Well, one is close. It's red with polka dots. But the other one is a black sheath. I do go to funerals sometimes."

Savannah was shaking her head. "We are *so* ordering you some new clothes, but tonight, the funeral dress will have to do. Is it at least above the knee?"

"At the knee." Taylor went to her closet and rummaged through to the back. She pulled it out and held it in front of herself. "There. Or I could just wear pants."

Savannah studied the dress. "With a belt, that'll work."

"I don't even own a—"

"We'll use a scarf if we have to. Sit down. We're doing your hair and makeup first."

As Savannah went to work, Taylor felt something inside her relax. She and her sister hadn't ever had much time to be together as sisters, to bicker and laugh and tease. This was nice. "So, tell me what's going on with you, since I have to hold still."

Savannah shrugged.

"Tell me what's going on," Taylor repeated.

"Well," Savannah said as she swabbed foundation onto Taylor's forehead, "Rupert found me."

"What?" Taylor squawked, causing Savannah to run the foundation through her eyebrow.

"Be *still*. It was fine." Savannah blotted at her eyebrow with a cotton ball.

"How was that fine? I got the impression he was evil."

"Stop talking so I can do your blush." Savannah selected a large, fluffy brush from a case and started stroking it over Taylor's cheekbones. "Hank did some kind of martial arts move on him and then ordered him out of the house."

"*Hank* did that?" She'd had the impression of him as a scholarly, slightly nerdy guy. "I'm impressed."

"So was I," Savannah admitted.

Something about the way Savannah said it made Taylor's antennae twitch. "Are you and Hank…involved?"

"No!" Savannah's own cheeks were redder than Taylor's made-up ones.

Taylor put out a hand to still Savannah's, which was fumbling through the makeup brushes. "Tell me."

Savannah hesitated. "I like him," she said finally. "And he's letting me stay, although I'm on probation, because I let Rupert in the house and because I'm a little too lax with Nadine."

"Is that true?"

"Sort of? I don't know. It's not like I had a normal childhood. Mrs. Williams was strict with me, but only about getting to pageants on time and sticking to my diet. Speaking of which…" She reached behind her to the table and grabbed a second scone.

"So you're working out the job side of things. That's good." But Taylor had the feeling there was more to it.

Or maybe she just had *more* on the mind due to her own feelings about Cody. "Do you find Hank attractive?" she asked bluntly. If Savannah did, that would be weird indeed. Savannah and Hank were even more of a mismatch than Taylor and Cody were, in the looks department.

"I find him attractive and I...well, I respect him." She paused, then added, "But nothing can ever work between us."

"Why not?" Taylor closed her eyes while Savannah did something uncomfortable with eyeliner.

"Well, because he *is* admirable. He's a solid citizen, a good dad. He's probably only had a couple of girlfriends, none after his wife left, according to Nadine. Whereas I..." She trailed off. "You know."

Taylor waited until the eyeliner was done and then opened her eyes and studied her sister. "Whereas you *what*?"

"I'm a...you know. A *tart*, as Aunt Katy would say."

Taylor's heart hurt as she studied her sister's gorgeous face. Savannah had, no doubt, been with more men than was good for her. "Do you regret your past?"

"Of course I do!" Savannah stared at her as if she were crazy. "Do you think I would've lived with Rupert, or the guy before that, or the guy before that, if I'd had a choice?" She shook her head as if she were impatient with herself. "But I did have a choice. Of course I did. I could've gotten a job early on and worked and saved and bought a bakery."

"No, you couldn't have. Stop." Taylor reached forward and brushed back her sister's hair. "You were in that world. Men were fawning all over you. You didn't get to have a part-time job in high school because you had to do the pageants, so you never learned to…" She trailed off.

"To work?" Savannah raised an eyebrow. "You're right, I didn't. Not in any kind of useful way." She selected a small silver container, opened it and leaned forward to brush at Taylor's eyebrows. "You really need to darken your brows every day. Look how it defines your eyes."

Taylor looked cautiously into the mirror and then stared. A happy feeling rose up in her. She looked good, and Cody would see her like this!

"All I know how to do is look pretty," Savannah said. "Which leads to living off men. Not exactly the best career move."

Taylor swung around. "No," she said. "You're so much more than your looks. It's just…hard to see past them, that's all." Two inspirations struck her at the same time. "You know, you're amazing at this makeup stuff. That could be the start of a career for you. Or…" She broke off, not sure how Savannah would take her other idea.

"Or what?" Savannah was standing behind her now, combing through her hair.

"You could let me do a reverse makeover on you."

"What do you mean?"

"You doll me up. I tone you down."

"Tone me down how?" Savannah pulled out a bottle of some kind of spray. "Stand up and bend over. We're going to make this hair bigger."

Taylor obeyed, shutting her eyes as Savannah sprayed the underside of her hair.

Finally, she stood. "One of these days," she said, "I'm going to make you look plain."

"Oh, yeah? That doesn't take a makeover. That's me when I get out of bed."

"I've *seen* you just out of bed, and you're still beautiful. Just a tiny bit less perfect. Does *Hank* ever see you looking that way?"

Savannah bit her lip. "No. I don't leave my room without makeup. I haven't for years."

"How about when you woke up in the morning with a guy?" Taylor was amazed.

"I got up first."

"Seriously." Taylor stared at her sister. "You got up first to fix yourself up?"

Savannah nodded. "All the models did. Well, most of us. The shock of someone seeing the real you…it's not a good thing."

Taylor frowned. "I think you should let me do it. The look-plain makeover, I mean."

Savannah shrugged. "Go for it. But not tonight. You only have…" she checked the time "…half an hour until Cody comes back to take you to dinner. Get your dress on."

Slightly embarrassed to undress in front of her bony sister, Taylor stepped toward the closet, dropped her jeans and unbuttoned her shirt, and started to pull on the dress.

"Wait! Wait." Savannah came over. "Is that the only underwear you have?"

"Well... I mean, I have my Sunday stuff."

"Put on your Sunday stuff," Savannah insisted. "You need to feel pretty and confident, and you can't do that in granny panties."

Taylor blew out a breath. "You're annoying, you know?" But she softened the words with a smile. Truthfully, she was touched that Savannah had taken all this time to make her prettier and more confident. She needed all the help she could get if she were going to survive an evening, even an evening to discuss how to get back on a professional footing, at the Rockfish Grill with Cody.

CHAPTER FIFTEEN

CODY KNOCKED ON Taylor's door, just three steps away from his own door, and waited on the landing. He ran a finger around the collar of his shirt and shifted his shoulders in the sport jacket and wondered whether the tie he'd worn was too much.

Probably not, for a place like the Rockfish Grill.

Taylor opened the door, and all the breath whooshed out of him.

Yeah, he'd been right to wear a tie.

She wore a black dress that was perfectly modest but showed her luscious figure. That was helped by the sexy shoes, high heels that brought her closer to his height and—he didn't gawk, he was proud of that, but he glanced—sure enough, her legs looked stellar. Her hair curled loose around her shoulders, and her eyes looked huge, her lips full.

She was a knockout.

How had he never realized she was such a knockout?

His mouth was so dry he had to clear his throat. "Ready to go?" he rasped out.

"Uh-huh." She slid on a coat and followed him downstairs. "Did the kids go with Nadine okay?"

"They were thrilled to go to play at Hank's. Apparently, there's an indoor gym where they can run around all they want. Plus a litter of kittens."

"Wow. So cool."

At the bottom of the stairs, he crooked his arm for her to take, walked her to the car and opened the door for her. When she climbed in, he caught another glimpse of spectacular legs.

How had he not noticed she had such great legs?

He hustled around to the driver's side and got in, jerking the car a little as he pulled out. *Steady, don't have a wreck here.* "Do you like this music? We can change it." He had on one of his regular playlists, pop alternative, but he suddenly felt like he should be playing jazz or classical.

"It's fine."

He drove to the Rockfish carefully, even though it was a five-minute trip over town roads with almost no traffic. He was acutely conscious of her perfume.

Why had she dressed up so much? How was she imagining this evening would go? It wasn't even how she looked. It was how she carried herself.

Like a sexy woman.

They were supposed to be discussing the awkwardness between them so they could get on with things at work on an easier basis. But when Savannah had texted him about switching to the Rockfish, he'd gotten curious. Had Taylor put her sister up to that text, and if so, why?

Probably she just felt like having good seafood rather than bar food.

But then she'd dressed like that and done up her hair and worn perfume. Why?

He felt like a teenager on his first date. No, scratch that. He'd *never* felt this way before.

They pulled up to the grill and parked. "Wait," he said. "I'll come around for you." Would she take that as an insult, an affront to her independence? He was sweating as he opened her door.

She emerged gracefully and accepted his help steadying herself on the icy pavement. Then she held his arm as they walked to the restaurant door. "This isn't a date," she informed him. "I just, I borrowed Savannah's shoes and I can barely walk in them."

If it wasn't a date, why had she dressed that way? "I understand. You look great in the shoes. You look... great." Cody was pretty sure he'd never been this awkward in his life.

"Savannah dressed me." She pushed back her hair, looked at him, looked away.

He was dying here.

The host in the restaurant knew her and was up-front in his feelings. "Girl, where have you been hiding yourself? You look amazing!" He led the way to a table with barely a glance at Cody.

He was pretty sure the host wasn't interested in her, romantically speaking, but the two men who checked her out as they walked across the dining room were a different story, even though they were each dining with their wives. There was a little sway to her hips, and her hair bounced and moved as she walked and...

wow. This was Taylor, but a different side of her, and longing hit him hard.

What if you had a woman who was gorgeous and could dress up like this and knock you out, but who could also work with you and talk to you, be a friend and a team player?

Not many men got so lucky, but if you did...life would be good.

The host pulled out her chair before he could, and then they were sitting across from each other. Candles on each table and low lights, quiet music, the murmur of voices. Very romantic. Not Cody's usual style of place, but with Taylor, he was glad to be here.

And he needed to stop. To rein in his feelings. No matter how sexy and kissable Taylor looked, she was still Taylor. She was the type of woman you committed to, not the kind for a fling.

And Cody couldn't commit. He never had. If a woman got too close, he ran.

He'd been called on it and psychoanalyzed for it by armchair psychologists in bars and by angry, disappointed women. There was no doubt it was all about his childhood, the not-so-benign neglect he'd faced, the way he'd been dumped into the foster care system.

He'd never regretted those aspects of his past so much.

Was there a chance he could get over it and learn to commit?

They ordered drinks—wine for her, a draft beer for him—and then she cleared her throat. "We should probably talk about what's going on at work, since that's why we're here."

"Right." *Was* that why they were here, though? He was confused.

"It's been awkward," she said firmly. "I don't want to have to walk on eggshells at my own bakery."

He pushed down his attraction and tried to focus on business. "Are you firing me?"

"No! Not now, anyway." She pushed back her hair with one hand.

That wasn't promising. He needed to clear things up with Taylor so that he didn't lose this job before he had something else in place, not that he'd been especially motivated to look for other work lately.

Right now, he was having a hard time focusing on work and professionalism and job security when she was taking his breath away.

"Any ideas on what went wrong and how to fix it?" he asked.

"We shouldn't have kissed," she said.

"Well, but—"

"It's awkward," she said. "I can't have awkward with my bakery. It means too much to me to succeed."

Ouch. Her bakery meant more to her than he did. "We can't reverse the past," he said. "Maybe there's another way to fix it." He was looking into her eyes, and he felt like he was hurtling into their depths, taking a dive into her heart. "Taylor, I…"

Their drinks arrived, the waiter stayed and chatted a moment, and Cody heaved a sigh of relief that felt a little like disappointment. The moment for declaring his feelings had passed, and that was a very good thing.

Wasn't it?

He watched her sip her wine. She sighed, smiled and stretched her neck and shoulders. "This is nice. I'm not good at relaxing, but I need to get better at it."

He wanted to help her do that. Declaring his feelings for her wasn't the way to go, since he couldn't do commitment, but maybe there was a middle ground. Maybe he could help her a little bit, as a friend. "Let's just take it easy while we're out tonight," he said. "We could both use some time to relax. Let's pretend there's no problem, and we're out on a fun date. Tomorrow, we'll have plenty of time to practice being chill around each other."

She looked at him over the rim of her wineglass. "You want to pretend we're out on a fun date."

"Yeah," he said. "Take it easy. Chat. Have fun. We could even…" He looked at the three-piece combo band setting up in the corner. "We could even dance. Let off some tension, and then maybe we'll be in a better place to laugh off any awkwardness. To go forward and make the bakery a big, big success."

She studied him, her eyes narrowing.

"Up to you," he said. "We can sit here talking it all through if you think that will help. You're the boss."

"That doesn't sound real appealing, does it?" She laughed a little. "I never did like the whole 'let's talk about the relationship' part of dating."

"Me, either," he said with feeling.

"So, okay," she said. "Let's just pretend it's a regular,

fun, *light* date—" she gave him a warning look "—and we'll start over tomorrow as fun, relaxed friends."

He reached across the table and shook her hand. "Deal," he said.

And then nearly reneged on it by clinging on to that hand, so slender, so work-hardened, so absolutely *Taylor*.

IT WAS THE most ridiculous thing she could ever have agreed to. It was *not* what fit in with her goals.

But somehow, the prospect of a fun, carefree date with Cody overcame all her wiser instincts.

And it *was* fun, more fun than she'd had in ages. Cody was charming, funny, a good conversationalist. And yeah, that made her a bit uneasy, because she knew he was super popular with the ladies, and this was why.

But she was going to relax and see what happened.

They finished delicious seafood meals, and Cody ate so much that she felt okay about eating a normal amount, not a delicate girl amount like Savannah undoubtedly would have done. Although maybe not. Savannah was changing her tune.

They were both too full for dessert, but as a bakery owner, Taylor felt like she had to try the cake, and Cody immediately agreed to share a piece with her. When it came with two forks, Taylor's heart skipped.

This was what women who dated, who had love and romance in their lives, experienced.

"Ladies first," Cody said, gesturing toward the cake.

She picked up a fork and tasted it. Carrot cake, which she loved. Her brain went into analysis mode while her heart registered the fact that Cody was watching her closely. *He* wasn't analyzing, she was pretty sure; he seemed to be enjoying watching her eat. Her chest heated.

Around them, the clink of silverware and the movements of waiters faded. Without looking away from her, he picked up a fork and tasted the cake, then raised an eyebrow. "Verdict?"

"You first." She needed time to catch her breath.

"It's good," he said. He took another bite, and savored it, and she watched his mouth, feeling the heat, now, in the pit of her stomach. "I think it's too sweet."

She felt as proud of him as if he were her star student. "Exactly. The cake doesn't need to be that sweet. It needs to be a contrast with the frosting, which should be cream cheese, by the way, not butter frosting."

The waiter overheard and stopped by, chuckling. "The cook knew you'd be critical. He's waiting back there to see what you think."

Taylor smiled. "It's really good. Everyone makes a recipe like this differently, but tell him we love it."

"But that if he ever needs a break, he can order cake from the Bluebird Bakery," Cody added.

"I'll tell him." He left and they finished the cake, slowly, savoring, dueling with their forks over the last bit of frosting.

Her heart galloped ahead. Maybe this could work, this whatever-it-was between her and Cody. She felt such a sense of possibility, although possibly that was just the wine.

But she was letting herself hope, and it felt so good.

The leader of the jazz band said a few words, and they launched into a song just as the dessert plate was taken away. "If we're going to have fun and relax, we should dance, right?" Cody asked.

"If you have time before the kids—"

He reached out and placed a finger on her lips. "Shh. There's time."

Oh man. The heat she felt was way more than what she'd get from wine.

He led her by the hand out onto the dance floor and surprised her by moving into a fast swing-dance style. Taylor loved to dance, or she had; she hadn't done it in ages, not since she'd started the bakery. She fell into rhythm with him and they met, and parted. For a few minutes, they were the only people dancing. The band leader praised their abilities and launched into a faster song, and they went hip-hop, and people clapped and joined them on the dance floor.

She was out of breath when the band moved into a slow song. There was a fraction of a second when they could have sat down, but instead, he pulled her into his arms.

He smelled good. Not all cologne-scented, but piney, with something heady and masculine that just seemed to emanate from him. She inhaled, her face in his neck, and felt almost dizzy. But he held her, strong, with those muscles she'd covertly admired ever since he'd returned from the service.

Her chest was rising and falling more rapidly than it should, but that was okay, because his breathing seemed a little ragged, too. He pulled her closer and ran a hand over her hair.

This was ridiculous, impossible, wonderful. Something tugged at her mind—something about how they shouldn't have kissed—but she pushed it aside and concentrated on the slow movements with him, swaying in her high heels, feeling pretty in her dress.

The world drifted away, but then again, it didn't. Because maybe this was real. Maybe there was a bright future where she got to have the man and the kids, love and a family. Maybe her dreams, even the secret ones, could come true.

When the song ended, she looked up at him.

He stepped back but kept his arm around her. "I hate to say it, but we should go. I told Nadine we wouldn't be late picking them up."

"Of course." She wrapped her arm around his waist. "This was fun. Thanks for suggesting we put work aside."

He squeezed her closer to his side. "The pleasure was mine. Believe me."

The ride home passed in a haze. They didn't talk, but they didn't need to. When the car stopped, it took a minute before she realized he'd gone to their apartments above the bakery rather than to pick up the kids.

What did that mean?

Once again, he came around to open her door and to help her out of the vehicle. With a couple of glasses of wine in her, she was glad for the help, especially since Savannah's tottery shoes had grown more uncomfortable as the night went on. She held his arm until they got to the stairs. Would he leave now to pick up the kids?

No. He followed her upstairs.

Taylor's heart thudded. He was going to try to come in. Would she let him?

Years of Aunt Katy's teachings and church lessons about chastity for singles warred with the warm, heavy feeling in the pit of her stomach. It had been a long time since she'd felt this attracted to a man. Maybe never. And never had a man looked at her and touched her with the kind of tender desire Cody had displayed when they'd danced.

So…maybe?

At her door, she turned to face him. He was *so* handsome, his brown eyes warm and soulful, his shoulders impossibly broad. He'd loosened his tie, and the slightly disheveled look suited him. Again she inhaled that distinctive, slightly piney scent. Her heart pounded, hard and rapid.

She put her arms around him. "Do you want to come in?" she asked in a husky voice she barely recognized as her own.

His eyes never left hers, but he didn't return the embrace. Instead, he reached behind himself and gently pulled her hands apart, bringing them around to clasp between them. "You're an incredible woman," he said. "And incredibly desirable. But this isn't the right thing to do."

Hurt and mortification slashed through her, sending the heat she'd felt for him into her face, morphing instantly into anger as hot as molten steel. How dare he turn her down in that patronizing way?

Go inside. Have some dignity.

But his kindly, friendly expression replicated the

looks she'd seen on the faces of most boys she'd liked, but ended up befriending. *Good old Taylor. Great gal. And you should see her sister...*

"You couldn't hold yourself back with Savannah," she spit out bitterly, "even when she was underage and it was *really* wrong. But it's pretty easy for you to do the right thing now, with me." Hot tears pushed at the backs of her eyes. She was *not* going to let him see her cry. She'd be an idiot to cry over a man.

He looked puzzled as he tilted his head and opened his mouth to speak.

She couldn't bear to hear whatever fumbling explanations he might have. She spun on her too-high heels, stumbling a little, went inside her apartment and slammed the door in his face.

Then she leaned back against it, sank slowly down to the floor and buried her hot face in her hands.

SAVANNAH LOOKED OUT the window on Saturday afternoon, eagerly awaiting Taylor's arrival. It was a gloomy day, with low-hanging clouds making the Chesapeake appear gray, too.

Yet she felt anything but gloomy. Instead, she felt excited.

Taylor was going to help her figure out how to tone down her looks and be more ordinary. She'd even promised to bring over ordinary clothes.

Nadine knocked, and then walked into Savannah's room.

"Don't bother Savannah, hon," Hank called from the kitchen. "It's her day off."

"It's fine," Savannah called back. "She's here as a friend, not as a job." She turned to Nadine. "Right?"

Happiness washed over Nadine's face. "Right," she said, and jumped up onto the bed.

"How are the kittens?" she asked Nadine. Hank wasn't the only one trying to set some boundaries. Savannah had forced herself not to go out and play with the kittens today, so that Hank and Nadine could have the chance to bond over them.

"They're adorable. Asleep right now. So, what are you doing today?"

"I'm getting a makeover from my sister," Savannah said.

"Oooh, can I watch?"

"Maybe for part of it." Savannah wanted to make sure she did more sisterly bonding with Taylor. That had been the best part of giving her sister a makeover yesterday. For once, she hadn't felt like a beggar and a failure around Taylor; she'd felt like she had something to offer.

She'd wondered if some of the makeover tips would carry over into Taylor's ordinary way of getting dressed, but now, as Taylor pulled up and trudged toward the house, she saw that wasn't happening. Oh, well. Change took time.

In fact, Taylor looked down in the dumps. "Give us some sister time first," she said to Nadine, "and then you can come back and watch my transformation, if you don't have anything better to do."

She hurried to the door and ushered Taylor inside,

sweeping her past Hank and into her suite. "What's going on? Are you hungover? How was last night?"

Taylor set down the bag she'd brought in and flopped onto the bed, just as Nadine had done. "I don't want to talk about it."

Uh-oh. "That bad?"

Taylor nodded. "I didn't want to come over, but he's in his apartment and I wanted to get away from him."

"We don't have to do the makeover," Savannah said. "We can just…go out for something to eat. Or stay in and watch mindless TV and eat junk." She went to her mini-fridge and pulled out a bottle of water. "Here, though. Drink this. You're probably dehydrated."

"Thanks. The makeover will be easy. I brought an outfit in there." Taylor nodded toward her bag. "Once you've put it on, I'll do your hair. Or undo it. You're not wearing makeup right now?"

Savannah lifted her hands, palms up. "I can't go out of my room without makeup. It's just eyeliner and eyebrow stuff and blush."

Taylor shook her head. "Off it comes."

Savannah hesitated, but then she remembered her goal. She had to see if she could be valued for more than her looks. It especially freaked her out to have a man—Hank—see her with absolutely no makeup. But that was part of what she was working on.

Anyway, she'd already established that Hank couldn't be interested in someone with her background. He wanted a smart, chaste type. He'd backed *way* off after the encounter with Rupert.

For whatever reason, that made her mad, and she

grabbed her makeup remover wipes and scrubbed off every trace of makeup. "There. Satisfied?"

A trace of a smile lifted the corner of Taylor's mouth. "You're not exactly hideous."

"Yes, I am." She knelt and dug through Taylor's bag. "These are the clothes?" She pulled out a crewneck sweatshirt and stiff, discount-store jeans.

"Uh-huh. Put them on."

Savannah checked the tags. "I have almost this exact same outfit, but in my size. I'll grab that." She dropped the clothes and stood.

"Nope. Part of the reverse makeover is wearing loose, baggy clothes that hide your figure. Put those on."

"Bossy." Savannah changed quickly, then looked in the mirror. "Wow. These are gonna fall off me."

"That's why there's a belt in there."

Reluctantly, Savannah pulled out the belt and put it on. The jeans were ankle-length, but not in a stylish way. They bagged in the seat and yet weren't high-waisted enough to nip in.

The crewneck shirt was orange, a shade that wouldn't suit anyone. "Where did you *get* these clothes?" she asked, turning away from the mirror.

"Back of my closet. They're too small now, but I hung on to them in case I ever get that thin—or that poor—again. Now, put your hair in a ponytail."

Savannah grabbed a puffy scrunchie, ran a brush through her hair and bent over. She pulled her hair into a high ponytail and turned to face her sister. "Like that?"

"Nope. That's too flattering. Do a low pony at the back of your head."

"I always look bald when I do that."

"But that's how three quarters of women with long hair wear it. You want to look ordinary, right?"

"Right," she grumbled. She redid her ponytail and glared at herself in the mirror. "I feel terrible. Truly ugly." She climbed up onto the other end of the bed. "So tell me what happened to make you so cranky. Didn't you and Cody get along? No spark?"

Taylor leaned back and stared up at the ceiling. "*I* felt a spark. He didn't."

"That's hard to believe." Savannah had been in the room when the two of them were there. Even when they were mopping floors and beating cake batter, the air was full of chemistry. And it definitely wasn't one-sided.

"I *thought* he felt something. When we were talking. And dancing."

"You danced? That's awesome! He wouldn't have done that if he didn't like you."

"Right?" Taylor sat up and wrapped her arms around her knees. "He's a *great* dancer. Fast and slow. And he, like, opened my door all the time and made me take his arm when I crossed the ice, because I was wearing those ridiculous shoes."

"He's into you for sure." Taylor looked at her own feet. "By the way, what shoes do I wear with this outfit?"

"Sneakers. Preferably not brand-name ones." Taylor held out her foot to show her own grimy-looking athletic shoes.

"Take those off. You're on my bed, for Pete's sake!"

"Sorry." Taylor took them off and tossed them to Savannah. "You can try these on, but I need them back to wear home."

Savannah pulled on the slightly sweaty shoes, hopped off the bed and looked in the mirror. Yes, that completed the doofus look. She turned away before she could get depressed. "So if there was chemistry, on and off the dance floor, why are you saying it didn't go well?"

Taylor heaved a huge sigh. "I made a move," she said, "and he turned me down."

"Aw, too bad," Savannah said. "But I'm proud of you for making a move. Did he give a reason for saying no?"

"Said it wasn't the right thing to do."

Savannah nodded. "That's so Cody. He probably just wants to take it slow."

"That's not so Cody. He's a player. I mean, he was with you."

Savannah frowned. "What do you mean?"

"When you were together that summer," she said. "When he, you know, went too far."

That seemed like such a long time ago, but still, the memory made Savannah's cheeks heat. "No, he held back then, too," she said.

"But you said—"

Savannah waved a hand. "I was embarrassed. I told it how I wanted it to be."

"What. Do. You. Mean." Taylor stared at her. "You told me you didn't use protection. You were worried about getting pregnant."

Why did Taylor seem so upset? Savannah had done a lot worse things. "That same night Cody turned me down, I sneaked out and met up with this other kid. That's who, you know…" She trailed off, unable to look at her sister. "That was my first time," she said finally.

"So it *wasn't* Cody who was your first?"

"No."

Taylor pushed herself off the bed and paced the room. "All those years, you let me think it was him? Let me be mad at him?"

"You were mad at him?" As Savannah recalled it, they'd left shortly after the non-memorable night when she'd lost her virginity. She'd had a couple of anxious weeks worrying about whether she was going to carry some virtual stranger's child, and then everything had turned out fine. Taught her a lesson. She'd never slacked off on birth control again.

"Of course I was mad at him! He took advantage! You were too young."

"That's what he said when he turned me down, way back when." Savannah nodded as the embarrassing moment came back to her. "I was annoyed with him. I felt grown at sixteen."

Taylor stopped her pacing and glared, hands on hips. "But I told him… Last night, when I yelled at him… Oh, man. Give me those shoes."

Savannah took them off and handed them to her. "You *yelled* at him? Why? And why are you so upset?" An uneasy feeling crept into her. She should have explained the real truth to Taylor, but they'd parted as soon as they'd left the island. Once her pregnancy scare was past, Savannah had put the whole series of events out of her mind.

Taylor put on the shoes and opened the door.

"Wait. Don't be mad." She'd just reestablished a good relationship with Taylor. She didn't want some minor incident from the past to destroy that fragile foundation.

Taylor started out of the suite, took a couple of steps and then turned back. She lifted a hand like a stop sign when Savannah tried to follow her. "You lied to me. And then you *forgot* to let me know the truth, even when we were back here on the island, the scene of the crime." She trailed off, waved an arm. "You made me wreck the best chance of a relationship I ever had!" Her voice rose, louder and shakier, as she spoke. "I'm done. I'm just done with you." And then she turned around and stormed out of the house.

Savannah's insides withered, a little more when she realized that Hank and Nadine were in the front room and had heard every word. "That went well," she tried to joke through a tight throat.

The two of them just looked at her. Stared, in fact.

She realized that she was dressed in the bad clothes, with the bad hair and no makeup.

She wasn't pretty and she was a liar, and they hated her for it. They'd only ever liked her for her looks, anyway.

The only person who did like her for more than her looks, her sister, now hated her, was done with her. Because she was a no-good person inside as well as out.

She felt like every bone in her body weighed a hundred pounds as she turned and made her way back into her suite, closing the door behind her.

THANK HEAVENS TAYLOR had gone out this afternoon. Cody would have gone crazy sitting in his apartment knowing she was next door, but that they were totally at odds. Yet he had to stay in his apartment for a video call with, of all people, his mother.

The kids' social worker had located her, and through a colleague, had put together a meeting. She, Cody and Mom were to talk through what should happen next with Ava and Danny.

The kids were spending the afternoon at Ryan and Mellie's place. No way was he going to upset them with seeing and hearing their mother unless she was truly committed to getting them back and taking care of them.

The thought of losing them after he'd just found them stabbed a hole in his heart. He'd come to love them so much in such a short time.

But love meant doing the best for the other person. Even if that meant letting them go.

A message popped up on his laptop. "A few delays, but the call should start in about ten minutes."

So… Cody was about to talk to the woman who'd birthed and abandoned him, for the first time in, what, fifteen years?

She'd shown up at his high school graduation, but his foster parents, Betty and Wayne, had policed their interaction since Mom was obviously high on something. He'd received a letter from her when he'd been overseas, a rambling diatribe against a boss who'd recently fired her and a request for money. He hadn't answered.

In no way did he want to start up a relationship with

her, especially on a day when he felt so raw emotionally. But for Danny and Ava, he'd do it.

He tapped on the table and checked the time. Eight more minutes. Eight minutes to try not to think about his disastrous date with Taylor last night.

He'd already gone over and over it in his mind. Of course he kept picturing how good she looked and remembering how easily their conversation had flowed, how well they'd danced together.

And then, when he'd made a superhuman effort not to kiss her and do all the other things he wanted to do, she'd turned on him and made some wild accusation about him and Savannah.

What did she even think he'd done to Savannah? As far as he recalled—and it wasn't all that clear in his mind so many years later—he'd just shaken his head at Savannah's immature efforts to seduce him and had gently sent her home.

But Taylor seemed to think, or assume, that he'd taken advantage of an underage girl.

Was that really what she thought of him? Did she consider him that much of a loser?

Dark despair washed over him, enough to make him realize how much better he'd been feeling in the past month since arriving on Teaberry Island. He'd thought things were looking up for him, personally and professionally. Thought he might stay and build a life here. Thought things were going to be different, that he could escape his nightmares.

But somehow, he'd managed to screw up his life here. Not just his relationship with Taylor—although that was what hurt the most—but also his living situation and his job. If this morning were any indication, he and Taylor weren't going to be able to work together anymore. She had refused to speak to him, period.

The whole plan for last night had blown up in his face. He and Taylor were supposed to talk about how to manage working together without awkwardness. Instead, they'd made everything worse. More awkward at best, completely broken at worst.

A video call buzzed into his phone. He accepted it, and there was Mom.

Just seeing her made his mood plummet further, and he'd thought he was as low as he could go.

Her skin was blotched, her hair disheveled. He knew for a fact that she was only in her forties—she'd had him so young—but she looked twenty years older. When she smiled, her blackened and missing teeth showed the telltale decay of an addict.

"Hi, Cody." The social worker's voice was brisk and businesslike. "To start off, your mother has something to say to you."

His mother's smile disappeared. She nodded. "I want to thank you for taking in your brother and sister. Mrs. Croft says they're doing real well."

"They're doing okay." He restrained himself from saying, *No thanks to you.*

"It's quite a commitment you've taken on," Mrs. Croft continued, adjusting the angle so both she and Mom could be onscreen. "We're wondering how you feel about continuing to be there for them."

"Of course I will," he said without hesitation.

"You'll take care of them? Raise them if your mother is unable? Assume full custody if things go that way?"

"Yes."

Mom's face contorted, and she sobbed for a full minute. Mrs. Croft turned the phone away so that Cody could no longer see his mother's face. "While your mother gets herself together, why don't you update me on your progress?"

Like *that* was clear in his mind. He steeled himself to the sounds of sobbing and sniffling and told the woman how the kids were doing in school and that they were making some friends on the island.

"I know they'll probably need therapy," he said, "but we're not there yet. I was thinking it's better they settle in before digging into...everything."

The social worker angled her head. "I understand your reasoning," she said, "but if they start having problems beyond what you can work with, therapy is your next line of defense."

The sobbing in the background was slowing down, and Mrs. Croft looked toward Mom. "What did you ask?"

"Did he...did Cody have therapy?"

"She wants to know if you had therapy," Mrs. Croft relayed, a touch of acid in her voice.

Mom was asking that now? "Several times," he said, keeping his tone even.

His mother came back on the screen. Looking at her was like looking at one of those mistreated animal commercials on TV. He felt impossibly sad, and irritated at being manipulated, and like there was no help big enough for the need.

She'd abandoned him, but he'd gotten through it and mostly over it. Worse, she'd abandoned his two younger siblings. He should hate her for it. He should cut her right out of his life and Danny's and Ava's, too. Write her off as a lost cause.

But this was his mother. He could remember loving her more than anything in the world. As a kid, he'd watched her face, trying to gauge her mood, and when she'd smiled, it had lit up the room, the whole universe. All his anger toward her couldn't sweep away that underlying love.

When she turned to accept another tissue from the social worker, he saw that she'd tied a ribbon around her ponytail, not a regular hair ribbon, but the kind you'd put on a Christmas package. For some reason, that pathetic effort on her part made his whole chest ache. "How about you?" he asked her gruffly. "Are you getting some help?"

She started to cry again.

Mrs. Croft spoke over the sobs. "She's attended two Narcotics Anonymous meetings."

Cody got the message: Mom was trying, but a couple of meetings was most likely too little, too late.

"He's a good man to ask how I'm doing, after all I did to him," Mom choked out. She held the phone closer to her face, like she wanted to see him better. "Or didn't do. And now he's taking care of his brother and sister."

"He *is* a good man," the social worker said quietly in the background.

"I always knew. I left because he was good, not because he was bad. He needed better than I could give him."

All of a sudden, Cody's throat was so tight he couldn't speak.

His first thought was for his siblings. Had she left them, too, because they needed better? And did they, like him, have no clue about that?

He realized that some part of him had always thought he was flawed and bad and unlovable. Being abandoned by a parent, by the mother who was supposed to love you best of all, had struck a huge blow to his developing ego.

To hear her say that he was good, to have the social worker agree with that…and not just because they wanted to make him feel good about himself, but for actual reasons…the warm wash of relief nearly drowned him.

And then determination straightened his spine like an order from a commanding officer. He was *not* going to get soft and emotional. He was going to rely on what they'd said, that goodness they apparently saw in him, to make a better life for his little brother and sister.

"C-c-can I see my babies soon?" Mom was wiping her eyes, trying to get herself back in control.

Cody could give in and let her see them, let them have some of the back-and-forth he'd experienced himself as a kid before he'd gone permanently into the system. Maybe a kinder, more compassionate man would do that.

But he knew what it was like to have mixed allegiances and to always hope that your mother would pull herself together enough to actually be a mom and take care of you. It tore you up inside.

Mom had had plenty of years to stand up and be responsible, and she hadn't done it yet. He saw her mouth working and her tears flowing, and he knew that there was some sincerity there, but also some emotional blackmail.

He wasn't going to fall for it.

"I'd like to work toward full custody of Ava and Danny," he said to the social worker.

Mom started shaking her head. "No. I need my babies."

"Your babies need a stable life." Again, he straightened his spine. He looked at her forehead so he wouldn't have to stare into the black holes of her eyes. "You can visit, supervised, if the court approves it. But I don't want them thinking you're going to take them back. You gave up that right when you stuck them under a table in a bakery and took off."

"We'll work all this out," the social worker said. "I think this has been a productive call."

"Take care of them," Mom said through sobs.

Again, his throat tightened. He nodded. "I will," he croaked out, and then ended the call.

He wiped his eyes and blew his nose and chugged coffee. And then, finding himself at loose ends, he started drafting a proposal to fund a support group for veterans on Teaberry Island.

An hour and a half later, there was a knock on the door.

No outsider without a key could get up here, so it had to be Taylor.

Taylor, who'd thought all along that he had taken advantage of Savannah.

Well, he hadn't. He wasn't perfect, but even his messed-up mother and some stranger who was a social worker thought he was a good man.

Taylor, who'd seemed like a friend, didn't think so.

He couldn't let that continue. He had to get better in his own estimation, work on himself so he could set an example for the kids and find work where he could make a difference.

He had done well in the bakery job. And he'd done well with the kids, at least somewhat. At least he'd taken on the commitment.

So maybe he *could* commit. Maybe he wasn't irreparably damaged from his childhood. Maybe he could achieve his dreams, some of them, anyway. But not with someone who thought the worst of him.

He strode to the door and opened it.

Sure enough, it was Taylor. She stood in the hallway, looking like she'd been dragged behind a cart, her eyes swollen, her mouth working.

Kind of like his mother.

"I need to tell you something," she said. "I was wrong to say the things I said last night."

He crossed his arms over his chest. "Yes. You were."

"I'm sorry. I learned more about what happened all those years ago, today, from Savannah."

"Oh, did you." He couldn't keep the sarcasm out of his voice.

"Yes. She told me she lied. See, she told me you and

she had…well, that you'd taken advantage, but today she let me know that wasn't true."

"But you believed it was true, all these years. And these past weeks while we've worked together."

"Well, yeah. I did."

He studied her. Even at her worst, she did something to him. He had a feeling he'd be a long time getting over her. "I can't work for someone who thinks the worst of me," he said. "I'm quitting the bakery, immediately. And I'll vacate this place as soon as I can find another home for me and the kids."

Her face started to crumble, and he couldn't watch it. Gently, he closed the door, blocking out her sad face and her manipulative tears.

CHAPTER SIXTEEN

TAYLOR SHOULD HAVE slept in on Sunday, the one day the bakery was closed.

Or, if she wasn't doing that, she should have gotten a jump on the week's baking, since her main assistant had just quit.

But she was too angry with herself to sleep in and too exhausted to start the baking. So she dragged herself to church and volunteered to help Mellie in the babies-and-kids room, overcrowded since the other Sunday school teacher was out sick today.

Maybe that would make her feel better and help some tired parents out in the process.

It worked for a little while. Three toddlers needed diaper changes at the same time and two kids—including Ava—got in a food fight.

But the relief was temporary. Every time she looked at Danny and Ava, a raw ache spread through her chest. There had been no back-and-forth between the two apartments this morning, no shared granola bars as they all rushed to get ready for church.

You don't know what you've got 'til it's gone. The songwriter had gotten that right.

"Hey," Mellie said when there was a calm moment,

"I'm glad you came, we needed you, but you look awful. Shouldn't you be recharging and taking care of yourself?"

Taylor had already told her the outline of what had happened between her and Savannah and Cody. Now, she swung over to sit on the floor beside Ava and Danny. They were engrossed in building a block tower, but they welcomed her help. Ava leaned against her, and she treasured it. "This is how I'm recharging," she told her friend through a tight, raw throat.

She wasn't going to be able to spend the kind of time with the kids that she had been, and that broke her heart.

Out of nowhere, she thought of her own mother. Birdy had raised them, haphazardly, through this phase and the next, had gotten them into their teen years, and then she'd abandoned them in the ultimate way, taking her own life. For the first time, she considered that from Birdy's point of view.

Birdy had loved them so much when she'd been in a good place mentally. Sure, she'd favored adorable Savannah in some ways; Savannah was the baby and so pretty. But she'd loved Taylor, too, and the three of them had had a cozy, wonderful life together at least part of the time. Taylor could remember a water balloon fight, building a snowman, stories at night.

And then things would grow dark, and they'd go for days without food while Birdy hid out in her bedroom.

Even then, Mom had loved them. And yet she'd left. How could she make herself do it?

Something she'd heard in a support group came back

to her: the suicidal person almost always thinks those left behind would be better off without them.

Remembering Birdy, setting aside her own feelings of anger and hurt, Taylor realized that thinking her girls would be better off was the only way Birdy could have taken her own life.

Taylor sighed. It hadn't been better, obviously. Losing their mother that way had left terrible scars on both her and Savannah.

She stroked Ava's hair. This innocent child would bear the scars of her mother's abandonment, too. So would her brother.

Taylor had played the mother role with them for a short while. Maybe, for their sake, Cody would allow a little friendship to remain. And maybe, the kids would help her find a way back to him, not that she deserved it.

Minutes later, Danny was leaning against her, too. It probably wasn't wise, but she let herself feel the maternal feelings and cuddle them close.

Behind her, she heard Cody's voice. It rumbled down her spine and sent electrical charges throughout her body. Was it possible that he wasn't mad anymore? Maybe he'd forgive her and they could go back to the way they'd been. Or forward into something better.

"Hey, Cody, there you are," Mellie said.

"Sorry I'm late. I had to talk to the pastor for a few minutes. Were the kids good?"

"As good as kids can be," Mellie said, which was tactful. "Ava got into a little skirmish, but no harm, no foul."

Ava climbed into Taylor's lap. Her eyes were sleepy,

her thumb in her mouth. The trust with which she snuggled against Taylor took her breath away.

She wanted kids so much. And not just kids. She wanted *this* child.

And Danny was older, but she wanted him, too. She reached out and ruffled his hair, and he grinned back at her before demolishing their block tower with a loud crash that made Taylor and Ava jerk out of their quiet cuddles.

"Danny. Ava. Time to go." Cody's voice behind her wasn't harsh, but it was firm and definite. Both kids scrambled to their feet.

"Clean up your mess," he ordered.

Taylor glanced up at him, and he beckoned to her. Hope blossomed in her chest. Until she saw his expressionless face.

"I'd rather you didn't try to continue having a relationship with them," he said. His voice was a monotone. His eyes didn't meet hers.

"Oh…" She couldn't restrain the little sound that came out of her mouth.

"I don't want them hurt any more than they already have been." He turned away from her and knelt to help the kids put the rest of the blocks away.

Taylor stood, hands dangling uselessly at her sides, trying not to cry.

"Let's go," Cody said as soon as the blocks were put away. He started ushering the children out of the classroom. "Thanks, Mellie."

"Brunch?" Ava asked, only she said it "bwunch." "Taylor come?"

Taylor's heart seemed to reach out of her chest. Toward the children. Toward Cody.

"Taylor can't come today." Cody's words were matter-of-fact, and the kids accepted it without question. A moment later, the trio was gone.

Taylor swallowed hard and marched over to the kids' bathroom, where she proceeded to scrub the floor on her hands and knees.

When she finished and went back out into the classroom, Mellie was waiting. Ryan and Alfie sat on one of the tables. All the other kids had apparently been picked up.

"You're coming home with us," Mellie said.

"No," Taylor said. "I'm going home to work on the books for the bakery." She didn't deserve friends or fun, not that she was in any shape to have fun today.

Mellie thrust her coat at her. "Come on. You're coming over whether you want to or not." She took Taylor's arm and guided her firmly through the church and out to their truck.

After a home-cooked meal of pot roast out of the Crock-Pot, complete with potatoes and carrots, bread and a green salad—of which Taylor ate two bites—Ryan took Alfie off somewhere. Mellie fixed tea and pointed to one of the chairs by the fire Ryan had built. "Sit," she said. "We're going to talk this through."

"Thank you for not abandoning me," Taylor said. "I don't need to talk, but thank you."

"You're welcome. And yes, you do need to talk. Spill it."

Taylor was too tired to stand up to her friend's in-

sistent support. So she fleshed out the details of what
had happened: how she'd disrespected Cody into quitting, and how she'd yelled at Savannah. "The bakery is
doing great," she said. "We have more orders and we're
in the black. Making a good profit, even. I have what I
thought I wanted. But I just destroyed what family and
friendships I have." She stared into the fire. "I have no
one to share it with."

"Black-and-white thinking," Mellie said. "You screwed
up, it sounds like. But is it really irreparable?"

"Cody quit. And you heard him. He won't even let
me hang out with the kids. And Savannah…well, I can
probably make it up with her, but…" The image of her
sister's stricken face wouldn't go out of her head. She'd
come down hard on Savannah for lying, back when they
were teenagers, and then forgetting it. But hadn't she
made plenty of mistakes herself?

Her goal of making a success of the bakery seemed
empty now. What was it worth if she lived alone above
the bakery, going upstairs to her empty apartment every
night, the eccentric small business owner who spent
every holiday by herself?

As for the goal she kept closer to her heart, that of
having a family…well, she'd just destroyed the two she
had. Savannah was all she had left of her family of ori-
gin, and she'd just kicked her sister to the curb. For…
well, for reasons, but were they good reasons?

And Cody and the kids, what she now realized was
her found family…that was gone, too.

She let her head sink into her hands, then propped
her cheek on her two fists and looked at Mellie. "I'm

too messed up to have a family, that's all. Our dad left, our mom died by suicide, and Savannah and I were separated. I always wanted to fix that and have a good family, but you can't build something when the basic materials are flawed."

Mellie threw up her hands. "Don't be ridiculous. Everyone's flawed. Cody's flawed. He's not blameless in this."

"Actually, he is."

Mellie shook her head. "One thing went wrong and he cut bait. How is that the right thing to do?" She shrugged. "It does make sense, considering his past. He had a rough childhood, and I guess maybe he doesn't know what he's doing when it comes to real relationships. He doesn't believe in himself. So he leaves."

"You're right, but that just proves my point. Two flawed people can't make it work together, and the stakes are higher now that he has the kids."

Mellie tilted her head to one side. "Ryan and I are both messed up from our pasts," she said, looking into the fire. "By rights, we shouldn't have made it. But I'm so glad we didn't give up."

Taylor didn't say anything. She couldn't. She was horribly jealous of her friend, and a little angry that Mellie thought her own situation comparable. Mellie had it all.

"I'm not making this all about me," Mellie said, uncannily reading her mind. "I'm saying you can do the same. You don't have to let a bad past ruin your future."

Taylor put her hands out toward the warm fire, but nothing could heat the cold in her heart. Mellie was

Mellie, she was amazing, but Taylor? She was anything but. She was hardworking, yes, but that was the only thing she had going for her.

Right now, having demolished her relationships with Savannah and with Cody, her soul simply ached. She felt like a down-on-her-luck convict, let out of prison but wracked by her own guilt, lacking the emotional skills to live in the complicated world of human relationships.

In a way, she understood her mother better. In this state of mind, with gloom pressing down on her, life felt uniformly dark.

"You can fix this," Mellie insisted.

Taylor leaned back, looking up at the ceiling to keep from shedding the tears that wanted to fall. "I just don't know if I have it in me to try. And I'm pretty sure Cody doesn't."

"Come on," Mellie said. "You're giving up that easily? The two of you are so good together, or you could be."

Could have been. Taylor's throat tightened. She wanted to be with Cody. Wanted it badly.

"Also," Mellie said, "it would be really, really good for the kids if you two were able to make it work. Just like it's good for Alfie to have both of us caring about him."

"But I'm not their mom." And having a relationship for the sake of the kids would never work.

Only it wasn't just for the sake of the kids. It was for her. Her and Cody.

"No, you're not their mom," Mellie said, "and Cody's not their dad. But their mom is apparently down for the count, so it's not as if you're taking them away from her. And those kids *need* a mom more than any kid I've ever seen, especially Ava."

Taylor remembered with a pang the feeling of Ava leaning against her, climbing into her lap. "I love that kid," she murmured, surprising herself.

"If you love her," Mellie said, "and you love Cody—"

"I didn't say that," Taylor interrupted.

"You didn't have to. And even if you're not there yet…give it a chance, will you? Maybe you can fix it. And you're not a quitter, you're a fighter."

Was she? She didn't *feel* like a fighter. Except when she thought of Danny and Ava. From the moment she'd seen them under that table in her bakery, heard Danny's brave little speech about how their mother had stuff to do, seen him pull out that pitiful baggie of sandwich crusts to mete out to his sister… Yeah. She didn't feel like fighting for herself, but for those kids, she might.

"This is worth fighting for." Again, Mellie uncannily echoed her thoughts. "You can do it, Taylor. You *have* to do it."

"Jeez, you're like a pro wrestling coach," Taylor grumbled. But she sat up straighter as energy materialized in her body.

Maybe it was true. Maybe she had a chance of fixing things, and even a small chance would make it worth the fight.

The question was, *how*?

SUNDAY EVENING, Savannah woke up from yet another restless nap, sat up and rubbed her eyes.

She could tell from the reddish light in the room that the sun was setting. That meant she'd been holed up in her suite at Hank's place for more than twenty-four hours.

Her hair felt oily, and her back ached from lying down for so long.

More than that, her heart ached.

She'd done a terrible thing to Taylor, something that had apparently affected Taylor's life and views and relationship with Cody. Savannah, of course, had entirely forgotten about the night in question until Taylor had brought it up.

Typical of her. The number of men and mistakes in her past was so high that they crowded each other out.

The repercussions were still rolling in, with Rupert's appearance last week as witness.

She pushed herself to the edge of the bed, forced herself to her feet. She took a shower and then put on jeans and a shirt—not the baggy ones Taylor had brought, but a similarly non-stylish pair of jeans and a plain T-shirt.

All was quiet outside her room. The mother cat and kittens were the only signs of life, and even they were sleeping.

Maybe Hank and Nadine had gone out. She should make a meal and leave it for them. If she was staying here, for the moment, she ought to earn her keep.

In the kitchen, she pulled out a bag of potatoes, celery and carrots and ham. Potato soup was comfort food. She'd always liked it when she visited Taylor at Aunt Katy's place, so she had gotten the supplies the last time she'd gone to the market.

As she peeled potatoes, she looked around the kitchen. It was so modern and full of fancy appliances, yet it felt almost like home. That was because she, Hank and Nadine had had fun here during the last month. They'd had family meals, some of them bad. She'd learned to cook.

It had been a good run. Whether she'd be able to stay here was up in the air, after what Hank had overheard, added on top of the many mistakes she'd made. He would be well within his rights to let her go.

She ought to be used to moving around, leaving one home behind for another, saying goodbye to people. It was how she'd constructed her adult life. She was the one who always had a bag packed, ready to leave on a moment's notice if things went south with any one particular guy.

She went still as she realized something. Here, with Hank and Nadine, she'd never packed a go bag.

It was the first time she'd even thought of it, even though normally, being ready to leave was a major part of settling into a new place. A fun part, even, or at least reassuring. It was always good to know you had an escape route.

But here, she'd really, really wanted to stay. She wanted to help Nadine.

She didn't want to examine the other reason she wanted to stay.

"What are you cooking?"

She jumped and dropped the knife, and it clattered to the floor. "Hank! You scared me! I didn't think anyone was here."

"Sorry." He came into the kitchen and leaned back against the counter. "How are you doing?"

"I'm okay."

"I… That was quite a fight you had with your sister. We didn't want to disturb you, since it's your day off, but I was worried."

"Thanks." His solicitous attitude made her uncomfortable; she didn't deserve it. "Where's Nadine?"

"She's off with her friends. Pizza night with the youth group at church."

"Oh." She put the potato and the peeler down. "Do you even want potato soup?"

"Don't go to any trouble. It's still your day off. I had a sandwich a little while ago."

She felt unaccountably hurt. He was rejecting her cooking. Rejecting *her*.

"Fine," she said. "I'm not hungry, either. I think I'll go watch some TV in my suite."

He looked like he was going to say something else, and then he hesitated. "I'll be in my study," he said finally. He was halfway out the door when he turned back. "Let me know if you want to talk."

He was probably going to fire her. He just didn't want to kick her when she was down. When she was un-made-up and dressed poorly and hadn't done anything with her hair. Yeah, she'd learned to cook, but she was still the same messed-up girl she'd always been.

Still, she wanted to stay. Wanted another chance.

She knew of only one way to make that happen.

She stuck the soup and ingredients in the fridge half

finished, remembering to cover the already peeled potatoes with water. Then she went back to her suite.

Moving fast, hating herself for what she was doing, she changed her clothes, made up her face, did her hair.

And then she walked into Hank's office. "I *do* want to talk," she said.

He looked up from his computer and then did a double take. "Are you going out?"

"No." She perched on the corner of his desk, causing her skirt to climb up her thigh. "I'm staying in. With you. This is all for you."

His eyes skimmed over her and darkened. He swallowed. "I don't understand."

She slid off the desk and leaned over him, trapping him in his desk chair. "There's been something between us since we met, and I think we should act on it." It was hard to meet his eyes, so she turned her face away and sidled into his lap.

She was crying inside.

"Savannah." He leaned back in his chair.

She took off his glasses and set them down, carefully, on the desk. Then she kissed him.

He was startled, she could tell that. But the heat of their bodies, pressed together for the first time, ignited something in him the same way it did in her. He lifted his hands to her face and kissed her back.

Yes!

She felt like pumping her fist in the air, but she was too occupied with his kiss. Because it was different from anything she'd had before, different from what she'd expected.

Hank was a nerd, a dad. But he was a *very* good kisser. He wasn't ravaging her mouth, wasn't biting her lips, wasn't pawing her. He was…tender. Intense, but tender.

He was giving her what any woman would want in a kiss.

His hands tangled in her hair now, and he rained kisses along her hairline. "Man, you smell good," he said, and he sounded like he'd just finished a race.

Wow. She hadn't realized exactly how much she'd wanted this, how attracted she was, but now…whether or not it worked—and it was the only thing that might— at least she'd have this one memory.

The light in the study was dim. Classical music played in the background, which was just so…so Hank. She ran her hands over his arms, loving how muscular they were. He didn't brag on his strength, but he *was* strong. He had an indoor gym, and he chopped wood, and he'd taken Rupert down without any problem. She relaxed against him, relaxed into the kiss.

He stroked her hair, touched her face. His breathing accelerated.

And then he made a tiny noise and pulled away. He literally lifted her off his lap and set her on her feet, and then he stood, leaving her chilled. She reached for him, not wanting it to be over, but he grasped her wrist and placed it back at her side.

He fumbled for his glasses and put them on. He stepped over to the window and looked out, running a hand through his adorably mussed hair.

It hadn't worked. She'd marshaled all her forces, used her heaviest artillery, and it wasn't enough.

Deflated, she straightened her clothes, pulling her skirt down from where it had ridden up, buttoning another button on her blouse.

"Savannah," he said, not looking at her, "what were you doing just now?"

"Trying to seduce you." What was the point in lying?

"Why?"

"Because I've wanted to since I met you," she said.

He did look at her then, his expression skeptical.

"And because I want to stay," she admitted.

He blew out a breath, turned and leaned back against the window. Keeping his distance. "What you just did makes it less likely you can stay, not more. I'm your employer. We're caring for a teenager together. We can't just…" He waved a hand at his desk, where she now saw the papers were awry and a container of pens and pencils had fallen to the floor.

It looked like someone had had a good time there, and they had. Well, she had. For maybe five minutes.

She knelt down and started picking up the pencils and pens, placing them carefully back in their holder. Then she set it down where it had been and straightened the papers on his desk.

She'd made everything worse, not better. She'd given it her best effort, and it hadn't been good enough.

Why should it be surprising that she'd screwed everything up? She glanced at him. His face was dear to her. When had he become so dear to her? Even his concerned dad expression almost made her smile.

Except for the fact that she wasn't going to see it much, if at all, in the future. She looked away, looked at the floor, and headed toward the study door.

She couldn't bear this constant worry that she'd be put out on the street, this constant reminder that she wasn't enough. She couldn't bear getting closer and closer to Hank and Nadine, all the while knowing that it couldn't last. "I'll start packing," she said.

CHAPTER SEVENTEEN

BY NINE O'CLOCK that night, Savannah had all her things packed when her phone buzzed with a text.

Here. Should I come in?

I'll come to the front door, she texted back.

She didn't want to disturb Hank, didn't want to re-awaken any drama with him lest she break down entirely. She was hoping Nadine would come home, though, in time to say goodbye to her.

If that didn't happen, she'd stay on the island until tomorrow after school and take Nadine over to the bakery, explain to whatever degree she could.

Savannah couldn't leave the island without saying goodbye to Nadine.

Leave the island! Just the thought of it twisted her stomach tight. Images played like a movie in her mind: arriving and seeing Taylor, so successful in her bakery. The cute little downtown. The icy, awe-inducing bay. All her cooking disasters. Helping Nadine get dressed up for a night out. The snowy evening they'd found the kittens.

Hank's kind face, the fine wrinkles that fanned out from his eyes. His low laugh.

His kiss, that blissful moment before everything had gone so terribly wrong.

Her throat tightening, she opened the door of her suite and headed toward the front door. *Just get out of here without breaking down*, she told herself. There would be plenty of time for emotions later.

She walked past the hallway to Hank's study, trying to be quiet, but it was as if he were listening for her; the study door opened. "Savannah. You don't have to leave tonight."

His concerned tone almost undid her. He was such a good man. "It's better this way," she said through a tight throat. "My ride is here." At her feet, two kittens batted each other and rolled around. She knelt down and petted them, getting her fingers scratched with their tiny claws. For the last time.

There was a knock on the front door.

"You're going to stay with Taylor?" Hank asked. "Did the two of you make up, then?"

Hank probably wasn't just pretending to care. He was the type who would try to make sure a woman was safe, even if he disliked her and wanted her gone.

"It's not Taylor," she said. "Taylor's not speaking to me. It's Cody."

"Cody!" The word seemed to burst out of Hank, overloud, propelled by what sounded like anger. He shook his head and looked away.

Instantly she saw what he was thinking. Heat rose to her face as she stood. "Yes, he's a kind man, and yes, he's one of my only friends on the island. But no, I'm not going to sleep with him." She went to the door and opened it, trying to stand up straight, to have some dignity.

Cody came in and looked from her to Hank. He lifted an eyebrow. "Cold night to put someone out," he said to Hank.

Hank took a step forward, his face reddening.

Savannah stepped in between them, holding out her hands, palms out, one for each. "You don't know the full story, either of you. It would help a lot if you would just chill."

Cody did some kind of bro-nod, and Hank kind of grunted. Then Cody followed her back to her suite and started carrying things out.

She picked up as big a load as she could carry and followed him out to the car. "I spoke with Mellie, and you can stay with her," he said. "It's close to the docks." He paused, then added, "Taylor's going to be devastated that you're leaving."

"Taylor hates me," she said. Suddenly, she saw a good deed she could do on her way out. "There's a reason for it. Do you remember that night when we were here in the summer and you and I went out and I…kind of pushed myself on you? Or tried to?"

"Yeah. Sort of." He didn't smile.

"Well, I told Taylor that you and I had slept together, that you were my first. But obviously that wasn't true. I was just trying to cover up the fact that I went off with some guy I barely knew." She sighed. "I'd forgotten what I said to her for years, until Taylor told me she didn't trust you because of what you did to me. I remembered then, told her the truth, but apparently it was too late." She put a hand on Cody's arm. "She's protective of me. She's always been that way. Don't hold it against her."

His eyes were crinkled narrow. "Thanks for telling me, but even though we didn't know each other for long, I would have thought she'd understand my character well enough to trust that I wouldn't have done that."

Hank came out carrying a load of her things. Just her luck, he reached them when she was talking intently to Cody and had her hand on his arm.

She wished Hank knew *her* character well enough to know she wouldn't go from seducing one man to seducing another all in the same night. Not nowadays. But why would he? He thought of her as the type who threw herself at men, and he had good reason for it.

She spun and walked back into the house and her suite, and only then did she realize that Hank was right behind her. She could smell his old-fashioned aftershave, and her fingers tingled with the memory of how it had felt to touch that cheek, bristly with evening stubble.

He looked at her with eyes as stormy as the bay. He reached out a hand to her. "Savannah—"

Her throat got impossibly tight, but she forced out words. "Don't make this harder," she said.

"Do you even have a place to stay?" he asked. "Are you staying with him?"

Of course he would think that, after how she'd acted, after the life she'd led. "I'm staying with Ryan and Mellie tonight and leaving tomorrow, after I say goodbye to Nadine."

There was a sound out in the main part of the house, a banging door. "Dad!"

Good, she was here. Best to get the painful stuff over with all at once.

Nadine rushed into the room. "Savannah, I need advice." She stopped abruptly and looked around at the two remaining boxes, the empty shelves. "What's going on?"

"I'm glad you got home before I left, honey. I have to move out."

"Did Dad fire you? Dad, don't! I need Savannah. I need to talk to her, like, now."

Cody walked into the room, took in the tableau of them and backed out, hands up like stop signs. "I'll be in the car."

"Say your goodbyes," Hank said, "and once she's gone, we'll talk, Nadine." He left the room.

"I'll fix it with Dad," Nadine said with confidence. "What happened, anyway?"

Savannah shook her head. "Grown-up stuff."

Nadine propped a hand on her hip. "Why don't you guys just admit you like each other?"

Savannah wasn't surprised that Nadine had suggested that solution. It was a good idea, if only it could work. But it couldn't, not after everything that had happened. "It's too complicated." She hugged the girl. "You're the best. I've loved getting to know you, and I hope we can stay friends. If it's okay with your dad," she added.

"You really are leaving." Nadine stepped back, her eyes shiny with tears, which of course made Savannah tear up, too. "I need to talk to you about Kevin," she choked out. "And other stuff."

"You can call me anytime. You have my number."

"It's not the same. I don't want you to go."

Now Savannah's heart was really breaking. She loved this girl. And yet she'd screwed up so badly. It was no one's fault but her own that she'd gotten kicked out of Hank's place. Her own completely inappropriate behavior had sealed her fate.

She squeezed Nadine's hand, picked up her last box and her purse, forced herself to walk past the kittens and away from Nadine. She climbed into Cody's car.

The moon went behind a cloud. How appropriate. It was a dark, dark night.

Darkness was spreading through her heart and mind, too, and for a moment, she held herself very still. She was used to finding ways to distract herself when depression threatened.

But this wasn't the kind of depression Mom had had, the black cloud that settled over her for no apparent reason. Savannah was blue because of real problems and losses. It was what the websites called *normal, appropriate sadness*.

As Cody drove across the island, she turned her face to the window and let her tears flow.

ON MONDAY AFTERNOON, Cody walked into the VA branch office in Pleasant Shores, a small town on the mainland. Weed was beside him.

He was tired, from having picked Savannah up late and helped her to get settled at Mellie and Ryan's place for the night. Then he'd had a brainstorm and asked if Savannah would stay, today at least, pick the kids up from school and day care and take them back to Ryan and Mellie's until he got home.

She'd quickly agreed, since she really wasn't ready to leave the island. Apparently the rift with Hank had happened rather suddenly.

Just like the rift between him and Taylor.

Taylor. He wasn't going to think about her.

He and Weed waited a short while, and then were beckoned into the office of an administrator who worked with outreach, volunteers and support groups. His office was typical VA: ancient, dented gray metal file cabinets, one with a drawer open and practically overflowing with files. An old-fashioned turquoise fake-leather swivel chair behind a battered metal desk. Two folding chairs in front of the desk. He took one, and Weed took the other.

"I'm interested in your suggestion that we form a support group on Teaberry," the man, whose name was Evans, said. "Would either of you consider being peer facilitators?"

Weed snorted out a laugh. "Nobody has ever asked me to facilitate anything."

"You'd be good," Cody said. "You know the community, and everyone knows you."

"Not always for the best," Weed said.

Evans looked at Cody. "You've had a variety of experiences in the military, including media work," he said. "That might be something we could use. And weren't you a squad leader?"

"Yeah." Cody didn't like to think about that because of how he'd left, not even saying goodbye to his men.

Evans stood. "I'd like for you to sit in on a meeting of one of our local support groups," he said. "I've okayed it with the facilitator, and I think it'll help you to see if you'd like to bring something similar to Teaberry Island."

They followed him into a tile-floored room set up with a circle of folding chairs. A table on one side held a large carafe of coffee and Styrofoam cups. Evans introduced them to the leader, who went by Tim. "We're all first names here," Tim said. "Make yourselves some name tags. This is an open group, so anyone can walk in and participate. So feel free to jump in if you have something to share. We can discuss how the group runs afterwards." He smiled at them and added, "I'm just a peer facilitator myself, a volunteer. It's worthwhile work. Not easy, but worthwhile."

Evans waved and headed out, greeting a couple of people on the way.

Men and women had been drifting in while they'd been talking. Now everyone sat down.

There was a bit of general talk, about whether a predicted storm would hit them, about the lack of cookies at today's meeting. Cody enjoyed listening, not least because he was successfully not thinking about Taylor.

And this thought conjured her up in his mind, of course. He couldn't forget the way she'd looked in that dress, how it had felt to kiss her. Couldn't forget, either, her abilities as a baker, her wicked wit when something went wrong in the kitchen and the way she'd cared for the kids.

The good memories made it all the worse that she'd judged him and found him wanting.

Tim called them to order and, once everyone had settled, asked how everyone's week had been. It was understood, apparently, that the question meant veteran-related issues, not what you'd had for dinner or done on the job.

His hunch was confirmed when a lanky redhead who didn't seem to be more than eighteen or nineteen shared an experience where someone had refused him a job on the basis of him being an unstable veteran.

"Illegal" was what several of the other participants said, immediately, but they didn't seem surprised.

"It's working with kids," the redhead explained. "They said they have to be extra careful with anyone who has a history of violence."

Tim tilted his head to one side. "Do you?"

"Nope. I have my clearances. But… I feel like I'll always be judged. Man, the recruitment commercials didn't say anything about this."

"Being a vet can be an asset as much as a liability," a woman said, and there was some general talk about job opportunities.

Cody wondered if he'd enjoy being a part of something like this, organizing it. Was there a possibility he could make a career out of it, or at least a part-time job? It couldn't hurt to do the free online training, which Evans had mentioned in passing.

Weed leaned over. "I know a few guys on Teaberry

who'd benefit from something like this. Not just guys. Couple of gals came back with horror stories."

Cody nodded, keeping it noncommittal for now. He did like the idea. His main obstacle was Taylor. Could he live on the island with her there, knowing what might have been?

Someone else shared a fight she'd had with her husband. "He got too used to being a single parent while I was overseas," she said. "Now he won't let me change anything."

"I hear that," another guy said. "My wife's the same way."

Someone shared good news, a promotion at his job, and everyone clapped for him.

A guy named Jasson brought things back to a serious level. "I just can't get over that blackout," he said, and the way the others nodded, he must have talked about it before. "Freaks me out I have no idea what went on, except that it was bad."

The words brought a sick feeling to Cody's gut. But if he was going to work with veterans, he'd need to be able to push through. So he listened to the blackout guy's story, his confusion and misery. Without planning it, empathetic words came out of his mouth. "I know. It's like a few days were cut out and you have the feeling something really bad happened, but you don't know what."

"Yeah. I had burns all over my body."

Cody had been badly bruised. A hematoma on his side had taken months to go away. He'd had injuries he didn't want to think too closely about.

And this was the question: Could he deal with that painful part of his life being reawakened? Did he want to?

"You may never know," Tim said. "And that could be a blessing. Your brain could be telling you you need to go forward without remembering the details of the past. Anyone else have something to share?"

A woman across the room started to speak, but the blackout guy spoke up again. "I just have a memory of crying like a baby from the pain. I don't think I revealed any classified information, but I might have."

A chill broke out over Cody's body, immediately followed by heat that brought beads of sweat to his forehead. He remembered crying, too. He remembered trying hard not to reveal anything. Had he succeeded? He didn't know.

No wonder he couldn't commit to anything. He didn't know what kind of a man he was.

He was still alternating between hot and cold. Dizziness took over as he started to stand, and he grabbed the back of his chair for balance. "I gotta go," he said to the group, and staggered out.

Out of the room, and out of the building, into the bright, cold, slightly salt-washed air of the bay.

But a part of him was back in the desert, where they'd all been constantly, miserably hot.

Weed appeared at his side, walking along, thankfully not saying anything. But a moment later, Evans walked up beside them. "How'd it go? Interested in starting something similar on Teaberry?"

Weed waved a hand.

Evans looked at him more closely. "What happened?"

"Flashback," Weed said.

It was such a small word to say to cover everything that had gone on, was going on, inside his head. The air felt cold on his face and he realized he was crying a little despite his efforts to block the tears.

It was the same effort he'd made back in Kandahar, when they threatened to kill a young American soldier he didn't even know, in front of him, to try to get him to spill state secrets.

It had started in a dark underground room that smelled of unwashed bodies and fear. He'd been stripped naked there, in a dirt basement lit only by a fire, terrified; his mind had raced as he'd scraped together a plan to try to save the kid. At first, God Himself had seemed to come to his aid, giving him a golden tongue, stories of plans that sounded plausible, tactics that made sense to the enemy, names and contact points that they seemed to believe.

Once they decided they'd gotten every detail he knew out of him, the commander had nodded.

They'd killed the kid, anyway, cut him off in the middle of sobbing out a Hail Mary. *That* was when Cody had lost it, tied to his chair, tears flowing, unable to stop the slaughter.

He'd known they would kill him, too. He'd been terrified. But he'd thought of his brothers and of Betty, how they'd grieve if he didn't make it home, and he'd pulled himself together enough to look past the young man expiring on the dirt floor. He'd realized he had to find a way to escape, or at least try to.

There'd been an explosion outside and his tormenters had scattered. The building had caught fire.

One of the men who'd guarded the door while all the torture and execution had taken place had rushed back in, cut his bonds with a knife, and pointed in the direction Cody should go before running back outside the burning building toward the shouts of his comrades.

Cody had checked the young man whose blood was draining into the dirt. No pulse. The flames had licked ever closer, the shouts outside becoming more desperate. There was some shooting.

And he'd run in the direction his unlikely benefactor had pointed, run until he could run no more, his mind already blurring the details of what he'd just witnessed.

He'd been fortunate; a small squad of US soldiers had found him. Though he'd had no ID, he'd remembered perfectly his name, his company, even their coordinates. But he hadn't been back with his company for an hour before they realized he'd lost his memory and was too messed up to serve, and he'd been honorably discharged.

He even had medals somewhere, or maybe he'd left them in a motel room. He'd never felt he deserved them.

Now, he couldn't stop shaking. Both with horror at what he'd finally remembered, and with relief that he hadn't done anything dishonorable.

He sank down onto a bench, and Weed sat beside him. Evans knelt in front. "We like your plan," Evan said, and Cody had a moment of confusion: What plan? Oh, right, the plan he'd written up for a support group on Teaberry.

"You need to work through your own issues first, though. You can talk to a counselor later today and tomorrow, get through this initial phase." He looked at Weed. "You'll stay with him?"

Cody frowned. He didn't know Weed well enough to ask that of the man.

"I'll stay."

"I have a buddy who can put you up," Evans said. "Former cop, had some PTSD himself."

Cody wanted to go home. Danny's and Ava's innocent faces seemed like the only thing that could save him. "I have kids," he said.

"You can't take care of those kids. You're a mess." Weed patted him on the shoulder. "See if Savannah can stay, another couple of days at least."

He didn't want to impose on her, but not having to deal with Taylor and his feelings for her would be a relief.

Weed handed him a bandanna and a bottle of water and walked down the street to have a cigarette. Evans went off to call his friend, to see if Weed and Cody could stay a couple of days.

Cody drank half the bottle of water in one gulp, scrubbed the bandanna over his eyes, and called Savannah. After he'd explained the situation, skimming over the details of his own meltdown, she said she was willing to help. "I'll pay you whatever Hank was paying," he said, "and you can stay at my place, where the kids are comfortable." He sucked in a breath. "If you can get Taylor to stop in now and then, it'll help the kids. They're crazy about her."

"I'll see what I can do," Savannah said, at which point Cody figured out that she and Taylor were still at odds.

"If Danny and Ava get too upset, I can be on the next boat back," he said. "They've been through a lot, and I don't want to set them back. It's just… I'll be able to take care of them better if I can get a couple of things straightened out."

As he ended the call, it occurred to him that he was showing every sign of being able to commit. To those two sweet kids, at least.

CHAPTER EIGHTEEN

ON MONDAY EVENING, Taylor was in Cody's apartment, and she was fuming.

She walked out of the little curtained-off bedroom Cody had rigged up for Ava and looked around the wreckage of the apartment. Pizza boxes, knocked-over drinks and scattered toys along with Savannah's open suitcase spilling clothes. The apartment wasn't big to begin with, and Cody usually kept it neat as a pin—a product of his military years, he said—but with two kids and Savannah here, the place had deteriorated quickly.

Taylor had come over the moment Savannah had called to see if she could help. She'd been listening from her apartment to the kids yelling and playing and, eventually, crying. She'd wondered what was going on.

Savannah's phone call had cleared it up, sort of. Savannah was staying here, taking care of the kids, and Cody was over on the mainland.

It hadn't taken long for the two of them to get together, Taylor thought bitterly as she found a garbage bag and walked around picking up trash. Last Friday, Savannah had helped Taylor make herself over, and she'd gone on that wonderful, awful date with Cody. Had Savannah even then been plotting to move in on Cody?

She stacked dirty dishes beside the sink and started running water. From Cody's bedroom, she could hear the rise and fall of Savannah's voice as she read Danny's favorite fantasy novel to him. When she'd come over and found Savannah trying to get two upset kids to bed, she'd immediately taken charge of Ava and left Savannah to handle Danny. Ava, though more upset, or probably because of that, had fallen quickly asleep. Danny seemed to be taking longer.

Taylor ought to just leave the mess and go back to her apartment. Now that she'd helped the kids, she needed to get out of here before a lot of emotion came to the surface. Get in, get out, avoid pain.

Things had finally seemed to be going great at the bakery, with the off-island orders coming just briskly enough. With Cody's help, they had been keeping up, though juggling night baking and daytime hours and child care was an ongoing challenge.

But then Cody had quit and she had fallen apart.

She could go downstairs and get started on tomorrow's baking. There was more than enough to do.

But she couldn't leave Savannah with this mess. No way could her sister handle it.

She'd gotten through half the stack of dishes when Savannah emerged from the bedroom and flopped down on the sofa, arm dramatically over her forehead. Typical.

"Who knew kids could be so exhausting?" she asked. "Give me a teenager anytime."

"Better get used to it if you're with Cody." Taylor banged the last of the dishes into the soapy water.

"Better get used to... Oh, my goodness, Taylor, you're such an idiot." Savannah sat up and ran her hands through her hair. Of course she looked gorgeous even after an evening of tangling with someone else's kids.

Not just someone else. Her new boyfriend. "For thinking that was a pretty fast transition, from Hank to Cody?" Taylor asked.

"No! For thinking we're together. Hank kicked me out, and the only person I could get a ride from was Cody, since *you're* not speaking to me. I went to Ryan and Mellie's at his suggestion—that's where he'd left the kids so he could come help me out. Turns out Cody had a thing at the VA over on the mainland, and Ryan and Mellie were busy, so I agreed to stay and get the kids after school."

"And you ended up back here at his apartment, why? When is he getting home?" That would be her worst nightmare, to still be around when Cody came home ready to enjoy his new girlfriend.

"Because Cody thought they'd be more comfortable here, with him away."

Of course. *Get used to it.* Savannah was what Cody wanted, always had been.

She sucked in deep breaths and let them out slowly and started drying dishes. She'd finish that and get out of here before she melted down all the way.

"I hope you're not planning on living here, full-time, you and him and the kids."

"No, dummy." Savannah came over to lean against the counter. "Good Lord, Taylor, if I weren't so tired I'd strangle you. Cody had a PTSD meltdown at this VA thing he went to over in Pleasant Shores. Didn't think he could care well for the kids, so he asked me to stay for a couple of days. For *pay*. He *hired* me. He wanted me to stay here partly so you'd be close by in case that would help out the kids."

"Oh." Taylor carefully put plates into the cupboard as her view of the situation reformed itself into a new pattern. Along with that came hot embarrassment. She'd misjudged her sister and Cody again.

A little flame of happiness sparked to life inside her, because Cody still thought of her as someone who could help the kids.

Savannah was still ranting. "Really, you and Hank both think I'd run directly to Cody's bed? I'm not even attracted to him!"

Savannah's vehemence, plus the absurdity of what she'd thought, made her believe her sister's words. "Oh. Wow." Saying she was sorry seemed so inadequate. Her heart hurt to think of Cody suffering. "Do you know anything about his meltdown over there?"

"He said something about a flashback," Savannah said. She dug through the refrigerator and found a mostly full jug of wine. She unscrewed the cap, sniffed it and pulled out two juice glasses. "Like I said, he suggested asking you to help. That wasn't my idea."

Taylor wiped her hands, hung up the dish towel and grabbed the glass of wine Savannah had poured for her. She took a couple of gulps. "I'm sorry. I obviously misjudged both of you. I'm…kinda screwed up about this whole situation."

"No kidding." But Savannah didn't sound hostile.

One great thing about Savannah: she didn't have it in her to hold a grudge.

Taylor went to the couch, sat down and propped her feet on the coffee table. "I really am sorry I blamed you. For tonight, and for what happened when we were teenagers who didn't know anything."

Savannah came and sat at the other end of the couch, tucking her feet under her. "I'm sorry, too. I'm sorry I lied to you back then and didn't take the whole situation seriously. I hope it didn't hurt things between you and Cody beyond repair."

"Me, too." They both drank more wine.

A sound came from Ava's bed, and Taylor went to peek in. Ava fussed a little, turned over and sighed herself back to sleep.

Taylor returned to the couch. "What happened with Hank? Why'd he kick you out?"

Savannah squeezed her eyes shut and then opened them again. "I was worried he was going to fire me— truth is I've been worried about that since I got there— so I put on fancy clothes and did up my hair and tried to seduce him."

"You're kidding!" Taylor couldn't imagine the confidence that would require. No way could she ever do something like that with Cody. Even the idea made her insides jump uncomfortably. "You said you tried. Didn't it work?"

"Nope." Savannah shook her head slowly. "It didn't."

"Wow." Taylor stared into her nearly empty glass. "If it didn't work for you, with Hank, no way could it work for me with Cody."

Savannah rolled her eyes. "Don't you remember how you looked on Friday night? You could have your choice of men, Cody included."

"No," she said, "it didn't work for me, either, remember? Not that I actually tried to seduce him, but...I did ask him to come in, and he wouldn't."

"Wow." Savannah went over and got the jug of wine, brought it back and refilled both of their glasses. "We're batting a big fat zero."

Taylor wanted to escape her own squirmy mortification, though admittedly, she felt better knowing Savannah had also struck out. "So...you must feel something for Hank. I don't believe you'd try to seduce him without any emotional attachment."

"Yeah." Savannah looked unseeingly across the room, a bleak expression on her face. "I'm kinda crazy about him. But it's not going to work. Not like you and Cody could work."

"Cody and I can't make it work."

"Have you tried?"

"Well, yeah. I put on a dress and danced with him and invited him inside."

"And then when he said no, you yelled at him and accused him of something he didn't do."

"Right." She wrinkled her nose at her sister. "Bad strategy?"

"Bad strategy." Savannah leaned her head back against the couch and stared up at the ceiling. "Even I know that Hank kinda wanted to get it on. He was just trying to be the bigger man and do the right thing. He's Mr. Honorable."

Taylor frowned. "I don't think that's why Cody turned me down."

Savannah held up a hand. "Cody *is* honorable. And he's nuts about you. It wouldn't surprise me at all if he said no because of respecting you and wanting it to be more than a fling."

Taylor thought about that. Manson would have seized any opportunity to make their relationship physical, no matter that he didn't respect her enough to offer something lasting. No matter that he'd barely complained when she'd turned him down the last few times he'd asked her out. Maybe Cody was different.

In fact, he was definitely different from Manson. Could Savannah be right about Cody's reasoning?

Taylor felt a surge of hope. "What should I do?"

"Um...apologize? Do something to show him you respect him? Just have an actual conversation?" Savannah yawned, found the remote and clicked on the TV. "Want to watch a Hallmark movie?"

"Sure. Maybe I'll get some ideas."

So they sat and half dozed through a movie. Taylor ran across the hall and found a bag of barbecue potato chips, their childhood favorite, a treat Birdy had bought them often because she loved them herself. After she'd died, on the rare occasions they'd been together, Taylor used to sneak them to Savannah, who was forbidden junk food on account of the need to stay model-slim.

"Remember eating these with Mom, watching movies?" Savannah held up a chip.

Taylor nodded, her throat tightening. Birdy had loved romantic comedies and had let them watch even the slightly-too-grown-up ones with her. Those movie nights, full of laughter, were some of Taylor's happiest memories. Birdy had laughed so hard, a contagious laugh that they'd all shared even when Taylor and Savannah were too young to get the joke. "She did the best she could," Taylor said, her voice catching a little.

Savannah reached out and squeezed her hand. "She did."

Finally, the movie ended and Taylor stood to leave.

To her surprise, Savannah stood too and hugged her. "Thanks for helping, sis," she said. "Make it up with Cody. He's a good guy."

Taylor nodded, feeling choked up. "Come over if you need anything," she said, and let herself out. Just as Savannah was starting to close the door, Taylor stepped back. "I hope you stay on the island," she said. "I'd miss you if you left. A lot."

"Aw, really?" Savannah's eyes looked shiny. "That makes two of you who've asked me to stay. I'll think about it."

As Taylor let herself back into her apartment, she felt much better. One half of her screwup was fixed. Probably the more important part, because sisters were forever.

But Cody, he wasn't fixed yet. What was she going to do about the situation with him?

On Thursday after she'd picked up Danny from school and Ava from day care, Savannah sat on a park bench, one leg tucked beneath her. Mellie sat beside her.

They'd met up in the town park accidentally, along

with half the island's residents, from what it looked like. It was a February warm spell, fifty-five degrees, sunny and breezy. People wore jackets but not hats, and there was much calling back and forth, the sound of shouting kids. The ground smelled rich, thawing from a snowy winter, and the breeze from the bay brought a salt scent Savannah was coming to appreciate.

She did love it here. Every time she thought about leaving, the island enchanted her anew.

Mellie stretched. "This is so great. I could sit here all day. I don't want to go home and fix dinner."

"You guys should come over. I put a chicken in the Crock-Pot before I left this morning. We'll just cook up some noodles or biscuits and we'll be ready to go."

Mellie pumped a fist. "Yes! Ryan's still away at his conference, so it'll just be me and Alfie." Then she tilted her head, studying Savannah. "I thought you couldn't cook. Should I be afraid?"

Savannah shrugged. "It's not gourmet, but cooking for Hank and Nadine was a crash course, and Taylor helped me."

"That's good." Mellie studied her. "She told me you two made up."

"We did. In fact, she'll probably be at dinner, too."

"That's great."

They watched the kids for a while and greeted other people from town—Linda the librarian, Mellie's grandmother, who ran the post office—and Savannah thought about Taylor, and Hank, and the week she'd had.

She'd been terribly upset about what had happened with Hank, and still was, in a way. But the immediate offer of work from Cody, and the business of setting up housekeeping in Cody's place and taking care of the kids, had kept her from brooding.

Taylor was a rock of support. She was busy, so Savannah had taken a couple of shifts at the counter and helped with some of the unskilled labor involved, boxing up Teaberry Island scones in a pretty way and getting them shipped to the mainland on time.

She was surviving. Scrambling, but surviving.

The problem was missing Hank and Nadine.

Nadine had called her twice already, and they'd spent more than an hour on the phone each time. Savannah had desperately hoped the girl would talk about her father, how he was doing, whether he seemed to miss her. But Nadine was caught up in her own social dramas and didn't mention him, aside from a quick complaint about his cooking.

The thought of Hank alone in that beautiful kitchen, trying to cook something Nadine would like, made her stomach twist.

She wanted to be there helping him.

But through her own foolishness, she'd cut that off from happening.

Or maybe not *just* through her foolishness. She'd reconciled herself to most of what had happened. She knew she'd learned and grown good at the job.

It was that last stupid attempt at seduction that had done her in.

"…when Cody is coming home?" From Mellie's quizzical expression, Savannah guessed that she was asking for the second time.

"Tomorrow," Savannah said. "The kids will be thrilled to see him."

"And you'll have to figure out what to do," Mellie said. "You're welcome to stay with us if you want."

"Thank you. I might take you up on that for a day or two." She'd actually heard about a tiny cottage for rent on the other side of the island and was planning to visit it tomorrow, but she didn't know how she could afford even the low rent of that, not working.

Ava ran over then and rummaged in Savannah's bag for a snack. She located a cookie and leaned against Savannah's leg, eating it.

"What's going on with, uh, employment options?" Mellie spoke carefully, probably so Ava didn't get wind of Savannah possibly making a change. The kid needed stability in her life, big-time.

Inadvertently, she looked in the direction of Hank's place.

Mellie read her mind. "Any chance of you getting that job back?"

"Pretty sure I burned that bridge." Through her own foolish mistake.

Ava spotted a day care friend and ran toward her, and the mom waved and walked the two little girls to the play equipment.

"I need to make a living," Savannah said, "but whether I could do that on the island, whether I want to…that, I don't know."

"What kind of work have you done in the past?"

Savannah pulled out the bag of cookies, offered one

to Mellie and then took one for herself. "I've modeled and mooched off men," she said.

"Oh. Well, you're pretty enough to get back into either of those gigs, if you want to." Mellie sounded surprised but not judgmental.

"Thanks. But I'm getting old to model, high fashion, anyway. And then there's my weight." She gestured at her body and waved off Mellie's automatic protest. "I know, I'm still thin, but not by model standards. And I'm not willing to give up these." She held up a cookie and took a bite, savoring the sweetness. "My sister's baking is way more of a pleasure than modeling ever was."

"I take it you don't want to, ah, mooch off men anymore? Because a few curves never seem to be a problem with them."

"Zero interest. I want to stand on my own two feet."

"Good." Mellie patted her arm, her expression approving. "You could work at the bakery, right? Taylor needs help."

Savannah laughed. "Temporarily, I can help her out. But I've manned the counter a couple of times in the past day or two, and I'm a disaster. Plus, Taylor and I are better, but I don't think working together would be good for us long-term."

"How about doing makeovers? Everyone on the island is talking about how Taylor looked that one night when you dressed her up. And I know Nadine's gotten a lot more polished because of your influence."

"Nah. I don't want to be all focused on looks. Mine or other people's." She smiled at Mellie. "I appreciate your suggestions, and I don't mean to be a negative Nellie about them. I'll figure it out."

"You will, for sure." She looked thoughtfully at Savannah and then at Danny and Ava. Ava had climbed into a swing, and as they watched, Danny broke off from a couple of other boys and came over to push her.

"They're such sweet kids," Savannah said.

Mellie snapped her fingers. "What about child care? There's always a need for that, and you're obviously good at it."

Savannah tilted her head to one side and drew her eyebrows together. "Really?"

"Yes, and with all ages. I hear Nadine and her friends love you. And it looks like Ava and Danny are starting to, as well. You hold the line with them without being mean, and Taylor says you're amazing at getting them to sleep."

Savannah snickered. "I've had my share of disasters with them. But that's something to think about. I do like kids." To her own surprise. She'd never thought of herself as the maternal type.

"Also," Mellie said, looking past her, "I don't think you burned the bridge you thought you did."

"What?"

Mellie gestured with her head. "Look behind you."

Savannah half turned, and then gripped the back of the bench, staring. Walking toward them was Hank with a huge bouquet in his hands.

"I think Ava and Danny would prefer to come to our house for dinner, after all," Mellie murmured behind her.

Savannah turned back and grabbed Mellie's arm,

suddenly terrified of what Hank's approach—with flowers—might mean.

"Talk to him. I'll take care of the kids." Mellie extricated herself from Savannah's death grip, waved to Hank and strolled over toward the play area.

Savannah turned back as Hank approached the bench, and this time, she focused on his face. His rugged, square-jawed face. Glasses, plain hair. He was wearing khakis and a sport coat like he always did.

She was melting inside.

He stood by the side of the bench Mellie had just vacated. "May I sit down?"

She laughed a little at his manners and nodded.

"These are for you," he said, nodding at the bouquet of riotously beautiful spring flowers in every color. There was a pretty vase holding them, too, and he set the big arrangement down on the concrete beside her.

She felt speechless and nervous, her usual confident act nowhere to be found. All she could think about was that she'd hit hard on this man, treating him like all other men, when he was actually so very, very different.

"I made a mistake, letting you go."

"Oh?" she choked out. Then, because his gaze was so intense, she looked away, looked down at the flowers. "Thank you. They're beautiful."

"I'd like to fix it," he said. "I…the place isn't the same, life isn't the same, without you there. Will you come back?"

It was what she'd dreamed of, sort of. She thought of returning to her little suite with Hank as her boss. It was appealing, but something about it didn't feel right.

It was too much like mooching off a man. Not really—she was a paid employee—but now that there was something between them, she couldn't do it. Slowly, she shook her head. "No," she said. "No, I can't."

His face fell. He looked out across the park, clearly trying to govern his emotions.

He had emotions. For her. He wanted her to come back.

And she knew, from the flowers, that it wasn't just as an employee. There was something more to explore here. "I'll date you," she said boldly. "And be friends with Nadine, even stay over when you're gone, but I don't want to live there anymore."

As soon as she'd gotten the words out, she knew they were right. Living with Hank was too much like what she'd done in the past.

"You'll…date me?"

She nodded. Looked at the flowers. "I mean," she said, suddenly insecure, "if you want that."

He was nodding, a smile tugging at the corner of his mouth. He reached out and touched her hair. "You're so beautiful," he said. "Way too beautiful for me, but I would be honored if you'd go out on a date with me. Or a lot of them."

She took deep breaths as his regard warmed her deep inside. Some of her hurt places, her jagged edges, started to come together.

Acting sexy right now might make that all happen faster, but it wouldn't be permanent. She wanted permanent with this man. "Looks aren't the important thing," she said. "Do you like the person I am, even when I'm not all dressed up and made up?"

He looked shocked. "Of course I do. How could you doubt it? You're fun and smart and kind, and more of a delight than any woman I've ever been around. I'd want my daughter to grow up like you." He waved a hand, laughing a little. "Of course, she's her own person. But you get my meaning."

"I think I do." Inside, bells were ringing and champagne corks were popping, and it was all she could do not to stand up and sweep him into her arms and make him dance. But not yet. "If we date," she said, "what I offered up before isn't on offer anymore. Not for a long time."

Disappointment flashed across his face.

"Change your mind?" She had to know. Too many men had wanted her for the physical side of things. She couldn't let that govern her relationships anymore.

"It absolutely doesn't change my mind," he said. "I'll wait as long as you need."

She looked into his eyes and believed him. She touched his cheek.

He pulled her closer. "May I kiss you?"

No one had ever asked her before.

"You can," she said.

And he did.

CHAPTER NINETEEN

As THE FERRY approached Teaberry Island on Friday morning, Cody stood at the railing, feeling as emptied out as a crab bucket in the dead of winter.

Seeing the island made him remember returning on the school boat each day, after he and Ryan and Luis had come here to stay with Betty. The novelty of riding a boat to school had never worn off, and the water stretching out in all directions had provided a soothing barrier against the uglier side of the world, a side they'd all seen way too much of, too young.

These past four days had brought him through another kind of ugliness and, he hoped, out the other side. He'd remembered much of what had happened in his captivity and had talked it through with a counselor and a support group, twice each. In the evenings, he and Weed and Paul Thompson, the former cop they'd stayed with, had sat around drinking beer and watching basketball. They hadn't talked much, nor deeply, but being around two guys who'd come through some hellacious stuff and kept on living had relaxed something in him, some fear that if he remembered, he'd never survive it.

He'd survived it. Was in the process of surviving it.

They'd all agreed that now wasn't the time for Cody

to start a support group, but he had committed to attending one in Pleasant Shores every week. As long as he was in the area, at least.

The trouble was, he had to find a place to live and a job. He was right back where he'd been when he'd arrived on the island as a half-homeless insomniac.

Then again, he wasn't the same. Because he'd gotten the responsibility of his two siblings, and he'd fallen for Taylor.

He had been right to quit the job, hadn't he? She'd basically admitted she thought of him as a scummy guy who'd take advantage of an underage woman, her sister. How was he supposed to go forward with her, as her employee or her tenant or both, knowing that?

Let alone go forward as what he really wanted to be, her lover, her partner, her man?

The irony of the situation wasn't lost on him. All his life he'd run from commitment. Now, when he'd finally worked through that and realized he did want to commit, he'd gotten into an impossibly tangled relationship with a woman who could never accept him as a true, equal partner.

The boat chugged closer to land. A couple of ducks flew in and careened onto the water, squawking with what sounded like indignation. No wonder. In February, the bay was cold.

After the boat was docked, he thanked the ferryman and started walking ashore. His responsibilities seemed to descend on him with each step. The kids. Work. A place to live.

He'd go to Ryan's, he guessed. Regroup a little, check

in, and make a plan for moving out of the apartment over the bakery.

Some kind of plan.

To move somewhere. But where, he had no idea.

"Cody?"

The voice was tentative, but he'd have recognized it anywhere. He turned.

Taylor stood on the docks, her hands twisting together.

"What are you doing here?" he asked.

"I was hoping to talk to you. And I need to do it at the bakery."

This was the bakery's busy time, although at midmorning they sometimes had a lull. "Surprised you could get away."

"It's important. Will you walk with me?"

His gut clenched. "Are the kids okay?" Savannah had reported in regularly. She'd assured him they were doing fine, although they missed him.

"They're doing well. It's a teacher's workday, but Savannah and Nadine are hanging out with them."

Come to think of it, Savannah was staying at his apartment. She might be there now. Maybe that was what Taylor was worried about.

He opened his mouth to defend himself against the wordless accusation and then closed it again. If she couldn't trust him, why would she trust anything he said?

They turned and walked toward the island's little downtown. The breeze tossed Taylor's braid, blowing loose strands of hair into her eyes, and she brushed them back with a quick, impatient movement.

"I want to apologize," she said. "I was wrong to be suspicious of you all these years. I should have questioned Savannah more before making a judgment about you. Should have trusted the man I could see with my own eyes was honorable and true."

Honorable and true. *Was* he that? He definitely liked the sound of those words on her lips. But was she sincere, or did she want something from him?

The weight of everything he'd been thinking and feeling over the past three days pressed down on him, crushing away his ability to understand the emotional subtleties of a woman. "That's fine, Taylor. I mean, great. Thank you."

She looked sideways at him as they passed half frozen ditches, straw-like weeds and vegetation, an old weathered oak tree. She let him be quiet, and was quiet herself, which was a very good thing.

But the quiet couldn't last. And he didn't really want it to.

"So, what went on over there?" She gestured vaguely back toward the dock and the bay and Pleasant Shores.

He lifted a shoulder. "Some of the stuff that happened to me overseas came back. It was…ugly."

She ducked her head and nodded and then glanced over at him. "Was it… Are you glad you know, or was it better when you didn't?"

"Good question." His steps slowed as he thought about it. "I don't like the images I'm going to be carrying around now. Except I guess they were in there somewhere, anyway, festering. So it's better to cut open the wound, if you want to get all metaphorical about it."

She raised an eyebrow. "I'd like to hear about it sometime, if you'd care to tell me."

He wanted to tell her, wanted her comfort. But knowing how she'd thought about him, he didn't quite believe in her.

They were walking through the little downtown now, mostly deserted at this time of the morning. As the bakery came into sight, she put a hand on his arm, stopping him. "I know you're out of my league, Cody," she said, "but I still would give a lot to try to…"

There was a high-pitched shout. Ava. "Here he comes!"

"Try to what?" he demanded.

"Try to…explore what's here between us." She stood on tiptoe, pressed a kiss to his cheek, and then took his hand and tugged him toward the bakery.

They walked in, and for some reason, everyone he knew was there: Ryan and Mellie, Hank, Savannah and Nadine. Alfie, the kids, the librarian, Weed… How had Weed gotten here ahead of him?

"Happy birfday!" Ava called out.

Danny clapped a hand over her mouth. "Taylor said we couldn't yell." And then they ran to him, and he knelt down, and they were all hugging as if they'd been apart for years, not just days.

Cody's eyes felt a little wet. To keep from breaking down in front of the inexplicable number of friends who were here, he looked around the bakery.

And saw that it was decorated for a birthday party. Happy Birthday, Cody, said a colorful banner.

Balloons, and streamers, and people singing "Happy Birthday" now, quietly in apparent respect for his fragile mental health.

For the first time, he remembered: today was his birthday.

His eyes sought out Taylor. She'd remembered that throwaway conversation when it had come out that neither he, nor Danny and Ava, had been to a real birthday party as a kid.

She gave him a crooked smile. "It was Ryan who told me today's your birthday."

"Because he remembers everything," Alfie said, looking up at his genius father. "And so do I, 'cept I didn't know it was your birthday today, but now I won't forget."

Cody's throat was too tight to speak, and the kids were getting wiggly, so he released them and stood, slowly.

"There's a cake here with your name on it," Savannah said. "Literally. Come see."

He walked across the bakery, thankful that people were starting to talk among themselves, taking some of the focus off him. When he got to the counter, he saw that there was, indeed, a cake. A beautifully decorated sheet cake with frosting balloons and flowers. Happy Birthday to a Hero, it said.

He ducked his head, embarrassed. "I'm not a hero," he said.

"Yes, you are," Taylor said firmly. "You're the most honorable and heroic man I know." She paused and looked around the little group: Hank, and Savannah, and Ryan. "I don't trust easy, like some of you know," she said.

Savannah snorted. "Understatement of the year," she said in an audible whisper.

"But," Taylor went on, "this man has won my trust. So…" She turned to face him and took his hands. "Will you come back? To live upstairs and work at the bakery?"

He looked into her eyes and knew that she was asking more than she'd said. He felt overwhelmed with it all, but her steady gaze made it better. "Think about it, that's all," she said. "No need to decide anything today."

Whew, that was good. Because it felt like saying yes meant committing to this town, and this life, and Taylor. And while that sounded almost perfect, there was still a kernel of doubt inside him.

Would he be able to do it, make it work, make it last?

IT HADN'T WORKED.

Taylor's heart felt bruised. Three days had gone by since Taylor had thrown the surprise birthday party for Cody. The apology party, really.

That had worked. He'd thanked her profusely for it, had told everyone that it was the first birthday party he'd ever had. He'd accepted her apology. And he was working and living at the bakery "for now."

But she was pretty sure he was looking for other work and accommodations. She'd seen him meeting with Rhonda Martin, who sold real estate on the island, and he'd made at least one trip over to the mainland, leaving the kids with Mellie. Beyond work, he hadn't sought Taylor out.

Business had been brisk on Saturday, what with Valentine's Day falling on a Monday. They'd made teaberry-frosted cookies in the shape of hearts, and little wine-infused cakes, in addition to their usual scones. Everyone raved—this was going to be great, it would make their sweethearts swoon. She'd also shipped a bunch of teaberry scones in pink-beribboned boxes to her growing body of mainland clients, many of whom had posted pictures on their social media pages.

Luckily, Lolly continued to want more hours and seemed to be enjoying the work more, which improved her customer service skills. Taylor had been able to focus on baking during the day, making up for the times Cody couldn't work nights due to taking care of the kids.

With some adjustments and maybe some new hires, she *could* manage the bakery without Cody.

But she didn't want to.

He and the kids had gone to church yesterday, but not with her. And then Hank had had a bunch of people over to watch the Super Bowl on his massive TV, and it had been fun. Cody had brought the kids, and there were other kids there to play with. Nadine's girlfriends had drifted in and out, making astute teen commentary on the commercials. Betty and Peg had arrived back from Paris in time to be invited and attend, and they'd been full of stories. Ruthie stood close by her mother most of the time—they'd missed each other a lot—but she also helped Savannah put out bowls of snacks. She'd developed a little more independence while Peg was away, which would be good for both of them.

It had been nice to see Cody's affection for his foster mother. Apparently, the family who'd rented the farmhouse had moved out, and Betty was back in. Maybe Cody and the kids would move in there, Taylor thought bleakly.

Despite her heartache about Cody, she'd loved watching Savannah and Hank's shy joy in their budding relationship. The blushes and light touches as they hosted together made Taylor happy for her sister. Savannah deserved a good man, one who adored her, and Hank appeared to be just that.

And Cody needed to process his past. She knew that. She wanted that for him.

But if he had any interest in taking their relationship to the next level, wouldn't he have said so?

With a sigh, she flipped the sign on the bakery door to Closed. She checked the window display, straightened a couple of Valentine's hearts. She'd leave up the display until tomorrow.

Then she walked through the quiet, fragrant bakery to her little office in the back.

She worked for a while on the books and the orders, did some planning. When dinnertime came, she went upstairs.

She wasn't hungry, but it was dinnertime. She needed to eat.

As she was debating between cans of tomato and chicken noodle soup, there was a knock on the door. "Miss Taylor!" came Ava's lisping voice.

She hurried over to open it. Ava was out there in the

same ballerina outfit she'd worn to the library. "Happy Valentine's Day," she said. "Eat pizza with us?"

"Sure." It was pathetic how happy the little girl's invitation made her. She plunked down the cans of soup on her coffee table, ran her fingers through her hair and followed Ava over to the other apartment.

Candy and valentines covered the floor. Danny was sitting there, stuffing chocolate into his mouth and sorting through his cards, putting them into stacks. "Ooh, yuck, Miss Taylor. Ceci Jones put a bunch of kiss stickers on my valentine!"

Ava had valentines, too, apparently from her day care. She kept throwing them up in the air, yelling, "Tines! Tines!"

Cody was sliding pizzas out of the oven. "I got those half-baked ones Mellie stocks at the market. I hope you like the Everything. Or else plain cheese."

"My two favorites," she said, ruffling Ava's hair. "How can I help?"

He smiled over at her. "Just sit."

So she did, although it felt awkward to watch Cody work in the kitchen without helping him. But pretty soon the kids were leaning on her, and she was able to keep them entertained while Cody got plates and drinks on the table. Ava sang out a prayer from her day care, and then they dug in. By the end of the meal, the kids were yawning. They all watched a Valentine's TV special.

She looked around, at the mess on the table, Ava's blond head leaning against Cody, Danny half watching the TV show, half playing with some little green soldiers he'd arranged on the end table.

This was what she wanted: a family. This would make meaning out of her work and her leisure. This would fill the hole she'd increasingly felt in her life.

She hadn't known if she could succeed at caring for a family. She had tried to fill the emptiness inside her with dedication to building the bakery into a big success.

But this—this man, these children—would make her life complete. She saw it clearly now, though she was pretty sure she'd botched her chance at having it.

Finally, Cody sat forward. "It's bedtime," he said. "It's a school night. Danny. I'll help you get started on your bath."

"I can help Ava change into pajamas," Taylor volunteered. "Then I'll head out."

"Don't," Cody said over his shoulder as he shepherded Danny out of the room.

She wasn't sure she'd heard him right, but he was busy running bathwater, so she took Ava into her little nook of a bedroom, found the pajamas folded under her pillow and helped her into them. By the time Ava climbed into bed, her eyes were closing. A short whispered prayer, two pages of a picture book, and she was breathing evenly.

When Taylor went back out, she busied herself cleaning up. That would be her excuse if she'd misheard Cody, if he really hadn't meant for her not to leave. The TV played in the background, another cartoon.

She was wiping the counters when Cody came out.

"Whew. It's a battle every night. You didn't have to clean up." He went to the refrigerator and pulled out a bottle of white wine. "Want a glass?"

"Um, sure."

"Good." He poured a glass for each of them, stoppered the bottle and gestured toward the couch. "Come on, let's talk." He clicked off the TV.

Uh-oh. Here it came. He was going to tell her he'd found himself and the kids another place to live and was leaving the island. She sat down on the soft old couch, stole glances at his handsome, serious face, and gulped wine.

A minute later, he took the glass from her hand and set it down, keeping hold of her hand in his larger one.

She could barely breathe for the pain in her chest.

"Listen," he said, holding her gaze, "I'm still pretty screwed up, and I don't know if I ever won't be." His thumb moved back and forth across her knuckles, gently stroking. His eyes seemed to burn into hers. "I keep trying to tell myself I need to work on my own stuff before sharing my life with anyone else."

When he paused, Taylor was aware of how hard and painfully her heart was beating. She wanted this moment to continue forever, because she was terrified of what would come next. At the same time, she had to know. She squeezed his hand. "Go on. I'm listening."

"Come here." He shifted to put his arm around her and tug her against his side. His warmth, the strength of his arm, the perfect way her head lay on his shoulder, cast a spell over her. She felt like she was watching herself from somewhere above. Watching this important moment that she would remember all her life, whatever he said.

He cleared his throat. "I got the feeling you might be willing to try something more with me. Taylor, you're beautiful and smart and...just good. And I love you."

She sucked in air and turned her face toward his. Now she really couldn't breathe, but it was because of her heart swelling with joy. "Did you just say...you love me?"

He nodded and brushed back a lock of her hair, his touch tender. "I did. I'm in no position to propose marriage..."

Fireworks went off inside her. He'd said the word *marriage*!

"I have problems. Money and career and PTSD problems," he continued, "but still, I want to commit to you. It's just too hard to imagine life without you. Will you try it with me, try to take things a step further?"

She'd dreamed of such words, but never expected to hear them from Cody. "I thought... You're way out of my league."

He looked astonished. "*I'm* out of *your* league? Oh, Taylor." He paused as if trying to figure out how to say something. "You've always outclassed me. I would be lucky to have you."

Looking into his sincere eyes, she realized that she believed his words. That old misconception that Cody was too good for her seemed to float upward with the sparks from the fire he'd built. Upward, and away.

Maybe she'd always been messed up about appearances. She thought of Savannah and Hank, who seemed deliriously happy. But Savannah was gorgeous even if she was wearing a T-shirt and jeans, and Hank was just an ordinary-looking man.

Until Savannah looked at him. Reflected in her eyes, Hank seemed like the most impressive man in town, on every level.

"I couldn't handle my feelings back when we were teenagers," Cody said. "They were too big, and I ran away. To Savannah, because I didn't have those feelings for her."

"Wait, what?"

He repeated what he'd said, in a patient voice. "I had commitment issues even back then, from how I grew up. That's why I couldn't handle what I was starting to feel for you."

Everything Taylor had thought she knew about the past took a different shape. He'd had feelings, big feelings, for her when they were teenagers?

Maybe she and Cody weren't so much of a mismatch as she'd thought. Certainly, the expression in his eyes made her feel like the most beautiful woman on earth.

She took both his hands. Her heart raced as she tried to find the right words to fit her feelings. An impossible task, though, when everything inside her was jumping and dancing and cheering madly. "I think I've always loved you," she blurted out.

As soon as she said it, she knew it was true. Even back when she'd pretended it didn't matter, that Savannah could have him, that she was only interested in a career, some deep part of her heart had been reserved for Cody.

Now she could let that part out, let it grow.

"Are you saying…yes?"

She nodded, her cheeks hurting from her wide smile. "Yes. I am. I'd like to try."

His eyes shut for a moment as a smile as big as her own creased his face. He pulled her close, and his arms around her seemed to make a promise: that the difficulties of life would be easier to bear, that the joys would be bigger and more lasting, because all of it would be shared, together.

EPILOGUE

ON EASTER AFTER CHURCH, friends and family gathered for a meal in the yard between the Forever Farmhouse and Mellie and Ryan's place.

Taylor walked in with Cody's arm around her, and nobody gave them a second glance. Everyone in town had quickly gotten used to their relationship; in fact, everyone claimed they'd expected it from the get-go.

She and Cody had spent every spare moment together over the past two months, getting to know each other. Cody had been faithfully attending counseling sessions and a support group in Pleasant Shores, and she could feel him becoming more open, and more comfortable with himself, every day. He still worked at the bakery, but he was talking to a man named Evans about a job with the VA support groups—a new one here and several on the mainland. The days of him working at the bakery would soon come to an end.

It was okay, though. Now that the bakery was getting more attention and obviously doing well, a couple of people had actually applied for jobs—one a local, and one who wanted to commute from the mainland. That was an option she hadn't considered until she'd seen how readily Cody went back and forth. Then it was like a light bulb went off. She'd posted ads and gotten several applicants.

In the end, she had hired a manager and a couple of part-time employees who'd increase their hours in the summer, along with Ruthie of course, and Lolly, who'd started coming in more regularly.

The good thing was, Taylor felt confident in Cody's love. She didn't need to have him by her side every minute to know he was thinking of her and caring about her. His frequent texts and the flowers he brought to her weekly were just two of the outward signs of his caring. They'd talked about marriage a lot, but she was in no hurry.

Except for the evenings, when it was hard to say good-night.

When the meal was over and cleaned up, the adults gathered around a bonfire while the kids and teens ranged over the shore. Everyone was glad for a warm day.

Taylor was about to sit down when Cody came over. "Want to go for a walk?" he asked.

She shrugged. "Sure. Are the kids okay?"

"Yep. Nadine's watching them."

They walked slowly into town, talking, holding hands. Taylor's heart felt full, like it so often did these days. This Easter, this whole year, felt like a resurrection for her.

When they got to the bakery, she stopped to look in the windows, reassuring herself that everything was okay. She always did that, and usually, Cody stopped with her, just as concerned as she was.

But this time he tugged her past it to the dilapidated Victorian next door.

"Notice anything different?" he asked.

She studied the structure. "Not really. Still with the great bones, but it's a mess." Then she looked around. "Wait a minute, the For Sale sign's gone."

"I bought it," he said.

Her eyebrows shot up.

"I started looking into it a couple of months ago. Between my veterans' benefits and this new job Evans just offered me Friday—"

"What?" She threw her arms around him. "You got the job and didn't tell me?"

He disentangled himself, laughing. "Shh. There's a whole elaborate set of things I need to tell you." He tugged her toward the old house. "So, I got the job, and I bought the house. Luis helped me finance it."

"Oh, really?" Cody's foster brother Luis was a millionaire businessman, so that part made sense.

But she was still trying to process what else he'd said. He'd *bought* the house.

"Yes, really. If you say yes." He pulled her to the dilapidated steps and pushed her shoulders gently, making her sit down. Then he knelt in front of her and pulled a small box out of his pocket.

Taylor's heart felt like a flying bird, nearly bursting out of her chest. She opened her mouth to speak but couldn't say a word.

He took her hand and met her eyes, his own gaze steady. His voice was sure when he spoke. "I know we've talked about getting married, and we've said we're not in a hurry. But I realized I am. I want to marry you."

Tears pushed at the backs of her eyes, and her throat felt too tight to speak, but she nodded a little.

"This is formal, a commitment. Taylor, I love you to the moon and back. You're my rock and my inspiration. Will you keep being that, for the rest of our lives? Will you marry me?"

Tears flowed now. "I love you so much," she choked out. "I'm so proud of you. So…impressed with all you've done. Marrying you…there's nothing that would make me happier."

He made a little sound in his throat as he moved up to the steps and pulled her into his arms. For a few moments, they just held each other while Taylor's heart sang.

Finally, he kissed her lightly and then brushed back her hair. "You know the kids are part of the deal. But it's been so great for them to be at the bakery, up and down the stairs. If we have this place, we can keep that. They can grow up at the Bluebird Bakery. We can connect it all."

"I'd love that."

"And maybe we can have more kids."

"I'd love that, too."

He pulled her close then, and she lost track of time, because she wasn't thinking, she was only feeling, full of joy.

The bakery, the kids, this man, their future together…she'd never dreamed a plain, ordinary girl like her could experience such bliss. But she believed in it now. She was living it. "I love you so much," she said against his neck, and kissed him again.

* * * * *

*Read on for a sneak peek at the next
Hometown Brothers book,*
The Beach Reads Bookshop, *coming in April!*

PROLOGUE

THE LITTLE BOOKSHOP, located on Teaberry Island on the Chesapeake Bay, had once been a fisherman's cottage.

In the 1950s, Tom Crockett bought it and made it into a bookshop. Located between the town's tiny business district and the harbor, it was central enough that it soon became a gathering place for the island's residents.

Its weathered porch held chairs and a checkerboard propped on old crab traps, and on warm afternoons as many as ten men would gather there, smoking and discussing the weather on the bay. Fishermen, primarily, but also teachers and shop owners and the town minister.

The women of the community tended to congregate inside the shop, drinking coffee from the percolator Tom kept on the stove and catching up on the latest news. More than one moonlit first kiss was shared on the porch, and at least three men were known to have knelt on the weather-beaten planks to propose to their sweethearts.

Inside, volumes of Chesapeake history filled the shelves, and nautical maps lined the walls. Regional cookbooks were popular with the island's few but loyal summer tourists. *Chesapeake* by James Michener was hard to keep in stock, and so was *Beautiful Swimmers*, the Pulitzer-Prize-winning study of the blue crab.

As the years passed, people grew busier, and Tom's bookshop clientele dropped off. Phone service came late to the island, but it did come, cutting down on the need for in-person sharing of news. People got their hit of history from television, and the old volumes that had once been treasured gathered dust on the shelves.

Tourists walked past the bookshop to trendier places on High Street. Friends told Tom, now nearing eighty, that he needed to modernize, but he resisted the notion.

His sons and granddaughters had bigger things to do than run a retail establishment that, truth to tell, hadn't turned a profit for years. And then Tom died, and the doors of the bookshop closed.

Winter after winter, storms took their toll on the sturdy structure. The weathered boards grew more weathered. Mice and chipmunks skittered across the floors, and a pair of barn swallows took up residence in the eaves. After a large bough from a nearby tree crushed one corner of the roof, rainwater dripped in, soaking some of the abandoned volumes.

One day, Tom's granddaughter Mary Beth, fiftysomething and hurting for money after a bad divorce, stuck a For Sale sign in front of the tumbledown building.

The local people were too kind to laugh, but privately, they shook their heads. Who would buy such a place? What was the good of a musty old bookshop full of musty old books? And indeed, the sign stood mostly unnoticed, rattling in rainstorms and bending to the ground when strong winds blew.

No one expected the bookshop's fortunes to change. But Teaberry had always meant refreshment and renewal for tourists, and sometimes the friendly community and natural beauty of the island had brought residents back from the brink of despair. Maybe the same could happen for a broken-down little bookshop...

CHAPTER ONE

"HAVE YOU EVER considered slowing down?"

The doctor's words were as out of place as his white coat in Luis Dominguez's busy corporate office. Mergers and acquisitions were what they did here, and at a fast pace. No one slowed down, ever.

"What are you trying to tell me, Doc?" Luis attempted to ignore the text messages that kept buzzing into his phone. "I'm only twenty-eight. I can't have something wrong with me."

Doc Henry fastened the blood pressure cuff on his arm. "My understanding is that you got dizzy at a board meeting. And that you live on coffee and nachos." He tightened the cuff, studied the numbers and frowned. "One thirty over ninety. That's concerning. Family history of heart or kidney disease?"

"I don't know." Luis didn't want to go into his family medical history, or lack of one, in the middle of a regular workweek in mid-April. "I'll try to take it easier. Eat better." Even as he said it, he knew it wasn't true, but he needed to get on with his day.

"I hope you will. Your board members are worried. Apparently, you're indispensable." The man patted Luis's shoulder. "I'll see you next week. We'll need to talk about medication, unless I see significant improvement."

"You'll see it," Luis promised. Ever the overachiever. He was a bit touched that his board of directors was worried enough about his health to set up weekly in-office checkups.

He'd built a life where no one had to worry about him, and he didn't have to worry about anyone else. That was how he wanted it, but every now and then, it was good to know someone cared.

He went to the door and gestured for his assistant, Gunther, to come in. "Everything ready for today's presentation?"

"Slides are all cued up, and people are arriving."

Adrenaline surged. "Good."

The doctor clicked his medical bag closed. "How about getting a hobby? Starting a family? Being married is good for your health, you know."

"Not gonna happen." Luis had already made peace with his single status, mostly. He was no good at forming and maintaining relationships. Didn't want the responsibility. Didn't want to *fail* at the responsibility, the way his parents had.

Plenty of women were up for a no-strings fling with a millionaire. The trouble was, that lifestyle had started to feel stale to him.

"Come on," he said to Gunther, heading for the door. "Let's get this party started."

The offices of Dominguez Enterprises buzzed with energy, people leaning over computers, the elevator buttons pinging, voices speaking rapidly into phones. *This* was Luis's hobby. *This* was his family. He was on track to reach his financial goals by age forty, but his lifestyle didn't leave room for coaching Little League or cutting the grass.

"Excuse me, Mr. Dominguez?" A gorgeous blonde woman came out of the lobby and intercepted him. She was holding a toddler dressed in pink, a bow in her dark curls. Cute. Luis liked babies. He reached out and tickled the little one's chin, clicking his tongue, and the child giggled.

"Can I speak to you for a moment, sir?" the woman asked.

He refocused on the blonde. "Not now." He gestured back toward the reception area. "Make an appointment with Mrs. Jackson there at the desk." He headed into the conference room, smiling at the sight of the business-clad men and women around the table. Men and women from whom he'd soon make a bundle of money.

Fairly and legally, of course. The small tech firm that was being acquired by the larger one would get a boost of capital and be able to keep all its employees on payroll, and the bigger firm would benefit from the diversification.

Luis loved brokering this type of merger. Ideally they'd all leave as happy as he was.

In fact, two hours later, they *did* leave happy. Everyone shaking hands, his own people congratulating him and him thanking them for their hard work.

Who'd have ever thought that a kid from his background would end up making deals with some of the most important businesspeople in Philadelphia?

Then again, maybe his career was at least a little

predictable. As a young teenager, he'd borrowed a few bucks from a friend and bought a case of high-caffeine soda, then sold it at a markup on test days. With the profit, he'd bought two more cases and expanded his business from the middle school to the high school. Of course, he'd had to skip class to do that.

"He's not the brightest kid, but he sure does have the Midas touch," the teacher who'd caught him had said to his foster mom.

And Luis had done his best to make the most of whatever talents and abilities he had.

Now, as Luis walked out of the conference room, the woman who'd approached him before came toward him, this time accompanied by Mrs. Jackson. The woman looked a little disheveled, blowing the blond hair off her face as she shifted the now-sleeping toddler in her arms.

She was still pretty, though. Maybe even prettier with her face flushed and her hair loose.

"I'm sorry, Luis," Mrs. Jackson said. "She wouldn't leave."

"I really need to speak with you." The woman's voice was low but determined. There was a sexy rasp to it.

He'd have blown her off if it weren't for those stunning slate-colored eyes that seemed to hold all kinds of secrets. But it had been weeks since he'd been out on a date, and he was feeling celebratory.

"Come on back. I have a few minutes," he said, gesturing toward the hallway that led to his office. He usually avoided women with kids. He definitely avoided women with husbands, so he stepped to the side and checked out her left hand as she passed him. No ring.

She wore a dark skirt and vest and a white shirt, and there was a slight swing to her walk.

He reached the office just behind her and held open the door. "Go ahead, have a seat by the window." He kept his voice low so as not to awaken the child. He nodded an *it's okay* to Mrs. Jackson, who tended to be a mother hen, and followed the woman inside. He knelt down by the mini-fridge. "Something to drink? I have water, soda. Juice if the kiddo wakes up."

Outside, he could hear people calling goodbyes to each other. He'd given everyone the rest of the day off. They worked late for him plenty of times, so he liked to offer perks when the occasion merited it.

"Water, please." The woman spoke quietly, too, but the child murmured in her arms and opened her eyes. "Juice, as well, if you don't mind."

He stood, holding two bottles of water in one hand and a juice in the other. He twisted the top off a water bottle and handed it to her, then did the same for the apple juice.

Sitting on the edge of his desk, he studied the woman. "So, what can I do for you?"

She sipped water, cradling the child in one arm, and then looked at Luis with a level stare. "I'd like for you to meet someone."

"Tell me more." Of course she had an agenda. Probably some project she wanted him to finance. Bringing her kid was a rookie mistake, but because she looked so serious and earnest, he'd let her down easy.

She nodded at the baby. "This is Willow," she said.

"Hi, Willow." Luis smiled at the little one, then sipped water.

The woman's skirt slid up above her knees in the low chair.

He lifted his eyes to her face. "What's *your* name?"

"I'm Deena," she said. "But Willow is the important one."

The baby held a small rubber doll out to Luis. He took it from her, hid it behind his back, and then held it out again, jiggling it, making her laugh. "Why is Willow the important one?" he asked.

"Because," the woman said, "she's your daughter."

THERE. SHE'D GOTTEN it out. Deena blew her hair out of her eyes and made soothing circles on Willow's back, holding the apple juice for her to sip. She inhaled the child's baby-powder scent and patted her chubby leg.

She loved the two-year-old fiercely, and she hadn't wanted to give up even the modicum of control that would come with rich Mr. Dominguez knowing he was the child's father. But she was pretty sure Luis wouldn't want much, if anything, to do with the baby. He was too rich and entitled.

To keep it all quiet, though, he would agree to pay child support. He wouldn't have a choice. And that would allow Deena to stop working so much, to spend more time at home and to get Willow the services she needed.

Maybe this would go okay. Luis Dominguez wasn't quite what she'd expected. True, he'd made her wait for two hours, but then again, she'd arrived unannounced. She'd heard him saying nice things to his workers, and he'd gotten her and Willow something to drink. So maybe he wasn't as uncaring as Willow's mommy had believed.

He was hot, too. Deena didn't do relationships, but if she did…well. Curly black hair, light brown skin, an athletic body, and a dimple in his cheek when he smiled… No wonder Tammalee had gone for him.

He took a sip of water, studying her. "I wouldn't have invited you in if I'd known you were one of those women."

"What women?" She bounced the baby doll in front of Willow, who laughed and grabbed for it, then held it to her chest in an adorable imitation of motherhood.

"Women looking to pin paternity on a wealthy man." Luis crossed his arms over his chest.

She raised her eyebrows. "That happens?"

"Pretty often." He took another sip of water and then put the bottle down with a thump. He looked oddly disappointed. "I'm not falling for it, so why don't you take your child and your scam elsewhere?"

"This isn't a scam. I'm serious."

"It's a new twist," he said in a fake-thoughtful way, "approaching a man you never slept with. Creative."

That made her cheeks heat. She didn't sleep with anyone, not that he needed to know that. "No," she said, reaching for her phone. "You slept with my roommate." She scrolled through her pictures, found one of Tammalee, and held it up for him to see.

He squinted at it. "Oh, yeah-h-h," he said, his brows

drawing together. "Sweet girl. But why are you coming here, not her, to claim this is my child?"

Deena glanced at Tammalee's smiling photo, swallowed hard, and slid her phone back into her purse. "Tammalee is dead," she said.

His eyes widened. "What? Really?"

She nodded. "An accident."

"I'm sorry to hear that." He stared at the carpet for a minute and then met her eyes. "You realize I'm going to verify all this?"

She blew out a sigh. "Look up Tammalee Johnson, obituary."

He studied her a moment as if wondering whether there were even a chance her story was true. She must have looked honest, because he walked around his massive desk, bent over the computer, and typed and clicked. He found what he was looking for and turned the computer so she could see.

The large picture of her friend, the one that had accompanied her obituary, made Deena choke up. And that made her angry at herself, and by extension, at this guy. Neither reaction made sense, but then, grief didn't make sense.

The baby stiffened in her arms, probably sensing her tension. Or maybe she'd spotted the picture of her late mother. "Shh, it's okay," Deena whispered, rubbing her back again. But this time, it didn't help; Willow wailed.

The high, keening cry was a sound Deena had heard daily for the past year and a half, but it still grated on her. "Okay. Okay, honey. Want more juice?"

Willow slapped the bottle away, spilling juice all over Deena and the guy's fancy carpet.

"Sorry." Although she shouldn't apologize for what his own kid had done.

She rocked Willow in the vigorous way that sometimes calmed her down, trying to gauge whether this tantrum was likely to be a long one. She looked at Luis from under cover of her lashes. Tammalee had been sure he wouldn't understand Willow, saying he only cared about money. Still, if this meltdown went on, he might require an explanation.

But first things first. She needed to get him to acknowledge paternity before going into Willow's issues.

Willow's cries were softening to Deena's experienced ear, but they were still grating.

Luis looked uneasy, his forehead wrinkling. "Can't you do something?"

"She's hungry and tired," Deena said by way of explanation.

"You could have found a better time to talk to me about this, when you didn't have to wait."

"You could have given me five minutes before your big important meeting."

But she could see that the baby's crying was impacting Luis, and she didn't want it to make him dislike Willow before even getting to know her. "We can leave," she offered, "but only when you agree to the next step."

"Fine. I'll do a DNA test." He sighed. "There's a doctor I can call."

"I have a test right here." She fumbled in her purse and pulled out the drugstore version. "You just have to rub the swab inside your mouth for fifteen seconds." It had cost $100, which was a hardship for her, but for Willow, it was worth it.

He was already opening it. "How long does it take?"

"Two days from receipt. You mail it in, so…next week?"

He pulled out his phone. "Mem? Hey, could you get a courier up to my office ASAP?" He listened. "Yes, I'm still here. I know. Soon." He ended the call and looked at Deena. "I'll have it sent to a better lab and try to get the results faster." He studied Willow, still crying, and shook his head.

She could tell he was hoping he'd get the good news that he *wasn't* Willow's father. Which, she supposed, was a possibility. Tammalee had enjoyed life, and men, and hadn't been particularly choosy about who she'd spent time with—in or out of bed. But she'd insisted that Willow's father was Luis, and Deena believed her.

She swabbed the baby's mouth, making her cry again. Handed Luis the swab, and stood. "She's a terrific kid and deserves the best," she tossed over her shoulder as she left.

Whether the best outcome would be having Luis as a father, or not having him, she didn't know.

CHAPTER TWO

CAROL FISHER SMILED reassuringly at the lanky college student now packing up his textbooks. "You did really well today. You'll handle the class fine as long as you come back to the tutoring center a couple of times a week."

"I will, Miz Fisher. Thanks." He smiled, waved and walked off.

Carol was gratified to see that his shoulders were straight, his walk brisk. A complete contrast to the way he'd come in, slow and slumped and discouraged.

Amazing what an hour of tutoring on an ordinary Thursday morning could do. She loved her job directing the tutoring center at Baltimore's Watkins College, even during the busy season people tended to complain about. Late April, the end of the semester, was when students needed them most.

She followed her student out into the reception area, and there was the part of her job she *didn't* love: her new assistant director, Deandra Gardener.

"Your next appointment is waiting." Deandra forked fingers through her half buzzed, half not buzzed hair and leaned closer to her computer screen.

Did it occur to Deandra to take the appointment herself? They were all supposed to be hands-on here. Carol looked up at the clock. Ten after ten. "I'm sorry to be late," she said to the student waiting for her. "Come on back."

"Excuse me, Carol, can I speak with you?" It was Carol's boss, Evie Marie, standing in the doorway of the center. Sweet, but inexperienced. Evie Marie had been at the college only three years, and was twenty years younger than Carol, and yet she was in charge of the entire student services area.

Still, a boss was a boss. "I have an appointment right now," she told Evie Marie. "Unless…Deandra, would you be able to take it for me?"

Deandra blew out a sigh and turned away from her computer. "Come on," she said to the student, who gave Carol a *save me* look.

Carol led the way back to her office. What did Evie Marie want now? Probably some kind of new initiative that involved collecting and submitting a ridiculous amount of data for every student they tutored. That was education these days. But Carol hated the time it took away from her real job, the students.

They sat at the little table in Carol's office. Evie Marie declined Carol's offer of tea. "There's no easy way to say this, Carol," the younger woman said. "We're not going to renew your contract."

Carefully, Carol finished pouring hot water from the old-fashioned hot pot she kept on her desk. She selected a tea bag from her caddy and plopped it into the water. Then she looked at Evie Marie. "Did you just tell me you're letting me go?"

Evie Marie nodded, her thin, folded hands wringing themselves over and over. "Your contract ends May 1, and we've decided not to renew it."

"May 1, as in...a week and a half from now?" Carol could barely take it in. She dunked her tea bag repeatedly, as if she could wash away the unbelievable thing that seemed to be happening.

"Yes. I realize it's short notice, but with two weeks' severance pay plus your accumulated sick leave—"

"But *why*?" Carol shook her head and pinched the skin on the back of her hand, hoping to discover this was all a dream. But no; it hurt, and the pinched skin went down slowly. A mark of age she'd read about and then noticed, starting around age fifty. Five years ago.

Evie Marie looked down at her notes. "We've talked about the tech issues," she said. "It's been noted as a problem at your last two performance reviews."

"But I work well with students. That's the important thing. At least...isn't it?" Carol's voice quavered, and she pressed her lips together.

"You do work well with the students, and they love you. But we want to take the center online, and you've been resistant. It's been decided that we need some new blood, new ideas."

"I'm resistant because the developmental students need in-person coaching, not just a face on a screen!"

Evie Marie didn't deny that. "I have my directive. We're a tech-savvy school. It's part of our image and our marketing."

"But the at-risk students—"

"—are *not* part of our image and marketing." Evie

Marie looked genuinely sad. "I'm sorry, Carol. I know you put your heart into your work, but you've never wanted to embrace the new."

"The new is overrated, especially if it leaves behind the students who struggle! You're the head of student services. Surely you understand that." She was waiting for Evie Marie to admit that letting her go was all a big mistake, even as the increasing heaviness in her heart told her this was no joke and she needed to accept reality.

"You're near retirement age," Evie Marie said in a soothing voice. "We can bill it that way. And there are your husband's needs. This way, you can spend more time with him."

Carol's stomach tightened. Spending more time with Roger was the last thing that would be a comfort. He'd be livid. They needed her benefits.

"You're serious about this, aren't you? Have you already started the search for my, my replacement?" Her tongue tripped over the word.

"We actually aren't doing a search," Evie Marie said. "Deandra has agreed to take the position."

"What?" Carol's jaw dropped as she stared at her supervisor. "You know her interpersonal skills are at the toddler level, and her work ethic—"

"The decision has been made."

The whole place had gone crazy if Deandra was considered a better head of tutoring than she was. "When do you want me out? Are you going to escort me to the door?"

"No, no. You don't need to work out the rest of the

month, but we'll of course give you time to gather your things. By the end of the day, or tomorrow at the latest." Evie Marie stood. "I know it's a lot to process. HR has been in the loop on this. They'll be able to talk to you about COBRA insurance continuation and unemployment. Why don't you take a few minutes, and I'll let them know you'll be over, say, after lunch."

Carol nodded, numb.

Evie Marie stood, opened the office door and stopped, waiting for Deandra and the student to walk by. Hadn't Evie Marie noticed that appointment, scheduled for an hour, had only taken twenty minutes? Didn't she see the miserable expression on the student's face?

Deandra looked in the door at her, and her lip pulled back in a strange kind of smile. She knew, obviously. Evie Marie had said it was all decided.

Carol was heartbroken for the students, but also for herself. What was she going to do?

LUIS WAS A FATHER.

He patted the DNA test results in his pocket as he headed toward his meeting with his child's guardian, Deena.

Though it was still April, DC was unseasonably hot and humid, especially in midafternoon. The faint smell of garbage and sweat rose in the commercial neighborhood, crowded on a Saturday. But Luis was too preoccupied to pay much attention. Ever since he'd gotten the results yesterday, his mind had been in overdrive, figuring out a plan.

Talking to his family, kind of a found family but all

he had, back on Teaberry Island had helped him make decisions. Actually made him a little bit excited about what was ahead.

He smiled as he walked into The Book Spot, a local independent bookstore where Deena had wanted to meet. That was one great thing about DC. It was a reading town. Half the people on the metro carried a book, and there were bookstores galore. He hoped to get this situation handled and then pick up the latest Baldacci thriller on the way out.

He welcomed the blasting AC as he strode through the shop and trotted up the steps toward the café. Deena was at a table in the back, set off a little from the others, reading.

She was *really* pretty. She wore the same white shirt and black skirt that she'd worn before, and he realized it must be some kind of uniform. Plain, but it couldn't make *her* look plain, not with those cheekbones and that curly blond hair escaping from the bun she'd put it in. Her cheeks were faintly pink, and she was sipping an iced coffee, engrossed in her book.

She looked up, saw him, and tucked a bookmark into her paperback.

It was one of the latest science-oriented award winners; he'd read it himself when it had come out in hardcover. None of his friends or colleagues had read it, and he felt a brief urge to sit down and talk to her about it.

But that wasn't why he was here. "Where's the child?" he asked.

"*Willow* is at child care." She emphasized the toddler's name, as if he might have forgotten it.

He took the seat across from her. "Like I told you over the phone, I got the DNA results, and they're positive."

"May I see?"

"You don't believe me?"

She tucked a curl behind her ear and gave him a steady, blue-eyed gaze. "Is there a reason I should?"

He guessed not. He'd barely been able to believe it himself. But even if she doubted him, it didn't make sense for her to fight it. It was in her best interest to believe that a wealthy man was the father of her friend's baby; she was likely to get some money out of it.

He shrugged and pulled out the paperwork, slid it across the table to her. She bent over it, and since she was obviously going to read every word, he went and got himself a coffee and her another iced coffee.

As he returned, she pushed back the papers, looked up at him, and lifted an eyebrow. "Okay. It all looks legit. Welcome to fatherhood."

Fatherhood. He tested out the word in his head. It didn't match his self-image, not by a mile. He was the hard-driving businessman in his family. His two foster brothers had settled down on Teaberry Island, where they'd all spent their adolescence, and both of *them* were raising children. Both of them had been surprised by it, too. Still, they seemed to relish the role and be made for it. Whereas Luis…wasn't. The little he knew about being a good father had been gleaned from his late foster father, but that had been about being the parent of teens. How to take care of a little girl…a little girl who was his blood…it didn't quite compute.

He had no delusions that he'd be good at this gig, not with his background.

Even so, he wasn't a ditherer. Being in business had taught him to take action. "I've figured out a plan," he said. "Obviously, I'm not set up for taking care of a young child here, so I'm going to take her back to Teaberry Island, on the Chesapeake, where I spent my teenage years. I have family there, people who can help me with babysitting and find a good child care provider. I'll have to be here in DC on weekdays, but I'll go visit her every weekend." He smiled at her. "You're off the hook, in other words. I can't tell you how much I appreciate—"

"No," Deena interrupted, cutting him off.

"What?"

"I'm not giving Willow to a complete stranger who only wants to see her on the weekends and who plans to pass her off to other complete strangers to basically raise."

"She's in day care right now," Luis pointed out.

Deena looked chagrined. "I know, and I'm not happy about that. That's why I contacted you. I'd like to see you pay child support. That would allow me to work less and spend more time at home with her." She paused. "You could visit her, of course. We could set up a schedule."

"Obviously I'll compensate you for the time you've spent—"

"That's not what I mean!" Her voice rose, and a couple other patrons glanced over. She leaned forward and lowered her voice, but it was still fierce and passionate. "I'm her guardian, and I love her."

For whatever reason, Luis felt that as an attack. Like

he didn't love his own daughter. Well, he didn't, not yet. He'd barely met her. "Love doesn't stand up in court."

She cringed. "Be reasonable. She can't be so easily moved."

"Why not? Kids adapt." He'd been moved too many times as a kid. It gave him a twinge, thinking he was doing the exact same thing he'd hated about his own childhood. But after this one move, he wouldn't do it again.

"Look, she has issues," Deena said. "She needs consistency."

"What do you mean, she has issues?" The child had looked fine to him when he'd seen her the other day. Beautiful, even. She'd been fussy, sure, but that was normal for a two-year-old. Wasn't it?

There was a pounding in his neck and chest, and his vision blurred. Had he taken his blood pressure medicine today?

"I mean," Deena said, and paused, as if debating with herself. She looked at him, her eyes narrowing, and then she spoke. "I mean, I'm pretty sure she has fetal alcohol syndrome."

Don't miss The Beach Reads Bookshop
by Lee Tobin McClain!

TAYLOR'S TEABERRY ISLAND SCONES

Ingredients

2 cups flour
¼ to ½ cup sugar, depending on your preference
1 tablespoon baking powder
1 stick butter, frozen or very cold
½ cup cream, milk, or Greek yogurt
1 large egg, beaten
1 teaspoon orange or lemon extract
(good with cranberries) or vanilla (good with any
kind of berries)
1-1½ cup teaberries, blueberries, dried cranberries,
or chopped strawberries (these will make your
scones pink, nice for Valentine's Day)

Directions

Preheat oven to 400°.

Combine dry ingredients in a bowl. Grate the frozen butter (Taylor's method) or cut cold butter into small cubes. Add to flour mixture and use a pastry cutter or your fingers to combine the mixture into a crumbly texture. Refrigerate.

Combine milk, yogurt or cream, egg, and vanilla or other flavoring in a small bowl. Add to flour mixture a little at a time, stirring lightly without overmixing. Add berries of your choice.

Make dough into a ball and then roll out into a circle about one inch high, adding flour if dough is too sticky. Cut dough into eight wedges, like a pie. Brush scones with milk or melted butter.

If time permits (*i.e.*, a handsome guy like Cody hasn't slowed you down), chill scones for 15-30 minutes.

Bake 18-21 minutes or until light golden brown on the edges.

If desired, make a glaze of 1 cup powdered sugar, 2 tablespoons milk, and a flavoring to match your scones. Cool scones for 5-10 minutes and then drizzle glaze on top.

Enjoy!

HARLEQUIN
PLUS

Try the best multimedia
subscription service for romance
readers like you!

Read, Watch and Play.

Experience the easiest way to get
the romance content you crave.

Start your **FREE TRIAL** at
<u>www.harlequinplus.com/freetrial</u>.